P9-CEI-709

Praise for the national bestselling
League of Literary Ladies Mysteries

"Logan has fun with this unusual story, intimate setting,
and feisty characters, and readers will, too."
—*Richmond Times-Dispatch*

"This is one of my favorite series. What could be more fun
than a mystery series that is about a reluctant book club? I
love how the mysteries run parallel to the book the League
of Literary Ladies is reading. Bea and her friends always
rally together to solve the mystery—especially if the accused
is one of their own. This well-plotted mystery will be a
delightful treat for cozy mystery readers. I found I could not
put this book down—I had to find out whodunit."
—MyShelf.com

"One of my favorite cozy mystery writers . . . What great
characters Kylie Logan has created." —Fresh Fiction

"Kylie Logan has created a cast of characters in whom readers will feel invested, as their histories are played out
throughout the series . . . The plot, a surprisingly complex
one in this third of the series, never suffers from the focus
on character development. Literature, the struggle of au-
thors, and friendship among women make this an absorbing
read—a spookily good book with an even greater mystery."
—Kings River Life Magazine

Irish
Stewed

KYLIE LOGAN

BERKLEY PRIME CRIME, NEW YORK

BERKLEY
PRIME
CRIME

An imprint of Penguin Random House LLC
375 Hudson Street, New York, New York 10014

IRISH STEWED

A Berkley Prime Crime Book / published by arrangement with the author

ISBN: 978-0-425-27488-0

PUBLISHING HISTORY
Berkley Prime Crime mass-market edition / May 2016

PRINTED IN THE UNITED STATES OF AMERICA

10 9 8 7 6 5 4 3 2 1

Cover illustration by Tom Foty.
Cover design by Sarah Oberrender.
Interior text design by Kelly Lipovich.

Penguin
Random
House

For the Airedale Terrier Club of Northern Ohio—
great dogs, great people!

Acknowledgments

Every year near Saint Patrick's Day, our family hosts a huge party. There's bagpipe music, of course, along with plenty of brothers, sisters, in-laws, cousins, and kids. Oh my, these days there are a lot of kids! There's also always a groaning board of food. Irish stew, soda bread, corned beef, and cabbage. We're in charge of bringing the colcannon and we make upward of fifty pounds of mashed potatoes as a basis for the dish. Delicious? You bet! And always a hit with the partygoers.

It was this sort of family tradition that gave me the idea for basing a mystery series on ethnic foods. To me, the foods traditionally served by family equal comfort food. In my own family, it's things like stuffed cabbage, pierogi, and that wonderful bread my grandmother made at holidays that we simply called Sweet Bread.

In other families (like my husband's), the comfort comes from the Emerald Isle. And that's what makes ethnic food so interesting. We each have our own memories and our own traditions and there's no better way to celebrate them than by honoring the dishes our ancestors cherished.

As with all books, there are plenty of people to thank for

help with this one, including my great brainstorming group (Shelley Costa, Serena Miller, and Emilie Richards), the folks at Berkley Prime Crime, and my agent. I'd also like to thank Georgia Schuff, my expert and go-to person when it comes to Hubbard, Ohio, and my family—all umpteen of them—for carrying on the tradition. *Na zdrowie* and *sláinte*!

Chapter 1

"I can explain."

At my side, Sophie Charnowski pressed her small, plump hands together and shifted from one sneaker-clad foot to the other. The nearest streetlight flickered off, then on again, and in its anemic light, I saw perspiration bead on her forehead. "It's like this, you see, Laurel."

"Oh, I see, all right." Good thing I was wearing my Brian Atwood snakeskin ballet flats. In heels, I would have tripped on the pitted sidewalk when I spun away from the building in front of us and the railroad tracks just beyond. When I pinned short, round Sophie with a look, I meant to make her shake in her shoes, and it gave me a rush of satisfaction to realize the ol' daggers from my blue eyes still carried all the punch I intended. Sophie flicked out her tongue to touch her lips, then swallowed hard.

While she was at it, I stabbed one finger toward the train

station and the sign that hung above the door that declared
the place SOPHIE'S TERMINAL AT THE TRACKS.

"This isn't what I expected," I said.

Sophie rubbed her hands together. "I know that. Really,
I do. I can only imagine how you must feel."

"No." I cut her off before she could say anything else
ignorant and insulting. "You can't possibly imagine how I
feel. I just drove all the way to Ohio from California.
Because you told me—"

"I wanted it to be a surprise." Sophie was a full eight
inches shorter than my five foot nine, and as round as I am
slender. She had the nerve to look up at me through the
shock of silvery bangs that hung over her forehead. Believe
me, the hairstyle wasn't a fashion statement. When I picked
Sophie up at her small, neat bungalow so we could drive
across Hubbard and she could show me the restaurant, I had
the distinct feeling I'd just woken her from an after-dinner
nap. "I knew once you saw the place—"

"Once I saw the place!" Was that my voice echoing
against the old train station and bouncing around the
semigentrified neighborhood with its bookstore, its coffee
shop, its beauty salon, and gift boutiques?

I was way past caring. "Sophie, you told me—"

"That I'm having my knee replaced tomorrow. Yes." She
took a funny sort of half step and pulled up short, one hand
automatically shooting down to her right knee. She kept it
there, a not-so-subtle reminder of the pain she'd told me was
her constant companion. "And that I need someone to help
out while I'm laid up. Someone to run the restaurant."

"Which isn't the restaurant it's supposed to be."

"Well, really, it is." A grin made her look so darned
impish, I almost forgave the lies she'd been feeding me for
years.

Almost.

"The Terminal at the Tracks has been a neighborhood gathering place for going on forty years now," she told me, and don't think I didn't notice the way she rushed to get the words out before I could stop her cold. "I always loved it here. We used to stop for breakfast on Sunday mornings after church. And after our Tuesday bowling league, we'd always get a bite to eat here. Only these days . . ." This time when she caressed her knee, she added a long-suffering sigh. "Well, I'm not doing very much bowling these days. But that doesn't change how I feel about this neighborhood. It's got the feel of history to it, don't you think?" Instead of giving me a chance to answer, she drew in a long, deep breath and let it out slowly while she swiveled her gaze from the train station to the tracks behind it and the boarded-up factory beyond.

"When I had the opportunity to buy the Terminal fifteen years ago, I just jumped at it. So there's my name up there on the sign." Sophie made a brisk ta-da sort of motion in that direction. "And here I am." She pointed at her own broad bosom. "And now . . ." It was spring and almost nine, which meant it was already dark. That didn't keep me from seeing the rapturous look that brightened Sophie's brown eyes and brought out the dimples in her pudgy cheeks. "And now here you are, too. So you see, everything is just as it's supposed to be."

Really? I was supposed to buy into this philosophical, all's-right-with-the-world horse hockey?

My pulse quickened and my blood pressure would have shot to the ceiling had we been indoors instead of outside in front of the long, low-slung building with a two-story section built in the middle above the main entrance. When that streetlight went off and on again, it winked against the weathered yellow paint and the dark windows of the restaurant.

I hardly noticed the sparkle of the light against the glass.

But then, I was pretty busy seeing red.

I would have leveled Sophie right then and there if she weren't thirty years older than me and limping, to boot. Instead, I followed along when she hobbled to the front door.

"What you did was low, underhanded, and dishonest, Sophie," I told her.

"Yes, it was." She didn't sound the least bit penitent. She stuck her key in the front door. "But now that we're here, you'll look around, won't you?"

I should have said no.

I should have put my foot down.

I should have opened my mouth and as so often happens when I do, I should have let what I was thinking pour out of me like the lava that spews from a volcano and incinerates everything in its path.

Why I didn't is as much a mystery now as it was then. I only know that when Sophie pushed open the front door and stepped inside the Terminal at the Tracks, I followed along.

"Welcome." She touched a hand to a light switch and the fixture directly over our heads turned on.

Sophie beamed a smile all around.

I did not share in her enthusiasm. In fact, I took one look around the entryway of the Terminal at the Tracks, and a second, and a third.

That's pretty much when I had to remind myself to snap my mouth shut.

What I could see—at least here in the fifteen-by-fifteen entryway where customers waited for their tables—was a mishmash of kitschy faux Victorian, everything from teddy bears in puffy-sleeved gowns to posters advertising things like unicycles and mustache wax.

And then there was the lace.

Doilies and rickrack and bunting.

Oh my.

Brand spanking new, it would have been overblown and downright dreadful. With fifteen years of service under its belt, the lace was yellow and bedraggled. The teddy bear propped on the old rolltop desk that also served as a hostess station looked as if it could use an airing, and what had once been a magnificent floor made of wide, hardwood planks was scratched and dull.

"I knew you'd love it as much as I do," Sophie purred.

Fortunately at that moment, a train rolled by, not twenty feet from the back of the restaurant, and the place shook the way LA had in the last earthquake I remembered. My sternum vibrated. My bones rattled.

By the time the train was gone and my body was done with its rockin' and rollin', I pretended I didn't even remember Sophie's last comment.

"There's something special I need to show you." She latched on to the sleeve of the silk shirttail tee I wore with skinny jeans and tugged me toward a glass counter with a cash register set on it.

"Right here." Sophie said, and tapped the glass next to the cash register. That's when her smile fell and her silvery brows knit. "Well, it was here." She chewed her lower lip. "It's always here. I must have left it"—she waved in some indeterminate direction—"in the office. I must have left it in the office when I took the day's receipts in there to file. You know, on Saturday, the last day the restaurant was open before I had to close." Another puppy dog look. "Because of my knee, you know. And my surgery tomorrow."

Sophie gave the counter another pat. "The receipt spike," she finally explained. "You know, the thin, pointy thing where we stick the receipts—"

"After they're rung up on the register." I'd worked in enough restaurants in my day; I knew exactly what she was talking about.

"This one is special," Sophie confided. "About yay high"—she held her hands ten inches apart—"and made completely of brass. It was Grandpa Majtkowski's. From his bakery shop in Poland. He brought it with him when he came to this country back in 1913. Imagine that, he came with one suitcase, one change of clothes, and less than twenty dollars in his pocket, and he still thought it was important to bring that receipt spike with him. And no wonder! It was all he had of home, all he had of the business he worked so many years to build, and—"

A tap on the front door saved me from any more of the history lesson.

Sophie didn't seem to mind. In fact, when she looked toward the front entrance, she grinned.

"It's Declan!" Quicker than a woman with a sore knee should have been able to move, she scooted over and opened the door. "It's Declan," she said again, and she moved back to allow a man to step into the Terminal.

Let's get something straight here—I had spent the last six years of my life working as a personal chef to Meghan Cohan. Yeah, that Meghan Cohan, the Hollywood megastar. I wasn't just used to catering to the culinary whims of the Beautiful People, I was comfortable rubbing elbows with them. When she was working on a film, I traveled with Meghan. All over the world. When she was bored, she'd take me along when she jetted to her place in Maui. Or the one in Tuscany. Or the villa in the south of France. I was in charge of Meghan's diet regimen, and her parties and the late-night soirees that sometimes ended up getting talked about in *Vogue* or *Elle* or *Cosmo*.

Meghan was powerful. She was gorgeous. And she allowed only powerful and gorgeous men into her circle.

I wasn't sure who this Declan guy was, but I knew that one look, and Meghan would have welcomed him with open arms.

Tall.

Dark.

I won't say handsome because let's face it, that's a cliché and Declan's looks put him far beyond platitudes.

His hair was a little too long and tousled just enough that had we been back in LA, I would have suspected he'd just come from some tony salon. He had an angular face defined by a dusting of dark whiskers, and he wore jeans and sneakers and a black leather jacket over a red plaid flannel shirt. Untucked. All of it was casual enough while at the same time it sent the message that whatever else Declan was, he was comfortable in his own skin.

None of which mattered in the least bit.

Not to me, anyway.

No matter how handsome the locals might happen to be, I'd already decided there was no way I was staying.

Declan came inside the Terminal and closed the door behind hm.

"I saw the light on," he said to Sophie, "and no one's usually here this late at night. I just wanted to make sure everything was all right."

"Aren't you just the best neighbor ever!" Sophie twinkled like a teenager. "Declan's from the Irish store." She looked out the window and I saw the lighted windows of the gift shop that was across the street and kitty-corner to the restaurant. From here, it was impossible to see exactly what was in the display windows on either side of the front door, but there was no mistaking the crisp green colors touched with a smattering of orange, or the wooden sign that hung above the front door, a gigantic green shamrock.

"Of course, everything's fine. I was just showing off the place." She closed a hand over the sleeve of his jacket and piloted him nearer. "Declan Fury, this is Laurel Inwood."

Add a thousand-watt smile to that description of Declan. And a handshake that was warm and firm enough to send the message that he was no-nonsense, practical, and far more sure of himself than 99 percent of the actors (yeah, even the ones who play tough guys in the movies) Meghan had introduced me to over the years.

"So, you're finally here." Declan had a baritone voice that managed to caress even the most ordinary greeting. "I know your aunt's been looking forward to your arrival."

I'm afraid my smile wasn't nearly as broad as his. Or as genuine. I refused to look at Sophie when I said, "She's not really my aunt."

"Oh." Declan pulled his hand back to his side, not as embarrassed as he was simply curious. "I guess I'm confused because Sophie always refers to you as her niece."

This time, I did take a second to slide Sophie a look. I wasn't surprised to see something like contrition in her pursed lips and her downcast eyes.

Which didn't mean I believed it was genuine.

"That makes me wonder why Sophie was talking about me at all."

Contrition be damned! Just like that, Sophie was back to her ol' grinning self. "You know we're all just as proud as punch of everything you've accomplished." She patted my arm. "Laurel's famous," she told Declan, and then, because she apparently saw the sparks shooting from my eyes, she was quick to amend the statement to, "Well, practically famous."

Maybe Declan was also a better actor than most of the ones I'd met out in LA. He pretended not to notice the undercurrent of annoyance and avoidance that flowed back and forth between me and Sophie. In fact, when he turned back to me, it was with a smile sleek enough to send prickles up my spine.

Not that it mattered, I reminded myself.

Since I wasn't staying.

"Well," he said, giving me a quick once-over from toes to top of head and apparently approving of what he saw since his smile stayed firmly in place, "it's nice to know there will be a practically famous chef holding down the fort while her aunt is in the hospital."

He had a short memory.

And he smelled like bay rum and limes.

I shook away the thought and the way the scent always made me think of tropical islands and warm sea breezes.

"Sophie's younger sister, Nina, was my foster mother for four years," I told him. "So you see, Sophie and I, we're really not related."

His smile never wavered. "Except you don't have to share DNA to be family, do you?"

"I'm just showing Laurel around," Sophie said, and she wound an arm through mine. "You know, because I'll be gone six weeks and someone needs to run the place."

"That doesn't mean that someone is going to be me." I untangled myself from Sophie's grip when I said this, the better to look her in the eye so she knew I meant business.

"We obviously need to talk, me and Laurel," she told

Declan. "There might be some rocky road ice cream in the freezer, and I don't know about you, but I think heart-to-heart talks always go better over rocky road."

Declan stepped toward the doorway that led into the main part of the restaurant. The woodwork around it was painted dusty blue, like the trim on the outside of the station, and there were lace curtains in the doorway that were tied back on either side with purple ribbon. He poked a thumb over his shoulder into the darkened room. "If you like, I can take a look around before you settle down for your heart-to-heart."

"No need!" Sophie's warm laugh bounced up to the ceiling fans that swirled overhead. "You know this is a safe neighborhood."

Declan leaned forward just enough to take a peek beyond the entryway and into the pitch-dark restaurant. "Maybe so, but it is late and—"

"And you need to get back to whatever it was you were doing before you took the time to come over here and check on an old lady like me." Sophie led him back to the front door. "A good-lookin' guy like you, you must have better things to do on a warm spring night."

Declan tipped his head, and when he smiled, the air between us sizzled. "Then I'll just get back to the shop. I've still got some work to finish. Good night, ladies."

"Isn't he the dreamiest?" Sophie giggled once he was gone.

Her back was to the door. Otherwise, I wondered if she'd still think he was dreamy when she realized that Declan didn't go across the street to the Irish store. In fact, he walked along the front of the Terminal, turned at the far corner, and headed into the side parking lot.

Once he was out of sight, I turned back to Sophie and

was just in time to see her shuffle her sneakers. "Rocky road?" she offered.

I let go a sigh of pure frustration. "You're not going to bribe me with ice cream, Sophie. I told you, I don't appreciate being lied to. All those years, you came to California to visit and you showed me and Nina—"

"Pictures of the restaurant." She looked up at me through those unruly bangs. "Yes, I know."

"But it wasn't this restaurant."

Sophie's cheeks flushed pink, but I wasn't about to let that keep me from saying my piece.

"You showed us photographs of a lovely place out in the country. Linen tablecloths, soft lighting, a fabulous wine cellar. That's the place I thought I was going to be helping out with while you were recuperating. This place—"

"This place is all I have."

Yes, her comment would have tugged at my heartstrings. If I had heartstrings.

Unfortunately for Sophie and lucky for me, I didn't.

That didn't mean I was completely insensitive. "I said I'd take you to the hospital tomorrow morning, and I will," I told her.

"And you said you'd be running the restaurant after that."

"It's not going to work."

Her shoulders drooped. "I know. I guess I knew all along. But still, you're here. Let me show you around." Her limp more pronounced than ever, she walked through that lace-curtained doorway and turned on the lights in the main dining room.

What I saw was pretty much what I expected.

Five, six, seven, eight . . . I counted . . . tables lined up against the far wall next to the windows that looked out over the railroad tracks. None of them covered with linen. Four tables to my left and two doorways, one marked KITCHEN and the other, OFFICE. To my right, six more tables, more lace, more kitsch, and once I skirted the jut-out wall that marked the back of the waiting area, windows that looked out at the street and gave a bird's-eye view of the light that shone on that green shamrock across the way.

And one customer.

I froze and looked at the man lying facedown on one of the tables.

"Uh, Sophie." She was already shuffling back to the kitchen in search of ice cream, and when I called out, Sophie hitch-stepped back the other way. "There's a guy here."

"A guy? That's impossible. That's—"

She got as far as where I stood and she froze, too, looking where I did, at the table against the wall where a man in a brown jacket was slumped, his head on his arm.

And that receipt spike of Grandpa Majtkowski's sticking out the back of his neck.

"Oh my goodness!" Sophie wailed.

If I didn't act fast, I knew I'd have another problem on my hands, so I pulled over the nearest chair and plunked Sophie down in it before I dared to close in on the man in the brown jacket.

From this angle, there wasn't much to see. In the light of the faux Tiffany chandelier directly above the table, his neck looked as pale as a hooked fish. Well, except for the thin river of blood that originated at the spot where the receipt spike was plunged into his spine.

I dared to put a finger on his neck, but even before I did, I knew I wouldn't find a pulse. His skin was ice and there were tinges of blue behind his ears and on the fingers of the hand that hung loosely at his side.

I fumbled for the phone in my pocket and dialed 911, hoping that when the dispatcher answered, I could make the words form in a mouth that felt suddenly as if it had been packed with sand.

And all I could think was the one thing I knew I wouldn't dare say to Sophie or to the cops—this gave a whole new meaning to the word *terminal*.

Chapter 2

"**O**h my goodness, it's the Lance of Justice!"

When Sophie shrieked out the words, I turned away from the cop who'd been taking my statement and toward the paramedics just as they lifted the dead guy from his chair and placed him on his back on the floor. As if they'd choreographed the move, Sophie and everyone else standing in a half circle around the table took a step back, their mouths open and their eyes bulging.

"It *is* the Lance of Justice," one of the uniformed cops gasped. "Hey, Oberlin!" He waved toward the detective who'd cornered me as soon as he learned I was the one who found the body. "The dead guy here, it's the Lance of Justice!"

If the look on his doughy face meant anything, Detective Gus Oberlin was not as surprised as the rest of them. Or as impressed, either. He scrubbed a hand under his wide, flat nose and looked up from the notebook where he'd been writing down what I told him, and he narrowed his eyes and looked past me and over my shoulder. They were small, dark eyes, the kind that took in everything and revealed little. Though he didn't say a word, I could tell he was cataloging the scene: the body bag the paramedics had set out and unzipped; the blank look on the victim's face as he stared, unseeing, at the ceiling; the astonishment that made the cops and the paramedics and Sophie, too, look as stunned as if they'd had a camera flash go off too close to their faces.

The dead guy was the Lance of Justice.

"Who's the Lance of Justice?" I asked Detective Oberlin.

He rolled the toothpick he was chewing from one corner of his mouth to the other. Oberlin was six foot four and weighed well over three hundred pounds. The buttons on the white shirt he wore under a nondescript blue suit jacket gaped just a little and there were spits and splots of tonight's dinner—spaghetti and meatballs, if I was any judge—on his sky blue tie.

"The Lance of Justice!" Oberlin didn't so much say the words as he crooned them. As if he'd just realized that what he thought was a pretty ho-hum murder (is there such a thing?) was suddenly delicious. The toothpick in his mouth twitched when he said, "Well, ain't that just a kick in the pants?"

"And this Lance of Justice guy, who—"

Without giving me a chance to finish, Oberlin waved one meaty hand at the nearest cop. "Get these witnesses out of here for now. We'll finish taking their statements when we're done looking over the crime scene."

With that, Sophie and I were escorted back to the restaurant waiting area and left with the dusty teddy bear, the rolltop desk, all that lace, and—

I looked out the front windows and blinked in astonishment, then realized I really shouldn't have been surprised. Six years in Hollywood, remember. Somehow, though, I

never associated the words *paparazzi* or *feeding frenzy* with
Hubbard, Ohio.

It couldn't have been more than twenty minutes since I'd
called 911 and already, the street in front of the Terminal
was packed with police cars and ambulances, their red and
blue lights pulsing through the night. That, of course, was
to be expected. But beyond the perimeter that the cops had
established in front of the restaurant, I saw knots of people
gathered as well as three trucks from TV stations in
Youngstown, the area's biggest city. One of them over on
the right had a powerful light shining on the front of the
restaurant and a woman in a neat black suit stood in its glow,
a microphone in one hand.

I swear, the chick must have had a sixth sense about these
things. She caught sight of me and Sophie, scurried over,
and tapped on the front door.

"It's me," she said, and she pressed her face to the glass
in a way that was supposed to make her recognizable and
instead just made her blue eyes look sunken and her nose
appear way too shmooshed. "Kim Kline!"

Sophie hurried to the door and took a close look. "It is
Kim Kline!"

"Do you really think we should—"

I was too late with my protest. Which probably didn't
matter since I was pretty sure Sophie wouldn't have listened,
anyway. She opened the door and Kim Kline slipped inside
the restaurant.

"Is it true? What can you tell me? What do you know?"
Kim was a petite woman and about as big around as a strand
of angel-hair pasta. Her hair was dark mahogany and it hung
over her shoulders in perfectly placed and very glossy
ringlets. Now that she wasn't face-to-glass, her eyes didn't
look nearly as beady, but her nose . . .

She'd never make it in Hollywood, that was for certain.
Honker.
Schnoz.
Beak.

Had I been pressed for a description, I would have said that Kim's nose—there was a rather large bulge at the bridge of it—gave her otherwise average face character, but back in Hollywood, they would have had a lot to say about it, and none of it would have been complimentary.

In one swift movement, Kim reached behind her and opened the door for the cameraman who waited outside. She cleared her throat, settled her shoulders, and signaled, and he switched on a blinding light and started rolling.

"So, what can you tell us?" she asked, her microphone poked in Sophie's direction. "We know there's been a murder and we've heard rumors. Our viewers want to know the truth. They deserve to know the truth. Is the victim really the Lance of Justice?"

Sophie blinked into the bright camera light. "Well, it's . . . That is . . . We saw—"

"What exactly did you see?" Kim was enough of a professional to realize she wasn't going to get anything out of Sophie. She spun my way and stabbed the microphone in my direction. "You two were here first on the scene. At least that's what we've been told. Take me through what happened, step by step."

Unlike Sophie, I am not camera shy. Paparazzi, remember. Meghan. Hollywood.

And if there was one thing I'd learned through it all, it was that sometimes it's best to keep your mouth shut.

Oh, I wasn't worried about tainting evidence. Or giving out too many details before the police were ready to have them released to the public. And heck, I sure wasn't worried about the Lance of Justice because so far, no one had bothered to tell me who he was and why everyone cared so much.

But I did have my reasons.

No comment meant no TV coverage. At least not of me. And no coverage meant my face wouldn't be plastered on the news and my name wouldn't be splashed across the screen and on the Internet if anyone bothered to search, and the people back in Hollywood who I thought were my friends until they proved they weren't would never have to learn that I was here in Hubbard, Ohio, in a sorry excuse for a restaurant and suddenly embroiled in some flashy little local drama.

It was too terrifying to think they'd learn how far I'd fallen.

"No comment," I told Kim.

A quick hand signal from her and the cameraman stopped rolling. Her top lip curled. "You're kidding me, right? Are you telling me you don't want to be on the local news?"

"I don't want to be on the local news." I stepped toward the door and since she was directly in front of me, she had no choice but to step back. "You'll have to leave."

She tried Sophie again. "Ms. Charnowski, there's got to be something you can tell me. Have the police demanded you keep silent? Is there some sort of cover-up involved?"

She was slow on the uptake, so I took another step toward her.

Kim fell back. So did her cameraman.

"Out," I said.

"It's not your restaurant. Ms. Charnowski—"

"Out."

Remember what I said about the daggers from my blue eyes?

Kim got out, and she took her cameraman with her.

That bit of excitement over, Sophie fluttered around like a bird before she finally dropped into one of the chairs against the wall.

I took the one next to her. "Who's the Lance of Justice?" I asked.

"The Lance . . . the Lance of Justice?" A hiccup punctuated Sophie's words and a tear trickled down her cheek. She didn't bother to wipe it away. "Jack Lancer. That's his real name. He's on TV. Channel WKFJ. Just like Kim Kline. He's a real celebrity. A star. You know, one of those investigative reporters."

This, I did not know. But then, I'd only just arrived in Hubbard and had yet to have the pleasure of checking out the local news. It did explain the crowd outside.

"So he was a reporter. What was he doing in the restaurant?" I asked Sophie.

She pressed a hand to her heaving chest. "I . . . I can't imagine. I . . . I don't know. I . . . I have no idea."

"Especially since the restaurant was closed."

She nodded. "It has been. Since Saturday after the late lunch crowd left and I locked up. And now it's . . ."

I couldn't hold it against her for not remembering instantly. It's not every day you find a body in your restaurant with your grandfather's receipt spike sticking out of the back of its neck.

"Monday," I reminded her. "It's Monday."

"That means he could have been here . . ." She squeezed her eyes shut, no doubt trying to banish the same image of the Lance of Justice that flitted through my mind. Eyes wide open. Staring. Cold.

Or maybe she was just trying to work out the math. "Do you think he could have been here that long?"

Something told me this wasn't the time to mention that if he had been, the Lance of Justice wouldn't have been in nearly as good shape as he was when we found him. It's not like I'm a forensic expert or anything. Far from it. But Meghan had once starred in a thriller that included espionage and murder and I'd been on the set every day to make sure the food she was served was locally grown and 100 percent organic. I couldn't help but pick up on what the writers went through over and over in regards to the minutiae of the script. Even if I hadn't, I'd seen enough of the crime scene shows on TV. I knew the basics. The Lance of Justice couldn't have been dead all that long. He was well preserved, not swollen, and he didn't smell.

The murder had been recent.

"So how did he get in the restaurant?" I asked no one in particular.

But of course, Sophie was the only one there, and she assumed the question was meant for her. She shrugged. "The police will find out. He must have . . ." She swallowed her tears. "He must have broken in."

"The front door wasn't messed with."

Sophie's gaze darted that way. "It wasn't."

"But we never checked on the back."

"We didn't have time."

"So, for all we know, this Lance character could have broken in." It made sense, at least until I took the thought to the next level. "Why break into an empty restaurant on a Monday night? That seems a little weird."

"Well, he is on TV." This, apparently, was enough of an explanation for Sophie.

It did little to satisfy me.

Before I had a chance to think about it, Detective Oberlin stepped into the waiting area and crooked a finger in my direction. "We need to know which lights were on," he told me. "And if the door was locked when you got here."

Automatically, I nodded. "It was. Sophie unlocked it. And the lights . . ." I thought back to what had happened just an hour earlier. It seemed a lifetime ago. "No lights." I knew this for sure because I had a clear image in my mind of Declan Fury coming in the front door to the waiting area, then peeking into the main room of the restaurant where it was dark. "No lights," I told the detective. "Not until we walked in there and turned them on."

He nodded, but I had no idea what that was supposed to mean. Something told me he wouldn't have bothered to explain even if he'd had the time. The way it was, before he could say another word, a fresh-faced cop poked his head out from the restaurant.

"Hey, Sarge," the cop said, "Lantana says you should come back in here right away. The window on the back door is smashed in. That's got to be how the killer and the victim got in here. But this is weird. The door that leads from the outside directly into the basement has been broken into, too, and it looks like someone was down there trying to swipe the copper."

Detective Oberlin had been taking notes about what I'd told him about the doors being locked and the lights off, and now his mouth pulled into a smug smile. He flipped his spiral-bound notebook closed.

"So that explains it." He tucked the notebook in his pocket. "The Lance surprised someone who was here to steal the copper. The thief knew he'd been seen. He killed the Lance to keep him quiet."

"But what was the Lance doing here in the first place?" I asked him. "And how did he get in? The restaurant's been closed since Saturday. You don't think he's the one who broke in the back door, do you?"

"Huh? What?" Oberlin's shaggy brows veed over his eyes and that smile of his faded in an instant. When he turned to head back into the restaurant, he was grumbling.

And I was left feeling just as confused as I had been since I found the Lance of Justice.

I sat back down next to Sophie, but she was so busy craning her neck to see what was going on out on the street, I wasn't sure she noticed. That is, until she provided the narration to the scene outside the Terminal's front window.

"There's Kitty from the beauty shop," she said, pointing to a woman whose hair was the same honey blond as mine and who was wearing a pink smock. "And that's her husband, Pat. The big guy with the broad shoulders who's standing next to her. Nice people." She slid me a look. "Kitty and Pat Sheedy are Declan's aunt and uncle."

I might have asked what on earth that had to do with anything, especially a murder investigation, but she didn't give me the time. "And there's Kim Kline. She's still here." Sophie rose out of her seat, the better to get a gander at the reporter, who had a microphone in her hand and was back in front of a camera. "I guess I should have been more prepared, huh? But when I knew the camera was filming, well, I just couldn't get any words out of my mouth." She swiveled around in her seat for a better look. "I thought she'd be taller. And look . . ." She pointed to the far end of the dead-end street and a redbrick building with a canvas awning over the front door.

"That's John and Mike from the bookstore." She was referring to two middle-aged men who might have been clones. Both were tall and thin, both had receding hairlines and wore wire-rimmed glasses. They watched the proceedings at the Terminal, worry etched on their faces.

"Carrie's already gone for the day, of course," Sophie

said, turning from the bookstore to look across the street at a place called Artisans All. "The arts and crafts crowd," she confided. "They don't shop late. And then there's Barb and Myra and Bill, of course."

For a moment, I thought I must be imagining things. Was that really perpetually cheerful Sophie sounding as sour as if she'd just bitten a lemon? I looked where she was looking, at the store just to the right of the empty storefront next to Artisans All where three people stood just inside the front door, coffee cups in their hands and their gazes trained on the Terminal.

"Caf-Fiends?" I read the name painted on the front window.

Sophie sniffed. "Stupid name for a coffee shop, isn't it? New in the neighborhood. I don't know about you, being from Hollywood and all, but I have to say, I don't trust people who charge three dollars and fifty cents for a cup of coffee. Three dollars and fifty cents!" Another sniff emphasized her outrage. "It ought to be illegal."

"We're going to have to talk to each and every one of them."

Sometime while I'd been looking out the window, Detective Oberlin and the young cop had come back out to the waiting area, and at the sound of his voice, I turned in time to see the sergeant send a laser gaze around the neighborhood. "Who saw what, where they were, what they know about the deceased. You know the routine. Statements, contact information, blah, blah, blah. And when you're done with that—"

Before he had a chance to finish, the front door of the restaurant opened and Declan hurried over. He crouched down in front of Sophie and took her hands in his.

"I saw the police cars. Is everything all right?"

"Obviously not." I shouldn't have had to point that out, so really, I didn't deserve the condescending little half smile he shot my way.

"Well . . ." Oberlin stepped back, his weight against one foot, and aimed a look at Declan. "Doesn't it figure? There's trouble, and look who's here."

When he got to his feet, that funny little half smile never faded from Declan's face. "Nice to see you, too, Gus. What's going on?"

"A murder, that's what's going on." Since they were pretending I was invisible, I stood up and stepped between Declan and Oberlin. "Some guy called the Lance of Justice."

Declan pursed his lips and let out a long, low whistle. "That ought to stir things up around here."

"You would know." Over my head, Oberlin glared in his direction.

Declan was nearly as tall as the detective, and though he was broad, he wasn't anywhere near as burly. That didn't stop him from trading the cop look for look.

"Just being neighborly," Declan said.

"As always," Oberlin shot back.

"Just like you were neighborly earlier tonight?" I asked, and don't think I didn't notice that this got Oberlin's attention.

He shifted his gaze from Declan to me. "What are you talking about?"

"He stopped in," I said, indicating Declan with the tip of my head. "About an hour ago. Right before we found the body. He said it was because he saw the lights on and he wondered what was going on."

"That would be because I saw the lights on and wondered what was going on." Declan crossed his arms over his chest and his black leather jacket creaked.

"He also said he was going to go back across the street when he left here, but when he did finally leave—"

The clink of metal on metal interrupted me as the paramedics wheeled a cart out the door of the restaurant. There was a black body bag strapped to the gurney, a round hump at the end where Jack Lancer's head was and the squared-off outline of his feet showing at the other end.

Instantly, the TV camera lights outside swung our way and we all squinted.

Except for Sophie. She looked like she was about to be sick.

"I don't suppose there's any way around this," Oberlin grumbled. "Vultures, every one of them."

He opened the door, then stepped back and out of sight of the cameras, allowing the paramedics to leave with the body. The cameras followed the gurney to the ambulance and when they did, Oberlin looked back my way.

"So what was it you were saying?" he asked me.

"I was saying that while you're taking statements, you might want to take his." I didn't have to point to Declan; he was standing right beside me. I looked up at him. "He was here earlier this evening, too. And when he left, he went—"

"I know you've got plenty to do." I would have thought Declan had forgotten me completely, I mean, what with the way he talked to Oberlin as if I weren't there, but his hand clamped over my arm. "And I'm sure you need to talk to Sophie and Laurel some more. But they're going to be in the way here and they don't need this crazy publicity." He tugged me toward the door. "I'll take them across the street and you can be sure I'll keep the newshounds away from them. When you need them, you'll find them over at the Irish store."

Chapter 3

Declan opened the front door of the shop and stepped back to allow first Sophie then me inside.

"Welcome to Bronntanas," he said.

I glanced up at the giant shamrock over the front door. The word he used—one he pronounced *BRON-tuh-nuss*—was nowhere to be seen on the sign.

"It means *gift* in Irish," he told me because he could either read minds or my look at the sign spoke volumes. "That was supposed to be the name of the place. But no one could remember it. Or pronounce it. So everyone just calls it—"

"The Irish store."

We finished the thought together and we might have laughed about it the way people do when they happen upon the same words at the same time if I could have gotten past that image of poor, dead Jack Lancer that was stuck in my head—and of the receipt spike that was stuck in his.

Another memory followed close behind. That one was

of Declan insisting he'd have a look around the restaurant before we found the body. And slipping into the parking lot on the side of the Terminal after Sophie told him we didn't need his help.

Maybe Declan was doing his mind reading thing again and knew exactly what I was thinking, because without another word he made his way down the center aisle of the small, well-lit shop and all the way to a counter where kilts and tams and tweed caps were displayed along with shawls and cabled sweaters. There was an open door behind the counter and when he closed it, I saw the white ceramic sign decorated with green shamrocks that hung from the door: OFFICE.

"What can I get you ladies?" he asked, and when Sophie answered, "Tea, if you have it," he ducked into another back room. While he rumbled around in there and she went to sit at a table next to the small sink and ministove and fridge where he prepared the tea for her, I took the chance to look around.

The Irish store (I'd never remember its real name or pronounce it properly even if I did) had a little bit of everything: jewelry in the front counter, including claddagh rings and brooches along with emerald-studded necklaces and earrings, paintings of quaint country cottages, T-shirts and sweatshirts that featured rainbows and leprechauns, teapots covered with shamrocks, and even a curio cabinet filled with Waterford and Galway crystal along with Belleek pottery.

The shop was spotless. The displays were tasteful and appealing, and there was an interesting mix of handcrafted and kitschy souvenirs.

It didn't strike me at all as the sort of place a man like Declan would work.

"So?" After he delivered Sophie her tea in a mug with a picture of a castle on it, he handed a similar mug to me. "What do you think of Bronntanas?"

"I think having a name no one can remember must cut down on your Internet sales."

I wasn't going for funny, but he laughed. "I don't much care for online sales. I think it's more important for me to get to know my customers, face-to-face. That way, I can learn what they like and help them make their gift choices."

"Like this tea?" I sniffed. The tea was dark and strong, and Declan had added milk to it.

"Let me guess, you like your tea to be herbal. And organic. Am I right?"

He didn't really care, so I figured I really didn't have to answer. Instead, I strolled over to check out a display of pretty painted pottery. "Is this your shop?" I asked him.

"It's a family business." He hadn't bothered with a cup of tea for himself. He leaned back against the nearest glass display case, his arms crossed over his chest. "I just keep things in order."

"So what did that cop mean? When he said when there was trouble, he wasn't surprised to see you around?"

A small smile played around his mouth. "You don't think gift shop managers can get in trouble?"

"I think trouble doesn't track with expensive crystal wineglasses and recordings of Irish folk songs."

"Ah, you've never heard some of the really good, old songs. They're all about trouble!"

A lesser woman might have been distracted by the heat of his smile and the way his eyes—as gray as the marble candleholders displayed nearby—crinkled up at the corners. I was immune. Six years with the Beautiful People will do that to a girl.

"It all must look incredibly boring to you."

There he was, reading my mind again even if he wasn't exactly accurate.

I sipped my tea and found it surprisingly delicious even though I wasn't used to sugar in tea or in much of anything else. "I'll come back someday and do a little shopping."

"But not anytime soon. If I'm not mistaken, the way you and Sophie were going back and forth over at the restaurant, it means you're going to walk out and leave that poor, dear lady high and dry."

I shot a look toward the back room. Sophie was still at the table, her feet flat on the floor in front of her, her eyes closed, her head back, and her hands wrapped around her tea mug.

"What I'm going to do or not going to do really isn't any of your business," I said, shifting my gaze back to Declan. "And your editorial comments aren't going to change my mind."

A lesser man would have taken offense. This one simply smiled. "You heading back to LA?"

I took another sip of tea, the better to try and drown the spurt of anger that exploded inside me when I thought about what Declan did—and didn't—know about me. "How much has Sophie told you?"

"About her wonderful, fabulous niece, Laurel, who she can't seem to ever get tired of talking about? Only that you're some Hollywood big shot. She mentioned some big movie star, but sorry, I'm not much into pop culture so I don't even remember the name. She also mentioned a cookbook. And a TV cooking show. Now, that I could get into. I love those shows where they go to firehouses and let the firemen do the cooking. Or the ones out in the wilderness where the host is forced to eat grubs and berries.

Something tells me that's not the kind of show you're going to be doing."

"I'm not going to be doing any kind of show." This was the truth, and I refused to elaborate. If I did, it would bring back the wave of disappointment that engulfed me every time I thought about how I'd had my dreams snatched out from under me.

"Sophie talks too much," I told Declan instead.

"She's proud of you."

"She has no reason to be."

"Not even the cookbook and the big-time movie star?"

"Ancient history!" Because I couldn't continue to stand there and pretend like it didn't hurt, I turned and strolled to a corner of the shop and a display of Irish-made beauty products.

"This stuff should appeal to you," he said, picking up a bottle with a distinctive blue and white label. "It's made with all-natural botanicals. Sounds like something a California girl would like."

"This California girl has plenty of skin care products, thanks."

"It's made with soy and wild oats," he said, giving the bottle a little jiggle. "Guaranteed to soothe and soften and firm. None of which you need because your skin is perfect."

It wasn't like I hadn't heard my share of compliments in my day. Still, I felt my cheeks heat, and before he could notice, I wandered toward the front of the shop and the windows that gave anyone in the Irish store a bird's-eye view of the Terminal.

The ambulance in which Jack Lancer's body had been placed was gone, but the police cars with their flashing lights were still there. So were the TV trucks and the gawking neighbors.

"Did you know this Lance of Justice guy?" I asked Declan.

He'd followed me to the front of the shop and I knew he was right behind me because I heard his leather jacket scrunch and figured he'd shrugged. "Everybody in this part of Ohio knows the Lance of Justice. He's a TV personality. Well, he was." He paused a moment, no doubt aligning his mind with this new reality. It wasn't *Jack Lancer* is *a TV personality*. Not anymore. From now on, anybody who talked about Jack would use the past tense.

"The Lance of Justice!" Declan's chuckle told me he didn't take the moniker 100 percent seriously. I couldn't blame him. Even to me, coming from LA, where hype was the name of the game and more often than not, people believed their own PR even when they shouldn't have, the name came across as overblown and self-important.

I wondered if the Lance was.

And if that was what got him killed.

"Jack Lancer was always on one crusade or another," Declan explained. "Sometimes, he'd do a story exposing public employees who weren't putting in their full day's work. Or he'd investigate companies that provided shoddy products or workmanship. You know, that sort of thing. Jack was big and loud and pushy. At least that's how he came across on TV. The fearless crusader. He was a publicity hound, too. He'd show up as grand marshal of local parades, or at the openings of stores. A local celebrity. He had a couple charities he backed, too. An animal shelter, the local food pantry. So I guess he wasn't all bad. Even small towns have hometown heroes."

"So do you think that's why someone would want to kill him? Because he was pushy and shamed people on TV?"

"I can't say." Declan stepped up beside me and I looked

up and to my left. From this vantage point, his profile was outlined by the pulsing lights outside. The red and blue flashing lights emphasized his firm chin and a nose that was well shaped and straight enough that some of the actors I knew would swoon with envy. Declan's gaze roved over the knots of people gathered out on the sidewalk, and I looked where he was looking, at the woman in the pink smock and the burly man who slipped his arm around her shoulders.

"Sophie says they're your aunt and uncle."

"Kitty and Pat Sheedy. Salt of the earth. Kitty and my mother are sisters. Pat and my dad . . ." He twitched his shoulders. "They love each other like brothers, but you'd be hard pressed to find two men who were more different."

"Different good? Or different bad?"

Declan laughed. "You'll see." He slid me a sidelong look. "If you hang around long enough."

Rather than get pulled into that conversation again, I watched the two uniformed cops who moved from person to person outside, asking questions and writing down the answers. For all I knew, the police already had a theory about the Lance of Justice's murder, and maybe it really did have to do with someone trying to steal copper out of the restaurant. If that was the case, though, and the theory of the crime was wrapped up in a neat package, those cops outside probably wouldn't have looked quite so worried.

"I imagine a man like Jack Lancer has plenty of enemies," Declan commented.

And I imagined he was right. I finished my tea, and when Declan held out a hand, I gave him the cup.

"What were you doing at the restaurant tonight?" I asked him.

I'd hoped for some other sort of reaction besides a laugh. "Now you sound like the Lance of Justice himself! What were you doing there? Why were you seen? What were you up to?"

"So . . ." I turned so I could face him. "What were you up to?"

"You don't believe neighbors should check on neighbors?"

"I don't believe in coincidences. You just happened to show up when we got there."

"Because you just happened to turn on the lights in the waiting area. Since Sophie isn't usually open late on Mondays, that seemed a little fishy to me."

"As fishy as you wanting to look around the restaurant?"

"I didn't like the idea of two ladies being in there alone after dark."

"Except we weren't alone. There was a dead body in the other room."

"And you think I knew something about it. You think that's why I wanted to get in there before you."

"That's one possible explanation."

"Are there others?"

I cocked my head and considered the question. "If you're the murderer, you might have been worried that you'd left something behind that would incriminate you."

"I hate the thought of being a sloppy murderer!" The way he shook those broad shoulders of his let me know he was kidding, but I didn't let that distract me.

"If you had some idea that the body was there and you aren't the murderer but you have an idea who is . . . well, maybe you wanted to see what you could see of the crime scene before the police showed up. You know, so you'd be one step ahead of them."

"Ah, I like that better. Makes me sound way smarter than I really am."

"Or you might—"

"Have been worried about two ladies all alone in the middle of the night in a closed restaurant. Especially when one of them is older and in pain and the other one is—"

"What?" I asked.

Declan stepped back and as he had over at the restaurant, he gave me a careful once-over. Just like then, he smiled when he was done. "The other one has the prettiest blue eyes I've seen in a month of Sundays, and I bet she knows her way around a kitchen."

It was my turn to laugh. "Is that a prerequisite of some kind with you? A woman has to know her way around a kitchen?"

"It helps. But then, I'm not very good when it comes to cooking. My talents lie in other places."

Oh, I bet they did.

Just like I'd bet that this wasn't the time or the place to think about it.

I nudged the conversation back to firmer ground. "And when you left the Terminal? You didn't come right back here."

The way he spread his hands was almost enough to convince me he was as blasé about the whole thing as he pretended to be. I might have been positive if a muscle didn't jump at the base of his jaw. "Did I say I was going to come right back here?"

"You went around the side of the building."

"I saw something move over there in the shadows and decided to investigate. You know, like the Lance of Justice would have. Turns out it was a cat. Has Sophie told you she feeds the neighborhood cats? And any lost dogs that come around, too. She's got a soft spot for strays."

He was getting a little too personal again, and I refused to be sidetracked. "Back at the Terminal . . ." As if he might actually forget the place I was talking about, I looked across the street. "You didn't like it that I mentioned in front of Detective Oberlin that you showed up earlier."

Declan puffed out a breath of annoyance. "Gus Oberlin is a bully."

"He said when there's trouble, you're always around. That seems pretty odd for a guy whose business is cute little stuffed leprechauns." Since there was one sitting on a pretty carved table nearby, I picked it up and wiggled it in Declan's face.

"Paddy." With one finger, he poked the leprechaun in the stomach. "He's sort of the shop mascot. And like I said, the shop itself, it's not exactly mine. It's a family business."

I patted Paddy on the head and put him back where I'd found him. "Detective Oberlin doesn't like you."

"And I'm not particularly fond of him. Which is why I didn't think you should mention that I'd been to the restaurant earlier tonight. Gus doesn't need any reason to believe things that aren't true."

"Like that you had something to do with Jack Lancer's murder."

Declan grinned. "Do I look like the kind of guy who would get involved in murder?"

"Do I look like the kind of woman who would believe a guy like you, just because you have a terrific smile?"

"Do I?" Yeah, like he hadn't heard that a thousand times from a thousand different women, Declan acted like it was news. "My parents will be thrilled. Seven thousand dollars' worth of orthodontia. But then, I played rugby in high school and college and some of these babies . . ." He pointed at his own wide smile. "Don't spread it around, because I'd hate to disappoint all the other women who think I have a terrific smile, but some of these choppers aren't even real."

I doubted it was true, but it made for a good story.

I wondered how much of everything else Declan said fell into the same category.

I, it should be noted, was not inclined to play such games. In the interest of full disclosure, I brought Declan up to speed. "Detective Oberlin thinks Jack Lancer's murder has something to do with somebody trying to steal copper out of the restaurant."

I thought that, like me, he'd see this as slightly preposterous. But the curse Declan grumbled told me that wasn't so. "Did he say who?"

"Not in front of me."

"He's probably just blowing smoke. Gus has that way about him. You'll see. Or you would, if you were planning to stick around."

"Which I never said I would."

He slid a look toward the back room. "She thought so."

"Sophie's an eternal optimist."

A slow smile brightened his expression. "Maybe she's not the only one."

"Maybe you both need to realize—"

What?

I never had a chance to tell Declan, and it was just as well. At that point, I wasn't sure what Sophie needed to realize except that I didn't appreciate the fact that she'd spent years talking up a fine-dining establishment that didn't exist.

As for Declan, what he needed to realize was a whole different thing.

Fortunately for my soul-searching, we heard a voice call from outside, "Hey, Sarge!" A cop ran out of that side parking lot where I'd seen Declan disappear just a little while before. "We got him, Sarge! We found him hiding in back of the Dumpster. We caught the killer."

The crowd surged forward and before I even realized it, I was out the front door and joining them. Declan was at my side. We pushed our way to the front of the crowd and we were right near the entrance to the parking lot when one of the uniformed cops came out of the shadows. He had a young man with him whose hands were cuffed behind his back.

The kid's shock of flaming red hair looked especially vibrant against a face that was as pale as a vampire's.

"Son of a—" Declan ground the words from between his teeth.

"What?" I looked from the kid to Declan. "What's going on? Who is that?"

"It's Owen Quilligan," Declan growled. "My cousin."

Chapter 4

"It's not much, but it's home sweet home." When I'd picked up Sophie to go to the Terminal, I only got as far as the front door of her house. Now she escorted me through the tiny entryway with its tile floor and hand-hooked rug and into a living room that was about the size of the closet I'd once had at Meghan Cohan's Italian estate.

The walls were a yellow that looked suspiciously like the yellow on the outside of the Terminal. The woodwork was painted white and the carpet had seen better days. My guess was that it used to be sky blue. These days, the color was worn and as tired-looking as Sophie was herself. Then again, it's not often (thank goodness) that a middle-aged woman finds a dead body in her restaurant. I couldn't blame her for the V of worry between her silvery eyebrows or the way her shoulders sagged.

When she shuffled through the living room and dropped her purse on the chair in the dining room, Sophie sighed.

She never even looked at me when she asked, "You're not staying, are you?"

"It's not that I don't want to." I guess I was tired, too. That was the only thing that would explain why I even bothered to try and soften the blow. Me? Worry that dancing around the truth was somehow going to stop reality from crashing down? That was a waste of time.

If there was one thing I'd learned from a lifetime in the system, it was that.

Still, there was something about the way Sophie shuffled into the pint-sized kitchen with its avocado-colored refrigerator that made me stumble over what I knew I had to tell her. "The restaurant is just not what I was expecting, Sophie. It's not what I thought I was getting into. Don't worry, I can still take you to the hospital in the morning, just like I promised I would. I'll just sleep on the couch tonight so I don't mess up a bed or anything."

"Don't be silly." She filled a teakettle and set it on the stove. "I've got your room all ready for you. I bought new curtains and had the room repainted. You know, because I thought you'd be staying the whole time I was gone."

It was my turn to sigh. "You're not going to make me feel guilty."

Her laugh was as weak as her smile. "I'm not trying to. I'm just telling you what I did. Just the facts, plain and simple. When I knew you were coming, I had the room painted. Orange. I thought . . ." She lifted one shoulder. "It seemed like a California color to me."

"I appreciate it. Really." There was a green Formica countertop and a sink along one wall and over the sink, a window that looked out onto a postage stamp–sized backyard. At a right angle to that was the fridge and stove and there was a door next to the fridge that was open just a tad and probably led into the basement. Across from the sink, there was a table big enough to seat two and I dropped into one of the wooden chairs beside it. "Nice paint and new curtains don't change the fact that you lied to me."

Sophie took a plastic container down from the cupboard and popped the top. "Oatmeal cookies?" she asked, holding out the container to me. "They're homemade."

Sweets don't fit in with the healthy lifestyle I advocate, and oatmeal cookies—homemade or not—don't provide anything but empty calories. Then again, on a night that included a dead body, a surly cop, and Declan Fury in all his exasperating glory, empty calories weren't such a bad idea.

I grabbed a cookie.

Sophie took two for herself and put the open container on the table between us, and when the kettle whistled, she poured two cups of tea and came over to the table to sit down.

"I was three years older than Nina," she said. "But Nina was always the one . . ." Sophie tipped back her head. "Nina was *that* girl. You know the one. I bet you met plenty of them in school."

"I never stayed in one school long enough to meet much of anyone," I told her. "At least not until Nina took me in."

"Well, that's just it, isn't it?" Sophie polished off a cookie in three efficient bites before she got up to add sugar and milk to her tea. She would have done the same to mine if I didn't shake my head. After a cookie and the tea I had at Declan's, the last thing I needed was more sugar.

She brought the tea back to the table—hers in a chipped china cup decorated with violets and mine in a mug that said *University of Youngstown Penguins*—and plunked down across from me. "Nina was just that kind of person, the kind who contacts a foster agency for no other reason than that she figured there was a kid out there somewhere who needed a home and some stability in her life."

I guess the bite of cookie I took was a little too big. That would explain why it was hard to swallow. I took a sip of tea. "She was right."

"Nina was right about everything. Oh, I didn't hold it against her!" Sophie laughed. "But she had that way about her. I was the older sister, but more often than not, Nina was the one who taught me what to do and how to act. She was the one with all the boyfriends. She was the one who was a cheerleader and the star of the high school plays. She was the one who joined the debate team just because it gave her something to do, and the swim team because it helped her stay in shape over the winter, and the high school newspaper because that way she could write about sports and meet all the football players." Sophie's smile said it all.

"Nina taught me to color my hair and she showed me the right way to wear lipstick and she took me for my first manicure. She had a spirit that couldn't be contained. I have to admit"—Sophie's cheeks darkened—"I was a little jealous. I always wished I could be more like her, and when she turned nineteen and announced she was moving all the way to California, well, I just couldn't wrap my head around news that momentous. As much as I wanted to be more like Nina, I would never have had the nerve to do something like that. Leave Hubbard! It's never going to happen. The Midwest is in my blood. But not in Nina's. Oh no! She was a real adventurer."

I'd lived with Nina Charnowski from the time I was fourteen until I graduated from high school and aged out of the foster system. She was a kind woman, and she'd taught me to appreciate hard work, good food, and the intricacies of cooking. Nina was the reason I went to culinary school and as I'd told her so many times over the years, I could never thank her enough.

Nina laughed loud and long. She bought bottles of wine she couldn't afford and enjoyed every last drop of every last one of them. She wasn't rich by any means. In fact, I would say she wasn't even financially comfortable. But she dressed well by adding pop to her wardrobe with just a few tasteful accessories.

Nina had style, and she was a good woman. But I'd never thought of her as an adventurer.

"She worked as a cook at Cal's Diner forever," I reminded Sophie. "She never talked about leaving."

Sophie reached for another cookie. "You don't have to wander to be an adventurer. Sometimes"—she tapped her forehead with one finger—"sometimes the adventure is all up here." She took a bite of cookie, swallowed, and washed it down. "So you see, that's why I lied."

"About the restaurant?"

Sophie nodded. "I'd go out to California and visit Nina, and I'd see that she was growing orchids. Or learning tai chi. Or taking tap dancing classes. And I'd feel so . . ." Her lips pinched. "I guess I felt inadequate. I could never measure up. Not to Nina. So when I bought the restaurant, all I told her was that it was a local place. I'm ashamed to admit that I never told her that it was the Terminal. If I did . . . well, the restaurant wasn't exactly first-class, not back when Nina and I used to go there for a bite on weekends. I wanted her to be impressed, and I figured I'd tell her the truth once I got the Terminal up and going the way I wanted it. That . . ." Sophie lifted both hands, then let them fall to her side.

"That just never happened. Every time I got up the

courage to tell her the truth, I realized that if it was her place, the Terminal would have a little more panache. So I'd decide to change something. Or paint something. Or renovate something. And I told myself that when I was finished, then I'd tell Nina that the place I owned was really the Terminal. She died . . ." Sophie cleared her throat. "Poor Nina died before I ever got up the nerve. So you see, when you were living with Nina and I came to visit, rather than show you pictures of the real restaurant—"

"You showed us pictures of the place with the candles and the linen tablecloths."

Sophie leaned forward, her elbows on the table. "I wanted to impress Nina. I wanted to show her I could be as exciting as she always was. So yes, I lied. For years. And lucky for me, Nina never came to town to visit or I would have had to confess. I'm not proud of what I did, Laurel, but I thought you'd understand. Haven't you ever wanted something so bad that you did the same thing?"

I had. In fact, I'd spent most of my life lying, trying to convince foster family after foster family that I was that ideal kid, the one they'd be crazy not to adopt.

"I get it," I admitted, and I don't think it was my imagination; some of the heaviness lifted from Sophie's expression. "But that doesn't mean—"

My words dissolved in a little whoop of surprise when the door next to the fridge popped open.

Sophie laughed. "Oh, that's just my little Muffin," she said." She leaned back in her chair. "Here, kitty. Here, sweet Muffin." When no cat appeared, she looked back my way. "I always leave the basement door open just a tad so she can come and go when she pleases. She must have run down when she heard us come in, and now she was coming up to see me. She didn't recognize your voice, though, and she's a little shy. I'm sure that's why she took off again. Don't worry. Once you're here awhile and she gets to know you better . . . Oh. Well." Sophie's nose twitched and her expression fell. "Never mind. Maybe you'll have a chance to see her before you leave in the morning. She's a darling little thing."

Sophie popped out of her chair and went into the living room. She was back in a flash, holding a framed photograph that she handed to me.

The picture showed a short-haired cat that was either black with white markings or white with black markings. Her face was half-and-half, divided almost exactly down the middle. One front leg was white and that foot was black. The other front leg was just the opposite.

"She's a sweetheart," Sophie said. "So gentle and well behaved. I hope you get to see her because you'll love her, just like I do. Of course . . ." When I put the photograph on the table, I saw that Sophie had her head cocked to one side and her mouth screwed up. "Now that you won't be here, I'll need to find someone to stop in and feed my dear little Muffin. But don't you worry about that!" She reached across the table to pat my arm. "Mr. Butcher down the street might be able to. Except on Wednesdays and Sundays, of course, when he's so busy at his church. Or Joanie Carlyle. She lives that way." She waved toward the backyard. "She might be able to come in the mornings, but I don't know about the evenings. And I would like Muffin checked on at least twice a day. That's the least we can do, don't you think, for the animals we love?"

Since I'd never had a pet, I couldn't say, but rather than be suckered in by the way Sophie's eyes twinkled in a way that told me she was trying to guilt me into staying, I decided to change the subject.

"Do you know that Owen guy?" I asked her.

It took her a moment. "You mean the murderer?"

"Declan told me Owen is his cousin. But his Uncle Pat and Aunt Kitty's last name is Sheedy and Owen's is Quilligan."

"Declan has a lot of cousins."

"And you've never met this one?"

Thinking, Sophie squeezed her eyes shut. "I don't think so. I would remember his red hair. Maybe he's just passing through."

"To steal your copper?"

"That's what the police said, isn't it?"

It was, but something about the scenario just didn't track with me. I considered it for a moment before I said, "I guess I can understand the part about stealing the copper, but why would this Owen character kill Jack Lancer?"

Sophie sniffled. "I guess we'll never know. Poor Jack."

"But what was he doing there?"

"Stealing my pipes, apparently."

"Not him." It was the same question that had been niggling at my brain all night. "This Lance of Justice guy. What was he doing in the Terminal tonight? The restaurant was closed."

Sophie took a minute to think this over, her fingers tap, tap, tapping on the wooden table. "The Lance has been coming in pretty regularly," she finally said. "Over the last few . . ." She thought some more. "I'd say it's been about three weeks. He's been coming in just about every day for three weeks."

"But never before that?"

"Oh no. I'd remember that. Jack Lancer is . . . that is, he was . . . he was a big TV star. Me and Denice and Inez—

Denice and Inez, they're my waitresses—we were just as pleased as punch when Jack showed up the first time. Imagine, having someone like him eating our pie and drinking our coffee! Then he came in the next day and the next and the one after that. I'll tell you what, he created quite a sensation with the regulars. Even had his picture taken with the boys. You know, Stan and Dale and Phil and Ruben, the guys who have lunch at table three every day. That Jack Lancer, he was just the nicest man. And now—"

I saw her tear up and knew if I didn't distract her fast, it would be too late. "How do you suppose he got in? Through that outside back door with the smashed window? And why was he there in the first place?"

Sophie snuffled. "Jack? Tonight?" Though this seemed like a critical piece of the puzzle to me, she had apparently not thought about it before. I could understand; Sophie was dealing with the shock and the surprise. She was intimately connected with the restaurant and since she'd met Jack Lancer and seen him on TV, there was a link there, too. One I did not share. To me, Jack Lancer's death was an interesting puzzler and thinking about it gave me something to do other than worry about where I was headed in the morning when I left Hubbard.

"Well, maybe . . ." Sophie considered my question. "Maybe the Lance of Justice and Owen, maybe they came in together. You know, to take the copper."

Though I had my opinions about how well-off TV reporters working out of stations in Youngstown, Ohio, were, I couldn't imagine one who would stoop to stealing copper to make ends meet. "Besides," I said as if Sophie were in on my thoughts, "if Jack and Owen were in it together, why would Owen kill Jack?"

Sophie laughed through her tears. "You're just as curious

as Nina always said you were!" Her smile settled. "She was very fond of you, you know."

I did, and I still felt guilty that three years earlier, I was in Morocco with Meghan when I heard about Nina's death and I didn't have the time to get back to California for the funeral.

I shook away the thought just in time to see Sophie's face fold into a mask of worry. "I hope people don't think that the Lance died because he was eating in the restaurant." Her voice rose and the words tumbled out and she came out of her chair. "I never thought of that! What if people think the food is bad. Or the place is dirty. Or—"

"All the details will be on the news," I assured her. "They're not going to leave out the part about how the restaurant was closed at the time. That's part of what makes the Lance's death a real mystery."

"Yes, of course. Of course, you're right." Sophie settled back down. "That would be terrible, wouldn't it? I mean, if people thought we did something at the Terminal to kill the Lance of Justice. My goodness!" She fanned her face with one hand. "That would be the most horrible thing. Of course, that might be the least of my worries. I mean, what with the time I'll be spending in the hospital, then the weeks in rehab. And the new coffee place down the street, of course, with their fancy drinks and their fancy sandwiches."

Caf-Fiends.

I rolled my eyes at the very thought.

"By the time I get back to work . . ." Sophie's sigh was monumental. "There probably won't be any work to get back to."

Really?

I bit my tongue, and while I was at it, I stretched a kink out of my back.

"Take another cookie. It will make you feel better," Sophie offered, and when I declined, she popped out of her chair. "Of course, you're tired! You drove a long way today."

I had.

For nothing.

The thought made me feel more exhausted than ever. I went out to the car for my overnight bag and came back in to find Sophie at the bottom of the stairway in the living room.

"Your room is up here," she said. "And there's a half bath, too. You know, so you can have some privacy. My bedroom is downstairs."

Limping, she led the way up the stairs and into a room that wasn't as much orange as advertised as it was cantaloupe. There were white café curtains on the windows and an old-fashioned white chenille bedspread on the double bed.

"You can hang your clothes in here." Sophie opened the door of a closet that smelled like mothballs. "Unless you don't even want to bother. I mean, if you'll be leaving in the morning, anyway. I need to be at the hospital at six and it's in Youngstown. We're going to have to leave early, I'm afraid."

"Not a problem." I plunked my suitcase on the bed. "I'm used to getting up early. Meghan always wanted her vege-table juice before she did her morning run."

"Meghan Cohan!" Sophie's eyes sparkled. "She's so beautiful and so talented."

And so unkind.

I shook the thought away. It might have been easier to keep it there if Sophie didn't ask, "What's she really like?"

"Like you said." How's that for vague? "Meghan is a beautiful woman. And she's plenty talented. She stars in

movies. She directs them. She's got her line of clothing and
yoga products, her perfume, her jewelry line."

"And she promised you a cooking show of your own."

I'd been looking out the window, but when I heard the
sudden metal in her voice, I spun Sophie's way.

She clutched her hands at her waist. "I read all about it.
In the tabloids. You were supposed to have your own
cooking show. Then that Meghan"—Sophie narrowed her
eyes—"she pulled the rug out from under you. Just like that.
The articles, they didn't say why."

"It's complicated." Truth be told, it wasn't. See, Meghan's
sixteen-year-old son had a nasty drug habit. And the media
got hold of the story.

Though it wasn't true, Meghan blamed me for the leak,
and once that happened . . .

Well, let's just say that if there's no fury like a woman
scorned, there's no holy hell like a megastar can create when
she feels she's been done wrong.

That cooking show, the planned cookbook, and my job
went up in a puff of smoke as big and as ugly as the ash
plume rising over a wildfire. As if that wasn't bad enough,
Meghan made sure I got blackballed and stayed blackballed
with her powerful friends who could afford personal chefs
and in every restaurant worthy of my talents.

Which explained Hubbard, Ohio.

And Sophie's Terminal at the Tracks.

And didn't change my mind one little bit about leaving
in the morning.

The thought firmly in mind, I took my cosmetic case over
to the dresser. There was a photo there in a frame studded
with gaudy "jewels" in shades of purple, red, and turquoise.

My stomach clenched. My jaw tightened. I recognized
the frame and the picture in it, and I didn't dare touch it.

Sophie had no such qualms. She grabbed the picture and turned it toward the light so I could get a better look.

"You and Nina." Sophie leaned over my shoulder and pointed at the woman whose crazy, curly hair was barely contained by the red bandanna she wore along with the apron from Cal's Diner. She was standing in front of the grill and I swear, even all these years later, I could smell the aroma of the onions she grilled to perfection and the burgers she piled them on. Before I met Nina, food was nothing more to me than a way to keep my body fueled. Nina had changed all that. She taught me to appreciate good food. She taught me to discipline myself enough to take my time and savor every minute I spent in front of the stove.

"You must have been about fifteen then," Sophie said, shaking me out of my thoughts.

"Fourteen," I corrected her, because I knew for sure that the photo was taken just a week or two after I'd gone to live with Nina, the first time I visited her at work. I'd just come from a placement where my foster parents were more interested in collecting money from the California Department of Social Services than they were in me. I could see the smudges of gray under my eyes, the results of the sleepless nights I spent listening to Bob and Marie argue. My hair was chopped and uneven, an act of defiance I thought would show them that I was my own person. Bob and Marie never noticed.

I looked really close and just as I suspected, I could see that my fingernails were broken down to the quick, the result of me spending a frantic weekend figuring out how to pick the lock on my bedroom door when they went on a jaunt to Vegas and figured I'd be "safer" if I stayed put.

I coughed away the sudden tightness in my throat.

Too bad I bothered, because the ache started all over

again when Sophie pressed the picture into my hands. "She wanted you to have this. Nina told me. You know, right before she died. She said when I saw you next—"

"Thanks." Without another look, I grabbed the photo and tucked it into my suitcase.

"So . . ." Sophie backed toward the door. "Good night, then. I hope you're comfortable tonight."

She didn't wait around long enough for me to tell her I was sure I would be. Sophie left the room and closed the door quietly behind her.

I sat down on the bed and though I tried, I couldn't resist dragging that photograph of me and Nina out of my suitcase.

I'd never cried when I heard Nina was sick or even when she died.

I didn't cry now.

What I did was got up and put the picture back where I'd found it.

I guess that was the moment I realized I'd really done it. I'd changed my mind.

I was staying.

Chapter 5

It was only until Sophie got back on her feet.

I told her that when I drove the twenty minutes from Hubbard to the hospital in Youngstown the next morning, and when I did, I refused to take my eyes off the road so I could pretend I didn't notice the way she twinkled like a beauty queen when she heard the news.

Just to make things perfectly clear, I mentioned it again while we sat in a bland and boring hospital waiting room with Monet posters on the wall, fake flower arrangements on the tables, and a variety of magazines to read, all of them at least three months old.

I would be sure to tell her again—just in case there was any way she could forget—that evening, once the Terminal was closed for the day and I could get back to the hospital and see how she was doing.

I would manage the Terminal only until Sophie was

feeling better. I would stick around only until she was fully recovered and up and well.

Then I was outta there.

It didn't hurt to remind myself, either, and I did just that when I parked my car in the side lot near where the cops had found Owen Quilligan hiding behind the Dumpster, and went around to the front of the building.

Declan Fury was at the front door waiting for me.

"Good morning!"

I dug the key out of my Prada bag. "Aren't you Irish gift shop types supposed to say *Top of the mornin' to ye* or something like that?"

His smile was as bright as the sun just skimming the roof of the boarded-up factory on the other side of the railroad tracks. "Sorry to disappoint you. My family came from Ireland something like a hundred and fifty years ago. We left our Lucky Charms accents back there."

I pushed open the door, but I didn't step inside. "What can I do for you, Mr. Fury?"

"It's Declan, and a cup of coffee would be nice. You do know how to make a decent cup of coffee, don't you?"

Truth be told, I make a stellar cup of coffee. Rather than mention it, I gave him my most sparkling smile. "I thought you were a tea drinker. Brewed in quaint little shamrock-decorated pots, of course, and served in charming mugs."

"That's only when I'm across the street and you know . . ." He gave me a wink and leaned a little closer. Just like it had the night before, the scent of bay rum enveloped me. That had to be the reason I felt a little light-headed, right? "I've got an espresso machine in the back room of the shop. If you're ever needing something a little stronger than tea, you can always stop in. I also happen to stock a nice variety of beer in the minifridge. Maybe some night after the restaurant is closed . . ."

Since he didn't finish the thought and I didn't want to think what that *maybe* might imply, I felt perfectly justified in not answering.

I stepped into the building and Declan followed me. "You're in a good mood for a man whose cousin was arrested for murder last night," I told him.

"Owen didn't do it," he said.

"Then who did?"

"Last night, you suggested that it might have been me."

"It was just a theory."

"And not a very good one." He closed the door behind us and we stood side by side in the waiting area.

"I can take a look around the restaurant if you like," Declan suggested.

"Just like you wanted to look around last night."

"Which doesn't make me a murder suspect."

"But it does make you look awfully suspicious."

He shot me a sidelong glance. "Truth?"

I wasn't sure this was the time or the place so I hesitated, and when I did, he took it to mean I wanted to hear more.

"I figured the kid might be in trouble," he said. "Owen, that is. He's from South Carolina, here to visit Kitty and Pat and the rest of the family."

"And you just naturally assumed that while he was in town, he'd be stealing the copper pipes from local establishments?"

"Owen is something of a hell-raiser. Always has been."

"And you wanted to keep him out of trouble."

"Keeping Owen out of trouble isn't always possible, but I wanted to try."

"And now he's been arrested for murder."

Declan muttered a word I couldn't hear but I could pretty well imagine. "Owen is a stupid kid and he was doing a stupid thing. There's no denying that. But the police don't have anything to connect him to the murder."

"Maybe he's too smart for that."

Declan chuckled. "You haven't met Owen." He stuffed his hands in the pockets of his leather jacket. "Even without any solid evidence, they're going to try like hell to get a conviction," he grumbled. "Gus Oberlin will see to it. Gus likes things wrapped up nice and quick. He sees one theory of a case and runs with it, even when he's running in the wrong direction."

I strolled over to the rolltop desk. "And you think that's what he's going to do this time."

"Absolutely. Gus is going to steamroll his way through this case. I just need to make sure that when he does, he doesn't flatten Owen in the process. You'll see I'm right. Owen might be a goofball, but he's not a killer."

I wanted to believe him. Not because I had any opinion— good or bad—about Owen Quilligan. As Declan said, I didn't know the kid. Still, I didn't like the thought of a young guy like Owen spending the rest of his life in prison. I didn't like the thought of Jack Lancer being dead, either. Or of finding bodies in restaurants. Dead instead of diners. Not a pretty thought.

I twitched it away and I'd already started through the doorway that led into the restaurant when Declan stopped me, his hand on my arm. "Don't you want me to go in there before you?" he asked.

I laughed. "What do you think's going to happen, the Lance of Justice's ghost is going to get me? Or do you think I'm one of those women who will dissolve into tears just looking at the place where the awful deed happened?"

One corner of his mouth twitched. "You're not?"

"I don't have the time. And I don't have the disposition.
So if you're waiting for tears, you're going to wait a long,
long while. It doesn't bother me to think that Jack Lancer
died here. I didn't know him. And I have no real connection
with the Terminal, either, so it's not like I think the murder
has somehow affected the ambience." I didn't mean to sigh.
Honest. But when I glanced around, I couldn't help myself.
"Let's face it, there's not much ambience around here to
begin with."

"Oh, I don't know." His lips pursed, Declan looked
around, too. "It's a throwback to another era and a time when
Hubbard was hopping. You know, before the factories closed
and the companies packed up and headed to warmer
climates. The place is charming."

"Are you looking at what I'm looking at?" Of course he
was, and of course he wasn't going to admit that he saw past
the lacy facade to the tiredness beneath. And even if he was,
I wasn't going to stand there and listen. I walked through
the lace-curtained doorway and into the restaurant.

Just like the night before, there were no lights on in there,
but this morning with the sun streaming through the
windows that looked out at the railroad tracks, Sophie's
Terminal at the Tracks was washed with golden light.

Sure, in a better, more perfect world (or maybe in a
Hallmark Channel movie), the sunlight would have accented
the Terminal's hominess, softening the rough edges of the
place and gilding everything from the yellowed lace over
the windows to the grainy black-and-white photographs of
trains and railroad workers that hung on the walls. It would
have made the dust motes that floated in the air into
sparkling fairy dust.

In reality, all the light did was accent the gouges in the

old floorboards, the smudges on the old wooden tables, and the fact that the windows needed washing. Badly.

"I can hang around until George shows up." Until he spoke up, I hadn't realized Declan had come to stand right behind me. Which was a funny thing, really, because anytime he was anywhere within five feet of me, I could feel the air heat between us as if tiny sparks of electricity crossed from him to me on invisible wires. "George, he's your cook," he added when I didn't respond to his offer. "Denice and Inez are—"

"The waitresses. I know." I spun away from the window. Too bad. Had I stood there a moment longer, I might have seen the freight train coming.

It rolled by not twenty feet from where I stood, and, startled, I gasped.

"People love it." Declan raised his voice to be heard over the rush of the train. "A lot of them come here just to see the trains."

Through the wall of windows at the back of the Terminal, I watched car after car streak past, fast enough to send a buzz of vibration through the old floorboards and just slow enough for me to see the brightly colored gang tags that had been painted on the sides of one car after another.

"Denice and Inez usually get here . . ." Declan pulled his cell phone out of his pocket and checked the time. "They'll be here by seven. Denice is usually first through the door."

I turned from the windows and the train smoothly streaking by and headed for the kitchen. "And you're usually up and going this early, too?"

He scrubbed a hand across the dusting of whiskers on his chin. "Actually, I haven't been home. Been dealing with the cops. And Owen, of course. Kid's got a head as hard as a coconut."

I pushed open the swinging door that led into the kitchen.

"I can't imagine there was anything for you to eat at the police station."

"There's a vending machine and, hey, I'm used to Fritos at three in the morning."

I glanced over my shoulder at him. "Spend a lot of time in police stations, do you?"

"Unfortunately, yes."

The kitchen was small, but thankfully tidy, and there was a coffeemaker on the stainless steel counter between an oven and a deep fryer. First things first: I got the coffee going, then checked out the walk-in cooler at the far end of the room. "How do you like your eggs?" I called out to Declan.

"Over easy, if it isn't too much trouble."

I got the grill started and found a loaf of bread and popped a couple slices into the toaster.

"You're not a vegan?" he asked, watching me crack the eggs. "Organics only? I expected more from a California girl than fried eggs and white toast."

"I'm used to cooking whatever my employer wanted to eat."

"So what do Hollywood stars eat?"

I grabbed a spatula and flipped the eggs. "Meghan's taste in foods depended on her moods. And on what just happened to be the latest food fad. So yeah, we went through a vegan phase, and we went all organic for a while, too. Superfoods, gluten free, Indian. You name it, I've cooked it."

"So you'll fit right in here." Declan grabbed a menu from a nearby stack and flipped it open. "Burgers and fries. Fried bologna. Swiss steak. Rice pudding. I happen to love Sophie's rice pudding, by the way, so if there's ever any left over, I'll be happy to take it off your hands." He slapped the menu closed and returned it to the pile so he could take a plate from me with three perfectly cooked eggs on it, and when he did, he breathed in deep and whispered a few words I couldn't hear under his breath. "Thank you," he added.

"No problem." I dished up the eggs I'd scrambled on the other side of the grill for myself and leaned back against the counter to eat. "So why did you come back here this morning?" I asked him.

He'd just taken a bite of toast and he chewed and swallowed before he answered. "You don't believe in being neighborly?"

Okay, I take it back. That really wasn't an answer.

I polished off a couple more bites of eggs. "You want to have a look around."

"There could be something the cops missed."

"Something that will prove Owen didn't do it."

He sopped up egg yolk with a piece of toast. "He didn't. And so if you'd just let me look things over . . ."

I finished my eggs, then took his plate and mine, and set them in the sink. "Be my guest," I told him. "While you're at it, maybe you'll be able to figure out what Jack Lancer was doing here last night."

"It is kind of freaky, isn't it?" I poured coffee and, mug in hand, Declan led the way out of the kitchen. Together, we stepped into the restaurant and walked over to the table where I'd found the Lance of Justice's body less than twelve hours earlier.

According to the phone call Sophie had gotten from Gus Oberlin before she went in for her surgery, the cops had stayed at the restaurant until the wee hours of the morning, checking every nook and cranny, dusting for prints, and generally leaving the basement, the back door, and the area around where Jack Lancer had spent his final moments a mess. They were done with the crime scene phase of the investigation, Gus told her. There wasn't much left to do except get a confession out of Owen and move on.

I set my coffee on a nearby table so I could prop my fists on my hips and look at the trails of fingerprinting dust some careless technician had left on the floor, the tables, and the nearby chairs. "We'll need to clean."

Declan wasn't listening. With a look, he asked which table Jack was sitting at, and when I pointed, he cocked his head and did a slow circumnavigation of the table. "Facedown or faceup?" he asked me.

It didn't take long for me to catch on to what he was talking about. Some things—like corpses—are hard to forget. "Facedown. On the table. On his arm." I put my forearm to my forehead to demonstrate.

"Blood?"

"Not much." I didn't add *thank goodness* because then Declan would think I really was one of those women who dissolve into tears, when actually I was thinking more blood would have meant getting a professional cleaning crew in there. I closed my eyes and pictured the scene the way I'd discovered it the night before. "The blood had trickled down the back of his neck," I said, demonstrating the path with one finger against my own neck. "It soaked into his shirt collar."

Declan steepled his fingers and tapped his top lip, his gaze moving from the table to the nearby windows that looked out at the street and the Irish store.

"Not the smartest place to kill somebody," he said.

"Because someone could have seen something." I nodded. "You were in your store. Did you notice anything?"

"We were closed for the day, and I was back in the office doing paperwork. Even if somebody came to the restaurant— and they obviously did—there's no way I could have seen anything."

"But you knew when Sophie and I got here."

It wasn't my imagination—his shoulders did get rigid. "I did," he admitted. "But only because I happened to go up to the cash register to check on the day's receipts and I saw the lights turn on."

It was certainly an explanation. And a mighty convenient one at that. I told myself not to forget it and said, "There were no lights on when we got here. Which means Jack Lancer was here in the dark."

"In the dark. With a killer." Declan gave this some thought. "It doesn't make a whole lot of sense."

"It does if Jack and whoever he was with didn't want to be noticed. But why here?" As if it might actually help me make sense of the situation, I looked all around, but there was nothing in the faded decor that explained why a TV reporter would break into the Terminal in the middle of the night. "Why did you think Owen might be here?" I asked Declan. "I mean, besides the fact that he's a troublemaker. Why here?"

Declan walked along the front of the restaurant. Here, there were three tables in front of the windows that met the wall of the waiting area. There were another two tables against that wall and two more across from them. The one nearest to where I stood was where I'd found Jack. Just like in the larger part of the restaurant, there were more posters on the walls here, more photographs, and an old railway timetable that had been matted and framed. When Declan got as far as the waiting room wall, he swung around and came back the other way.

"The last place I saw Owen yesterday—I mean, before I saw him being led away in handcuffs—was at Kitty's," he said. "That was around six in the evening. He'd spent the day with me over at the shop unloading a truck and helping me check in some new inventory. He was supposed to leave

my place, stop and say good night to Kitty, then go to my
parents' for dinner, and when he didn't show up, my mother
called. She was not a happy camper. She'd made salmon
because she knows it's Owen's favorite and she said the meal
was time-sensitive and that's why she was worried, but I
knew the real reason she called. She knew Owen not
showing up meant he was in some kind of trouble. He's that
kind of kid. I walked down the street and didn't see any sign
of him in any of the other shops. Honestly, I thought he
might be out boosting cars. Or doing some serious underage
drinking. When I saw you and Sophie come into the Terminal, I wondered if you'd gotten a call about a break-in and
I figured it was worth checking to see what was up."

"Owen must have still been hanging around when Sophie
and I got here." This was a no-brainer, but I mentioned it
anyway. Talking through the scenario helped me keep it
straight in my head. "Otherwise the cops wouldn't have
found him hiding out back."

"Agreed."

"And Owen admits he was here for the copper?"

Declan made a face. "Owen doesn't admit anything. But
he doesn't deny it, either."

"Did he happen to say if he ever came inside the
building?"

"He said he might have taken a look around. His words
exactly, 'I *might* have taken a look around.'"

It was all I needed to hear. I started back to the kitchen.

When I found the door that led into the basement, Declan
was right behind me. There was an old umbrella stand in
front of the door and I tried to lift it and realized that it
weighed a ton. Together, Declan and I dragged it to one side
and scrambled down the steps.

According to the historical marker sign out front, the

Terminal was built in 1889 and my guess is that nobody had bothered to update—or for that matter, clean—the basement since. It was a big, rectangular room built from huge sandstone blocks that held in the cold and the moisture.

I shivered and hugged my arms around myself and the leopard-print top I'd worn that day with black pants.

There were narrow windows at ground level and shelving along every one of those walls. The shelves were mostly empty and there were boxes and discarded restaurant equipment here and there on the floor. Most of it looked as if it had spent the better part of my lifetime right where we found it. I skirted a coffee urn and a piece of copper tubing that had been dropped nearby and made my way over to the deeper shadows along the far wall. Just as I suspected there would be, there was a stairway there, and at the top of it, a door that led to the outside. The window in the center of the door was broken.

"That's got to be how he got in," Declan said. "And don't think Gus didn't notice it. I'm sure they took pictures, and see"—he pointed to smudges on the wall—"they dusted for prints down here, too. Owen doesn't have the brains God gave a goat. He'd never think to wear gloves. I have no doubt some of those prints belong to him. With that bit of information, Gus will have no problem making a case for Owen leaving here, going upstairs, and killing Jack."

"Really?" I looked at him long and hard and when that didn't work, I pointed back toward the stairway where we'd come down. "You think he really broke into the basement, started taking the copper, left it where he dropped it, then broke into the back door upstairs so that he could kill Jack Lancer? That seems awfully complicated."

"Like I said, Owen's not the brightest bulb in the box. Maybe he just came up the basement steps and—"

"Did you see that old umbrella stand in front of the door that leads down to the basement from the kitchen? No way Owen opened the door from this side with that thing in front of it."

"Unless he put it back when he was done."

"From this side of the door?"

"You're right." Declan pulled out his phone and headed back to the stairway. Upstairs, he slid the umbrella stand back where we'd found it and took a few photos.

"You'll sign an affidavit, right? I mean, if Gus asks. You'll say that the umbrella stand was—"

"Right there. Right where you just put it. Yes, of course. When we came in, that's exactly where it was."

"Great!" He sent the pictures he'd just taken over to Gus Oberlin and while he was at it, I strolled back into the restaurant.

The first thing I did was swipe a doily off the closest shelf where it shared space with a doll dressed in Victorian clothing.

Too many knickknacks and too little ambience, and a menu that if what Declan had read to me about burgers and rice pudding meant anything, lacked not only imagination but any food actually worth eating.

And none of it mattered, I reminded myself, dropping into the nearest chair.

Because I was staying until Sophie was better and then I was gone.

Where?

I had no idea, but I knew it wasn't going to be Hubbard, Ohio.

Or the Terminal at the Tracks.

As far as I could see, the restaurant was as terminal as its most famous customer.

Chapter 6

When I heard a sharp rap on the front door, I hurried through the restaurant and into the waiting area.

Face pressed to the glass.

Beady blue eyes.

Scrunched-up nose.

I might not know local news, but I'd recognize Kim Kline anywhere.

Apparently, so would Declan.

Though I hadn't realized he'd followed me, he reached around me, yanked open the door, and barked, "Ms. Inwood has no comment."

Really?

I wedged myself between Declan, the door, and Kim, who had retreated and was toeing the line between the front walk and the restaurant. "I can tell her that myself," I grumbled, before I turned to the reporter and said, "Ms. Inwood has no comment."

"But—"

Whatever she was going to say, I cut off Kim when I shut the door.

"I don't need a keeper," I said, and I marched through the waiting area and back into the restaurant. If Declan and I were going to go at it, the last thing I needed was a media audience. I made sure we were far from the front windows before I turned to him. "I can take care of myself. Which means I could have told her myself that I had nothing to say."

"You did tell her, and you handled it well." How Declan could stand there and smile when my blood pressure was about to shoot through the roof was a mystery to me. "I forgot you had the whole Hollywood thing going for you. Apparently, you've stared down the paparazzi a time or two."

"Or three or a dozen or a hundred times." I didn't need the reminder of my former life. Not when my current life was turning out to be so complicated. When we looked over the crime scene earlier, I'd left my coffee cup on one of the tables, and I snatched it up and again walked far enough away from the windows to be sure Kim couldn't see us, even with her nose pressed to the glass. I held the coffee cup in both hands against my chest. It wasn't much in the way of a shield but only an idiot could miss the symbolism. I doubted very much that Declan was an idiot, but just in case, I thought it only fair to tell him, "I don't like pushy men."

"Neither do I," he confided. "Though I do confess I have something of a soft spot right about here"—he laid a hand over his heart—"for pushy women."

I bit back the reply I was tempted to hurl at him and matched him smile for smile. "Well, then, it's a good thing I'm not a pushy woman, isn't it?"

"Jury's still out on that." He laughed and his eyes sparkled with way more mischief than anyone should have been able to muster at that time of the morning. "I'm not about to pass judgment, because I don't know you well enough. Not yet, anyway."

I puffed out a sigh of frustration. Or maybe I was just trying to catch my breath. "You're exasperating."

"And you're intriguing." He took a couple steps back, the better to look me over as he had a time or two before. This time, just like those other times, heat raced up my neck and into my cheeks. "When are we going to have dinner together?"

I hesitated. But then, being blindsided will do that to a girl.

"I'm free tonight," Declan said.

I shook myself back to my senses. "I've got to go to the hospital tonight. To check on Sophie."

"Tomorrow, then." He turned and headed for the door and called back over his shoulder, "Unless you still think I'm a murderer!"

"I never said you were a murderer. I only said it was a possibility. And I didn't agree to dinner," I added. I shouldn't have bothered. By the time I got to the front door, Declan was already out on the sidewalk and ignoring her when Kim Kline scrambled over, tape recorder in hand.

"Pushy and exasperating," I grumbled.

That is, right before I smiled.

Just in case Declan might see, I spun away from the door.

And spun around again when there was another tap on the window.

This time when I grumbled, it had nothing to do with the handsome gift shop manager. I opened the door a crack. "Really, Ms. Kline, there's nothing I can tell you about Jack Lancer and even if there was—"

Like a bolt out of the blue, an idea hit. I was being perfectly truthful; there was nothing I knew about the dead TV star.

But that didn't mean Kim Kline didn't know plenty.

I swallowed my words, and when I opened the door I took a step back so she could walk into the restaurant. "Would you like a cup of coffee?" I asked her.

Don't worry, I hadn't forgotten the pledge I'd made to myself the night before: I would stay far away from the cameras, and there was no way I'd let myself be quoted and thus end up with my name plastered in the newspapers and on the Internet.

"This is off the record," I told her before she could open her mouth and say a word. "If you promise not to quote me—"

"You're an anonymous source." Kim actually crossed her heart with one finger. "I appreciate your help. This is the most exciting thing that's happened around here in a long time. Jack and I worked together, and when I got this assignment . . ." Her cheeks flushed. "Well, this is the biggest break I've had in my career. Anything you can tell me will put me one step ahead of the competition."

I led the way into the kitchen and when we got there, I dumped my cold coffee, refilled my coffee cup, and poured a nice, hot cup for Kim.

"So what do you think Jack was doing here?" Kim asked.

"I was about to ask you the same thing."

She flinched. "You mean you don't know? You mean . . ." As if she might actually see something interesting in a kitchen that was so far out of date I wondered how anyone could cook anything in it, she looked around at the fryers and the grill, at the tiny salad prep station, and out the pickup window where Sophie's one and only cook passed food through to the servers. "Do you believe what the police are saying, that Jack Lancer actually broke into the restaurant with the guy they arrested, the one who was stealing copper in the basement?"

I didn't think it fair to reveal what Declan and I had already determined. Someone broke into the basement, all right. But chances were, that someone wasn't Jack. Whoever was downstairs had never come upstairs. Which meant Jack couldn't have gotten up here from down there and the person who was down there—Owen—could never have been up here. Jack must have come in through the back door. But why? And if he was with Owen, why wouldn't the two of them just come in together?

I finished my coffee and set down my cup. "Do you believe it?" I asked Kim.

"The kid could have been desperate," she suggested.

"Desperate enough to kill? To cover up his copper stealing?" I shook my head. "Even if he was, from what I saw of Owen Quilligan, he was young and fit. Jack would have been no match for him. To me, that means if he ran into him and wanted to keep him quiet and get away, the kid could have punched Jack in the nose and run. Or whacked him with a piece of copper tubing, knocked him out cold, and gone on stripping the copper out of the building. But he didn't. He didn't even finish stealing what he started to take. The kid is the one who ran, and he left the copper where he dropped it. Seems to me, the question has to be why."

A new thought hit me. "Did he carry a weapon?" I asked Kim.

"Jack?" She had just taken a sip of coffee, and she swallowed so hard, I heard the gulp. "I don't think so. I don't think . . ." She made a face. "That just doesn't seem like the Jack I knew. And even if he did carry a weapon, why would he bring it here to your restaurant?"

Just hearing the words, a prickle of annoyance shot over the back of my neck. "If you're going to get your anonymous source right, you can start there," I told her. "It's not my restaurant."

"Of course not. You're not Sophie. Not that I know her or anything," she added. "Until I was assigned Jack's story, I'd never been here before. I mean, why would I be? It's not like it's a dinner destination. I mean, for anyone."

She was working her first big story so I guess she was allowed to be a little nervous and a little thoughtless, too, so I cut her a little slack.

A little was all I ever cut anybody.

"So what kinds of stories was Jack working on?" I asked Kim.

Her shrug was noncommittal. "From what I could see when I went back to the station last night and looked through his files, just the usual. Something about school cafeteria lunches not being nutritional enough. Something about the local food bank Robin Hood, too, though that file was so slim, I have a feeling it was initiated by a tip and then Jack discovered there really was nothing to the story. I mean, really, how interesting could it possibly be to do a story about somebody who leaves anonymous donations at the St. Colman's food pantry now and again?" It wasn't and Kim knew it—that's why she rolled her eyes. "There was a file about some car repair place, too, a shop on the other side of town that charges for parts they don't really install."

"Nothing about the Terminal at the Tracks."

Another shrug told me all I needed to know.

"So why Jack? Why here?"

"Maybe . . ." Kim finished her coffee and set her cup on the stainless steel counter. "Maybe he was just in the wrong place at the wrong time. Maybe the cops are right. He ran into that Quilligan kid and the kid killed Jack to keep him quiet."

"If that's true, it would be the wrong time, but what about the place? It was a place he had no business being."

Since this was obvious, Kim didn't bother to answer. Fine by me. That gave me a chance to ask, "Could he have been meeting someone?"

Kim's cheeks paled. "Like the Quilligan kid?"

"Forget the Quilligan kid!" I controlled my temper. Just barely. It wasn't Kim's fault that I knew about the umbrella stand and she didn't. "Let's try out some other theories," I suggested from between gritted teeth. "You know, just in case the cops find out they're wrong about Owen."

I guess Kim had never even considered the possibility, because she wrinkled her nose and cocked her head. "Okay." She didn't sound sure of this at all. "So let's start with Jack's files. The school cafeteria story . . . You people here at the Terminal, you don't have anything to do with the food provided to the local school district, do you?"

As far as I knew, the restaurant didn't, and I told her so. Right after I reminded her—again—that I was not in any way, shape, or form to be included in the "you people."

"Then what about the church food pantry?" Kim's nose twitched. Since it was such a big nose, it was hard to miss. "If you donate leftover food—"

"We do. That is, the restaurant does," I corrected myself. This anonymous source wanted to make sure she stayed clear of any close association with the restaurant. After all, she wasn't sticking around. "Sophie told me that on Fridays and Saturdays, any food that's left over goes to the homeless shelter downtown. And she says if there's ever any canned goods that are about to expire, she sends them to the food bank because she knows that over there, they'll give them out right away and the food won't be wasted. I can't imagine knowing something like that is the kind of thing that gets a man killed."

That morning, Kim had her glossy ringlets pulled back into a ponytail. She was wearing the same black suit she'd worn the night before when she tried to push her way into the restaurant, and now that I thought about it, it was probably because she'd been working nonstop since she heard Jack was dead; she hadn't had a chance to change.

That would explain why there were bags under her eyes, too. And why Kim put a hand to her mouth and yawned.

"Sorry." She apologized instantly. "It was a long night."

"Then you're probably anxious to get going." I led the way out of the kitchen and, as weird as it seems since I was reluctant to let Kim in, now I hated to see her go. She hadn't told me anything, not anything useful, anyway.

Maybe she was feeling the same way about me.

Kim paused outside the kitchen door. "Can you show me . . ." Her eyes positively gleamed when she glanced around. "Can you show me where he . . . I mean, where it . . . Sorry!" As if to gauge whether I was thinking less of her, she gave me a quick look. "I've never worked a murder before. Could you show me where the body was found?"

As far as I could tell, it wouldn't hurt. And it would give me a few more minutes to question Kim.

I led her to the part of the restaurant where those few tables were wedged between the front windows and the wall of the waiting area. From there, it was really a no-brainer to determine where Jack had been killed; the table, the chair, and the floor around both were still sprinkled with fingerprint powder.

"Oh, right here!" With two fingers, Kim touched the back of the chair where Jack had spent his last moments on earth. "Was there a lot of blood?"

I hoped my quick smile told her this was something I would rather not discuss. "I'm sure it's all in the coroner's report."

"And you can be sure I'm going to get my hands on that as soon as I can, but until then—"

I headed her off at the pass. "Until then, tell me about Jack. We've talked about how he might—or might not—be somehow connected with Owen Quilligan. We've talked about the stories he was working on. But what about him? What kind of person was this Lance of Justice?"

Kim's shoulders shot back just a tad. She stood a little straighter. When she spoke, even her voice was different. It rang with conviction, like she was in front of the TV cameras.

"Jack Lancer was a mainstay of this community. A man of integrity and mettle. He stood up to corruption. He refused to back down from controversy. He was a hero."

"Great. Fine. Wonderful." I waved away her words at the same time I swiped at a dust mote that floated by. "But what kind of person was he?"

She gave me a sidelong glance. "Truth?"

"I wouldn't expect anything less from you."

Kim leaned nearer. "Professionally, Jack had it all going for him. He'd been at the station for, like, forever, and he had all the perks that went with his job. You know, wardrobe allowance, primo parking spot, more days off than anybody else on the reporting team."

"And were the other reporters jealous?"

She thought about this for a moment. "I don't think so. I mean, most of us, we weren't even born back when Jack started at WKFJ. And most of us . . ." One corner of her mouth pulled tight. "There aren't many people who are happy staying at the first station where they get a job after college."

"Like you."

"Like anybody who has an ounce of ambition. Don't get me wrong, I'm grateful for this opportunity at the station. But I've got bigger plans. You know, bigger markets. Network news. There must have been hundreds of reporters who've come and gone since Jack started at the station. And I can't imagine any of them were jealous of a guy who sank into a rut and settled there. They all moved on. Just like I'm going to do."

"Which makes me wonder why Jack never did."

"Hey, the guy was a hometown legend. He cut the ribbons when buildings were opened, and he wrote books that were published by some small, local press. You know, about his exploits as an investigative reporter. He even had a wall calendar he sold every year and he donated the money to charity. The Lance Gives Back, he called it. Corny, but people around here, they loved it. So why would he move somewhere else? Big fish, small pond. The Lance liked being the center of attention and he got plenty of it around here."

"So the guy was at the top of his profession. You still haven't told me what he was like, personally, I mean."

"Personally?" Kim picked a thread from the skirt of her black suit. "Well, I didn't know him all that well. I mean, why would I? This is my first job since I graduated from Kent State. But I'll tell you what . . ." She looked left and right and out the front window. A TV sound truck from another station had just pulled up and as if there were any chance the people inside could hear, Kim lowered her voice.

"Professionally is one thing. But I hear that personally, Jack was a scumbag."

This was something. At least more something than the nothing I'd already gotten from her. I inched nearer and lowered my voice, too, the better to make it seem as if we were trading confidences. Would she open up? I was about to find out.

"A scumbag, like a scumbag who cheats on his taxes? Or shoplifts in the grocery store? Or—"

"Women." Kim's lips pinched. "A couple ex-wives, a couple girlfriends and, from what I heard, the wives and the girlfriends all happened at the same time. If you know what I mean." She winked.

"So you think one of them might have a motive to kill Jack?"

"You mean, if this Owen guy didn't do it." She considered this for a moment before she scooted a little closer. "There were plenty of fights. And I'm not just saying that because I got some information from somebody who knew somebody who knew somebody. I heard a couple of them myself. You know, the phone would ring in Jack's office and he'd pick it up and the fireworks would start."

"Who was he fighting with?"

"From what I heard, it had to be one of the exes. It was always all about money. How Jack still owed and Jack didn't pay and Jack had to abide by the decisions of the court. Only of course . . ." She looked away. "Of course, I didn't hear that part of the fight because that's the stuff the woman on the other end of the phone would be saying. I filled in the blanks. You know, the way you do when you're in on only one side of the conversation. Over in my cubicle, I only heard the fights from Jack's side of the phone. So I guess technically—I mean if I was reporting what I heard—I'd have to say it was more like Jack didn't owe a dime, Jack always paid on time, and he followed the letter of the law, well . . . to the letter!"

"You heard more than one fight like that?"

"Absolutely. But then, like I said, there's been more than one Mrs. Jack Lancer. I have no idea which of them he was fighting with."

"So at least one woman was angry with him." I made a mental note of this and I couldn't help myself, it brought back memories of all the high-powered, high-visibility, high-voltage Hollywood marriages I'd watched dissolve. Meghan's friends were a lot like Meghan herself: self-centered to the max. When their relationships imploded there was fallout of epic proportions.

I found myself thinking about the time an actor famous for playing superheroes (I'm not going to name names) showed up on our doorstep in Tuscany drunk as a skunk and crying like a baby.

Or the woman with three Oscars to her name who was so screwed up after her husband dumped her for a younger, more beautiful woman that she disappeared for six months and was found wandering the streets of LA and sleeping under a bridge. No, that story didn't make the tabloids. But then, the actress had a PR agent who was obviously worth his weight in golden statuettes.

Love did crazy things to people's brains.

Love gone bad only made things worse.

Suckers.

If they'd learned like I had—early on and with constant reinforcement—that nothing lasted forever, maybe they wouldn't have taken it all so personally.

Maybe Jack's ex-wives wouldn't have had those screaming matches with him on the phone.

"It really doesn't make sense, though," I said, more to myself than to Kim. "If one of those women was mad at Jack for not paying what he owed in alimony or child support . . . Well, he for sure couldn't pay if he was dead."

Something told me Kim had already thought of this. "I'm looking into his will," she told me. "You know, for my story. Jack, he didn't strike me as that stupid, but you never know, do you? If he married one wife and never took the other wife off as the beneficiary in his will—or of his life insurance policy—well, that would be a pretty good motive for murder, wouldn't it? I mean, if that Quilligan kid really didn't do it."

It would.

But not murder in a closed train station restaurant.

"Well, it looks like you're going to be plenty busy tracking down suspects." I ushered Kim to the door. "I'm sure you'll need to look into Owen's background, and then there are all those wives and girlfriends of Jack's. What did you say their names were?"

Her smile was as stiff as meringue. "I didn't. And I'm not going to. Not until I confirm my information and my sources. And not until the cops eliminate Quilligan as a suspect. It wouldn't be ethical, would it, to go chasing off after some grieving woman when there's no reason."

Ethics and local news?

I was stunned.

But not as stunned as I was when Kim opened the door, stopped, and turned to me one last time.

"You know," she said, "if you're looking for viable suspects, there's one you shouldn't eliminate from the list. In fact, I'd say his name would have to be right at the top."

"Somebody else?" I was thinking that it might have been easier to ask Kim who liked Jack rather than who had reason to want him dead. "Who? And for what reason?"

"It's my turn to be an anonymous source." Grinning, she stepped outside. "Just ask your cook."

Chapter 7

My cook was George Porter, who appeared at exactly the stroke of seven and filled the front door top to bottom and side to side. George had hands like hams and enough tattoos on his arms to cover nearly every inch of skin. Just for the record, that was a lot of inches.

Even though I insisted on "Laurel," he called me "ma'am," and when we spoke, he looked at the floor, the ceiling, and the train that whizzed by on the tracks out back. Anywhere and everywhere but at me.

I never had a chance to ask him what Kim was talking about when she dropped his name in connection with the late, great Lance of Justice because Denice Lacuzzo showed up hot on George's heels and as soon as she did, George melted into the background and hurried into the kitchen.

Denice watched him go. "You're lucky to have him," she said, though I was pretty sure I wouldn't know that until I tasted his cooking. "He loves this place almost as much as Sophie does. Been here nearly as long as I have."

"And you've been here . . ."

She was a short woman and so wiry, I could see the muscles bunch along her arms when she slipped out of her lightweight jacket. Denice's brown hair was scooped up into a ponytail and she wore black pants and a yellow polo shirt with the outline of the Terminal embroidered over her heart. She took her plastic name tag out of her pocket and pinned it beneath the embroidered picture. She smelled slightly of cigarettes. Believe me, once I got my footing and established my position, she would hear about this.

"I've been here twelve years," she said, and something about the way she shifted from foot to foot told me I was disrupting the morning routine. I motioned her away from the front door and followed her through the restaurant and into the kitchen, where Denice went straight for the coffee machine.

"Hey, you made coffee!" She poured one cup for herself and another for George and drank it while she wiped down the plastic-coated menus on the counter. Denice was quick and efficient. Done with the menus, she filled tiny cream pitchers, set them on a tray, and put them in the cooler. She looked over the recipe for the day's special—meat loaf—and helped George get ground beef and bread crumbs and eggs out so he could start mixing.

It wasn't until she was done that we heard the front door open and slap shut.

"I'm sorry, I'm sorry, I'm sorry." The woman who scurried into the kitchen was my age, with curly dark hair that hung over her shoulders and big, dark eyes. She peeled out of her jacket and hung it on a peg next to Denice's, then zipped over to the far end of the counter and started refilling sugar shakers even before she caught her breath.

"Mauro had a stomachache this morning," she said. "I had to wait to take him to day care. You know, to see if he was going to throw up. If he was really sick, I would have called my mom to come over and watch him."

Behind the woman, Denice rolled her eyes.

I stepped forward. "You must be . . ."

The young woman's mouth fell open. "I'm so sorry." She wiped her hands against the yellow polo shirt that matched Denice's. "I'm Inez Delgado and really, I'm not usually late. It was just my little Mauro. You know, because he wasn't feeling so good."

Denice whizzed by with an armload of loaves of bread and took them over to the grill for George. "Sophie's having her surgery this morning," she reminded Inez. "This is Laurel."

"Sophie's niece." Inez grabbed my hand and pumped it. "I'm so glad to meet you. Sophie talks about you all the time. And I'm really sorry I'm late. Really. I won't—"

"I'm sure it won't happen again," I said. "You know how important it is to keep everything on schedule in a restaurant."

"Oh yes." Inez nodded. "It's just that little Mauro, he's only three . . . and . . ." She glanced at George and Denice. "Well, I have to tell the truth. Mauro really didn't feel good this morning, but that's not the only reason I was late. I was up late last night and I slept in a little too long this morning. But I couldn't help myself. I was watching the news. I bet everybody else around here was, too."

Denice came back the other way and said, "Jack's murder. It's got everybody talking, that's for sure."

George grunted.

Deep down inside, I knew I'd have to have a conversation with the staff about the Lance of Justice, but truth be told, I'd been so busy since the previous night when I arrived and made the grisly discovery, I hadn't exactly thought about what I should say to them.

I thought now was as good a time as any to come up with something.

Apparently, so did my staff. Inez and Denice both stared at me, waiting to hear more. George, I noticed, kept his back turned. He grabbed a spatula and even though I'd left the grill spotless after I made eggs for Declan and me, George scraped it clean.

"Sophie and I . . ." I reminded myself that I had nothing invested in the situation. Not in the town, not in the restaurant, and certainly not in the life and untimely death of Jack Lancer.

Tell that to the sudden lump of emotion in my throat.

I cleared it with a cough. "Sophie and I were here last night," I told my staff, and though it was technically not true, since I was the one who'd rounded the corner and found Jack slumped over the table, I made the discovery plural. It helped defuse the creepy factor. "We're the ones who found the body."

Denice's cheeks paled. Inez's eyes filled with tears.

George grunted.

"He was a nice man." Inez sniffled. "For the last few weeks, he came in every afternoon."

"Coffee and a slice of pie." Denice nodded.

"Sometimes a dinner to go so he could take it back to the station with him," Inez added. "That is, if there was a special on the menu that he really liked. George's Swiss steak, that was one of his favorites."

George grunted and slammed the spatula down on the grill.

"Well . . ." I didn't want to pin George down about what Kim said, not in front of Denice and Inez, so I stuck with the first order of business. "I'm thinking what happened here last night might bring out the curious and the gawkers. We might be busier than usual today."

"So there would be another blessing to Jack Lance's death," George grumbled.

I pretended not to hear. "I'm going to ask all of you to not say anything, even if someone asks. The basic story has already been on the news; there's really nothing any of us can add to it."

"Since you found the body, you could," Denice said.

Inez's eyes glimmered. "Tell us!"

"There's nothing to tell." Technically it was true. Nontechnically . . . well, I didn't think this was the time to explain how, thinking about Jack, I'd tossed and turned all night and when I did fall asleep in fits and starts, I dreamed about a slim rivulet of blood, warm and wet against the back of my neck.

I shivered and hugged my arms around myself. "The police have asked me not to say anything." It actually might have been true. I couldn't quite remember. "So for now, that's all you need to know. Jack Lancer's body was found here. If anybody gives you a hard time and presses you for information, you can tell them that. Other than that, there's nothing any of us know about the man, right?"

As if they'd choreographed the move, Denice and Inez both stepped back and looked George's way.

So much for trying to be subtle.

An opening like that gave me the perfect opportunity; I stared at George, too.

He tugged at the gold stud in his left ear. "Hey, it's not like I killed the guy," he snapped.

"Nobody said you did," I told him.

"Yeah," Denice piped in. "They said on the news this morning that they caught the killer. Some kid who was in here stripping the copper."

"Well, that part's true," I told them. "About the copper, I mean. About him being the killer, well, I don't know. And I don't think the police know for sure, either. Not yet. But none of that matters," I assured George. "No one's saying you had anything to do with the murder, George. But I am curious. Kim Kline, she said—"

"That reporter is still hanging around out front." Though in the kitchen there were no windows that looked out on the front of the restaurant, George shot a look that way, and as if he could see Kim in her slightly rumpled black suit and didn't like what he was looking at, he narrowed his eyes. "She's gonna cause trouble. Mark my words. Reporters, that's what they do. That's what they live for. Causing trouble."

"Is that what Jack Lancer did?"

George's eyes snapped to mine. "I didn't kill him."

I sashayed closer to the cook. "Call me crazy, but something tells me, with the way you're talking, maybe you would have liked to."

"And nobody could blame you, George," Denice put in. "You just remember that. Everybody knows what the Lance of Justice did to you. Everybody knows none of what he said was true."

"Do they?" George stared down at the grill.

I made sure I kept my voice light and airy, the better to try and soften the tension that suddenly filled the kitchen like a grease fire. "Hey, everybody knows but me! Somebody want to fill me in on the details?"

Inez waited for Denice to say something.

Denice waited for George to speak.

George waited for . . .

Well, I don't know what George was waiting for and as it turned out, I wasn't going to find out. Not right then, anyway.

The front door of the restaurant opened and banged shut and we all flinched and sprang into action.

"Your turn to hostess today," Denice told Inez.

Inez grabbed a stack of menus and scampered out front.

I thought it only fair to follow her. After all, I'd already warned the staff that there might be gawkers and question-askers and nosy reporters around. If there were, it was my job to head them off at the pass.

As it turned out, the three people who stood in the waiting area weren't just gawkers, they were question-askers and reporters, too.

"We just need a few photos," a young man with dark, shaggy hair was telling Inez when I strode up to stand beside her. "If there's blood, that would make the most dramatic shot, you know? But even if there isn't—"

"Can Inez show you to a table?" I asked him.

He turned away from the waitress and blinked at me for a couple seconds, as though he couldn't quite bring me into focus, before he asked, "You mean for breakfast?"

"Unless you're ready for lunch. We can accommodate you if that's the case. Today's special is meat loaf. It might take a while since we don't have the oven going yet, but we can serve it up for you along with mashed potatoes and green beans. If you don't mind waiting, that is."

"I don't want to . . ." He exchanged looks with his companions. "That is, we aren't actually looking to . . . We just want to snap some pictures and get a couple good quotes to go with them. We already had our coffee and muffins over at Caf-Fiends. It's not like we actually want to eat here."

It wasn't Inez's fault that she was standing there slack-jawed and unsure how to handle things, but it was my responsibility to set an example. I snatched the menus out of her hands and tapped them into a neat pile against the rolltop desk. "Thanks for stopping in," I told the young man.

"You mean—"

"I mean, it's like that sign you see in so many places. 'No shirt, No shoes, No service.' Only here, we've added 'No loitering.' If you're not a customer, you're loitering."

"So you're going to blackmail us into buying the crummy food in this place?"

For all I knew, the food at Sophie's was, indeed, crummy. In fact, I suspected *crummy* was putting it kindly. That didn't excuse this guy for dissing the Terminal.

I backstepped him and his companions toward the door. "Thanks for stopping by," I said again. "We hope to see you another time."

They got the message and left.

I turned from the door and found Inez grinning from ear to ear. "That was really cool."

"It was really rude is what it was."

"Not on your part."

My smile matched hers. "No, not on my part."

"You think we're going to have to put up with that nonsense all day?"

I didn't think it, I was sure of it. I also knew one way we could at least reduce the possibility.

I called a quick staff meeting and told George, Denice, and Inez what I had in mind. Within minutes, Inez and Denice were giving the restaurant a quick cleaning, concentrating on the little jut-out area where Jack had been killed. Once the fingerprint powder was all cleaned up, customers could speculate all they wanted about where Jack had been killed. While they were at it, I had the two waitresses get rid of a couple dozen lace doilies, three cobwebby teddy bears that were so high up on a shelf I don't know how anybody ever saw them, and a giant china pitcher of fabric flowers that made it impossible for anybody standing in the doorway between the waiting room and the restaurant to see the people at the table in the far corner against the windows.

Three people came in, one at a time, while they were working, and the girls took turns taking care of them. I noticed that the two Inez helped turned right around and walked out again and when they did, I gave her the thumbs-up. She'd apparently been paying attention when I sent that photographer on his way earlier; she knew how to identify the gawkers and tell them (politely, I hoped) that they weren't welcome if they weren't going to order.

The third was apparently a regular and Denice got him a cup of coffee and pulled out her order pad. "Pancakes, bacon, and rye toast?"

The man nodded.

I just happened to be standing close by. "I'll put the order in for you," I offered and headed back to the kitchen. Of course I had an ulterior motive. In addition to seeing how the orders were handled and how George prepared the food, it gave me a chance to finish the conversation we'd started earlier.

He looked up at me over the pancake batter he was whipping. "You didn't come back here just to watch me work."

"No, I didn't," I said. "But I do need to get used to the

routine around here. It's important for me to know how orders are prepared."

"Not much to makin' pancakes." He scooped up batter and dropped it on the hot griddle, waited for precisely the right moment, then flipped the four hotcakes. He already had bacon sizzling on the grill and he turned each strip over.

"I knew Lou would be here," George commented. "Always here this time of day. Always orders the same thing."

"So that's all taken care of, and we don't need to talk about Lou. But we still need to talk about Jack Lancer," I said.

George shot a look at me over his shoulder. "Do we?"

I shrugged like it was no big deal when actually, I was beginning to think it was. "I hate being left out of the loop. And I am the boss."

"Only until Sophie comes back."

I couldn't agree more and I nodded to prove it. "Only until Sophie comes back. But right here, right now, I'm in charge. And today's going to be a crazy day what with the media circus and all. Which means if I don't know what's going on—"

"Nothing. Honest." George slipped the pancakes and bacon onto a plate and rang a bell to tell Denice to come pick up the food. After she was gone, he turned to me.

"It happened a long time ago," he said. "Before I came to work for Sophie."

"Denice says you've been here twelve years."

"Nearly." He leaned back against the counter. "Before that, I had my own place. George's Country Diner. South of here. Over near Struthers."

I wasn't surprised to hear George had once owned his own restaurant and now cooked for Sophie. This is a tough business, and restaurants open and close at the speed of light. Sometimes it's because a place stays hot for a while, then falls off customers' radar. Other times, it's money problems that make a restaurant close its doors. Often, people who get into the industry picture themselves meeting and greeting patrons, sipping wine in a corner, and watching the cash roll in. Long hours, staff problems, hot kitchens, and soaring food costs have a way of wiping that fantasy off the map!

"Jack Lancer, he lived over near Struthers then," George said.

My head came up. "You knew him from your restaurant?"

George grumbled a word I couldn't quite hear. "Thought he was God's gift to the world. The Lance of Justice!" He spun to face the counter, his palms braced against the stainless steel. His shoulders heaved. "He used to come into my place once in a while, and you know, that son of a gun expected a free meal every single time. Because he was some big shot TV star!"

He spun back the other way, threw out his hands, and let them drop to his sides with a slap. "That guy's got a plum job over at a TV station and he expects free meals out of a guy who was working sixteen-hour days and barely making ends meet. Can you believe it?"

I could. I'd seen that sort of attitude of entitlement—and worse—from the Hollywood crowd.

"And you know, the first time he said something about free food and how he'd spread the word around about my place and he gave me that smile of his and a big wink . . ." I got the feeling that if we weren't in the restaurant, George would have spit on the floor. "The first time, I fell for it. I was only too happy to give him a free burger and fries. After all, he was the Lance of Justice!"

"But it happened again, right?"

"And again and again and again. And then the Lance, he'd bring his wife in and expect her to get free food, too. Or one of his girlfriends."

The fact about the Lance's affairs jibed with what Kim had told me about his private life, so I wasn't surprised.

"I just couldn't do it. I had rent. And utilities. I had suppliers to pay. I told him that, too, and you know what the Lance did?"

"Said bad things about your food?"

"Worse than that! That no-good, lowdown scumbag had the nerve to do a piece about my restaurant. You know, one of those ex-po-sés talking about how the service was terrible and the food was rotten."

"Was it?"

Fire in his eyes, George shot me a look and pushed away from the counter. Good thing he realized I was just playing devil's advocate because had he come at me, I wouldn't have liked to think about defending myself with nothing but the loaf of white bread on the counter nearby.

"George's Country Diner wasn't no five-star restaurant, but it was clean and the food was decent and I didn't overcharge nobody. Not ever."

"Then the Lance of Justice couldn't prove all those bad things he said."

The sound that came out of George's throat reminded me of thunder. "That didn't stop him. He showed up at my restaurant one afternoon and even brought a cameraman with him. I tried to toss them both out on their keisters, and before I could . . ." It had happened twelve years earlier, but just thinking about it turned George's cheeks a color that reminded me of the trickle of blood on the back of Jack Lancer's neck.

"That creep had a little box with him, and he opened it up and released mice into the restaurant. Just in time for his cameraman to get shots of those critters running helter-skelter all over the place. The couple customers I had—they didn't see Jack spill the mice out of the box—they ran out of the place without paying and they never came back. And Jack Lancer"—George ground the name out from between his teeth—"that so-and-so ran a story on the news that night all about how my place was dirty and should be closed. He went to the health department and showed them the footage."

I guess George realized he had an ally when he saw the way my hands curled into fists. He shot me a small smile to thank me for the support. It didn't last more than a second. "Folks stopped coming," he said. "Just like that. Word spread and folks stopped coming and I had to close my doors."

"So you really did have a reason to want to kill Jack Lancer!"

To George's eternal credit, he did not deny this. In fact, he simply grinned.

It was so coldhearted a look, I swallowed hard. "The cops are going to find out that Owen Quilligan couldn't have killed the Lance of Justice," I told George without explaining how I knew. "My guess is when they do, they'll come around and talk to you. I mean, if they know about what happened in Struthers."

"Something you need to know about this part of the world. Nobody hardly ever leaves. Everybody's involved in everybody else's lives, and everybody knows everybody. The cops, they know what happened back in Struthers. Everybody knows."

"Then they probably will talk to you. You just need to stay cool and keep calm," I told George. "Just tell them the truth." A thought hit and I gave the cook a careful look. "You do have an alibi for last night, don't you, George?"

"Alibi? Sure." George went over to the grill and grabbed his spatula again. "I was out. All night."

"And not here."

He shook his head. "Not here."

"The cops will want to know where you were."

"I was—"

Denice poked her head into the kitchen. "Hey, George," she called, "Lou wants another stack of pancakes!"

He grabbed the mixing bowl and ladled batter onto the grill. "I was at my AA meeting over at St. Colman's Church," George told me. He didn't wait for me to ask for the details. "See, after I lost the restaurant, I kind of hit rock bottom. Found comfort in a bottle and hardly came up for air for months at a time. So you see . . ." He deftly flipped the pancakes. "My restaurant closing and my drinking . . . well, I got Jack Lancer to thank for ruining my life."

Chapter 8

When four men arrived at the door of the Terminal at noon and none of them were carrying notebooks, cameras, or tape recorders, I was encouraged.

Until Inez informed me that they were Stan, Dale, Phil, and Ruben, Terminal regulars who hadn't missed a lunch at Sophie's in three years, ever since the factory where they used to work closed down and they filled their weeks with passing the time, shooting the breeze, and wishing for the good old days when there was plenty of work on the assembly line along with overtime hours and health care benefits. Sophie's was their daily lunchtime stop, and they'd linger over coffee until nearly four, Inez said. On weekdays, Sophie's closes at five so where Stan, Dale, Phil, and Ruben went after they left the Terminal, I didn't know.

Not that I'm complaining. Customers are customers and these four were customers who knew exactly what they wanted.

It was Tuesday.

They'd have the meat loaf.

Inez put their orders in and stopped for a moment to press a hand to the small of her back. "I'm glad there's somebody here who didn't just show up to hear the gory details," she said.

I couldn't agree more.

All morning I'd fielded questions from both walk-in customers and the nosy reporters who gathered outside, and except for a quick visit from Detective Gus Oberlin, who came to check out that heavy umbrella stand in front of the basement door, then mumbled and grumbled and huffed and puffed while he wrote in a little notebook, things continued much the same way all that Tuesday and started out the same on Wednesday, too.

More gawkers.

More reporters.

Few paying customers, and the few who did show up read over the menu and whispered to one another about how the panini sandwiches, wraps, and smoothies over at Caf-Fiends looked a whole lot more appealing than our same old, same old burgers, our fried egg sandwiches, and the day's special, meatballs over rice.

By nine, I already anticipated another day of empty tables and loaded questions.

Bored and disgusted, I made my way to the tiny office next to the kitchen and honestly, I tried my best to accomplish something. I went through the latest invoices and checked off what had been delivered against an inventory list that Sophie kept.

"Cans of tomatoes. Check. A case of canned green beans. Check. Twelve cases of peanut butter." I grumbled the words and checked the inventory, but as far as I could see, there were no jars of peanut butter anywhere in the restaurant. And even if there were . . .

I grumbled a little more and wondered what on earth Sophie was thinking and how on earth she planned to use that much peanut butter, and while I was at it, I flopped back in the chair in front of Sophie's gray metal desk, where an old computer shared space with samples of to-go utensils, takeout cups, and paper napkins thin enough to see through. The pile was topped with a brown teddy bear that sat precariously at the peak, dressed in a purple Victorian gown.

I eyed the bear.

The bear stared back at me.

The bear won; I dropped my head into my hands.

This was what my life had come to. A dumpy restaurant. An unimaginative (not to mention unappetizing) menu. And teddy bears wearing clothes.

It was official: I had lived the high life and now I'd fallen as far as it was possible to go.

"But then, what did you expect?"

I listened to my own question echo back at me and felt the old, familiar weight of my past bear down on my shoulders. Those last years working for Meghan, I'd been able to put it all behind me. But then, great clothes, fine food, and a breathtaking view off a balcony in Tuscany will do that.

It only made me feel worse when I remembered that the night before, I'd visited Sophie at the hospital and—fingers crossed behind my back—told her business was good and that we were handling the rush well, but not as well as we would once she was back and in charge. How would I feel if one of these days soon I'd have to report to Sophie that under my management, the Terminal had gone down the tubes?

* * *

"I KIND OF wanted a burger today." Phil Plumline was nearing sixty, balding, and could stand to lose forty pounds. He wrinkled his nose and squinted at the handwritten page I'd passed out when he and his buddies came in for lunch later that same Wednesday. "What happened to the burger? Why isn't it on the menu?"

At the same time I made sure to smile when I looked at the men seated at the round table, I reminded myself of the pledge I'd made just a couple hours earlier when I was feeling down and dejected: I was going to turn things around. For the Terminal and for myself.

Starting here.

Starting now.

Starting today.

Things were going to change.

"We're trying some new things," I told our regular lunch bunch. "Just a couple entrées for now, but I promise as the days go by, we'll add to the list. I've got some exciting new dishes in mind."

"First Sophie has to go away for who knows how long. Then the Lance of Justice gets murdered here. Now this?" Phil slapped the menu down on the table and frowned. He sat next to Ruben, a forty-something guy with coal-dark hair and a scar on his left cheek. Ruben sat next to Dale, the oldest of the four regulars, a thin guy with a bent back and a quick smile. Dale looked at Stan, an African American with salt-and-pepper hair and dark-rimmed glasses, who slipped my new and improved (albeit abbreviated at such short notice) menu out from under Phil's hand, read it over, and shook his head sadly.

"No meatballs and rice?" Stan asked and added, "Alice is

going to her sister's tonight and she's not going to be home to make dinner. I wanted something nice and filling to hold me over. I had my heart set on meatballs and rice."

"But the lentil and quinoa salad is excellent," I told him, and pointed down to where it was listed. Between waiting for the food delivery from the supplier I'd made a frantic call to, listening to George grumble about how I'd lost my mind, and giving Denice and Inez a crash course in describing our new dishes, I hadn't had a lot of time. I'd handwritten fifteen entrée lists and instructed the staff that diners would have to share the menus just like Phil, Ruben, Dale, and Stan were. The menus were a little more informal than I liked, but my handwriting was decent, and the paper I'd chosen from the stack under Sophie's printer was crisp and blindingly white. The menu made a statement: casual without being fried egg sandwiches. Personal and fresh.

Just like I envisioned our new and very much improved menu.

"The braised salmon with leeks and sumac is fabulous," I told the four men, and hoped I was right. I'd left George in the kitchen with detailed instructions on how to cook the dish and trusted that when someone finally ordered it, he'd come through. "My supplier just delivered the salmon and it's as fresh as it's going to get in this part of the country and—"

Ruben drew in a long breath. "I can't help myself. I miss the smell of fried onions. George isn't frying any onions today. What's up with that?"

"It doesn't have anything to do with the Lance of Justice dying here, does it?" Dale asked. "Good man. Such a shame. You're not the one who found him, are you?"

"She's the one who changed the menu." Phil crossed beefy arms over his round belly. "I'm thinking that says something right there. Hell in a handbasket. The place is going to hell in a handbasket."

It was.

Precisely why I'd decided to switch things up.

"They got pastrami on the menu today over at Caf-Fiends," Ruben said. "Saw the flyer up in their window when I parked my car down the street. I don't know about you guys . . ." He pushed his chair back from the table. "But pastrami sounds better than this la-di-da stuff."

Truth be told, my menu selections weren't all that la-di-da. But they were, apparently, a deal breaker.

I hoped when I sighed I didn't sound as defeated as I felt.

My words clipped behind my gritted teeth, I informed our regulars that while our specials were what we were featuring that day, of course they could also order off the old menu. When I walked away, I heard them giving Denice their orders: one burger, one fried bologna with extra onions, two meatballs with rice.

The good news was that our four regulars were the beginning of a little minirush. The other good news was that the people who did show up had apparently caught wind of my new rule about loitering and not ordering. The bad news? Like our regulars, they turned their noses up at the new menu.

Three tables, three reporters at each. They ordered coffee.

Two other tables of elderly ladies, there to pay homage to Jack. They ordered pie.

A single man at a table by himself in the corner. I went over to see what I could do for him.

I saw that the man had the lentil and quinoa salad and breathed a sigh of relief. At least someone around here was willing to take chances, even if he had just picked at his lunch and half of it was left on the plate. He had his money counted out and on the table with his bill.

I reached for it. "I can take that for you."

He slapped a hand over the stack of singles. "Denice waited on me. I want Denice to get this tip."

"She will. I promise. I'm just helping out because she's busy right now."

As if to prove me right, Denice whizzed by with a tray full of coffee cups for our resident reporters. She called out, "Be with you in a sec, Marvin," and hurried over to the tables along the back windows.

Marvin glanced up at me. "I'll wait for Denice," he said.

It looked like he might have to wait for a while. Another man walked into the restaurant and didn't wait to be shown a table. He was young, maybe twenty, with thick, curly hair the color of beach sand, and he was slim and wiry. His tan Carhartt jacket was open over worn jeans and a white T-shirt. He sauntered over to a table in the corner and flopped right down.

Denice was busy. Inez was back in the kitchen. I went over to greet the young man.

"Can I get you something to drink?" I asked him.

"Waiting for . . ." He lifted a hand toward where Denice was refilling coffee cups at one of the tables filled with elderly women. "Uh, Denice. I just wanted to tell her . . ." The kid was obviously not used to casually shooting the breeze. In fact, he was so nervous talking to me, his voice rose just a tad. "I got a computer she's been looking at. I wanted her to know. You know, so she doesn't go out and buy one for herself. I got it," he said again. "And, Denice, I need to tell her that. She's . . . she's my mom."

"Oh." Not the most graceful of replies, but I had a good excuse. I'd known George, Denice, and Inez for a little more than twenty-four hours, and except to know that Inez's Mauro was three and inclined to tummy problems and that George hated Jack Lancer and had a tendency to tip the bottle, we hadn't gotten to the personal stage yet.

"I didn't know Denice had a son," I told the young man. "I'm Laurel."

It took him a few seconds to realize it was his turn. The kid scratched a hand along the back of his neck. "Ronnie," he said. His gaze followed his mom when she zoomed around the reporters' tables, refilling coffee cups and asking them (I knew it wasn't for the first time) if they'd like to look over the menu. "I'll . . . uh . . . wait for . . . uh . . . her."

Apparently, it was the theme of the day, because Marvin repeated his intention of waiting, too, when I went back to his table and told him I could get him his change while Denice was busy.

Fine.

I caught Denice's eye and pointed to Marvin so she'd know he was set to check out, and she'd just headed that way when Gus Oberlin walked in.

Three tables, three reporters each, remember.

That meant nine news-hungry types, and they all jumped out of their seats at the same time and hurried over to surround Gus. Phil, Dale, Ruben, and Stan didn't want to miss a thing; they got up and went over there, too, and the old ladies scraped back their chairs and bent their heads so they wouldn't miss a word.

Denice was trapped on one side of the restaurant and I was on the other, and I hated to make a customer feel trapped, too. I threw caution to the wind and scooped Marvin's bill up off the table, told him I'd be right back with his change, and squeezed through the crowd gathered around Gus and to the cash register in the waiting area. By the time I repeated the procedure in the other direction (squeeze, sidestep, squeeze some more), and got back to Marvin's table, he was gone. To the men's room, I imagined, since there was no way he could have gotten out the front door without me noticing. I left his $1.75 change near his coffee cup and, my mission complete, I strode over to break up the press frenzy.

"You're going to need to take this outside," I said, raising my voice to be heard above the questions the reporters threw at Gus. "This is not a press room, it's a restaurant. And you're disturbing our customers." (This, of course, was not precisely true since our few customers—except for the old ladies—were part of the crowd.) "Outside, people. Now."

Since it was the most I'd said to any of them since they'd walked in, the reporters (I noticed Kim Kline was one of them) apparently took this as a sign that I'd had some sort of change of heart. A couple of them turned to me, tape recorders on, pens poised above notebooks.

"Do you think he really did it?" a man asked. "Owen Quilligan, do you think he really—"

I spun away and found myself face-to-face with a woman in a pink suit. "Tell us what it was like, that moment of cold awareness when you looked into Jack Lancer's dead eyes and saw—"

When I turned away from her and found my nose pressed into a yellow-and-orange-striped tie stained with coffee splatters, I was actually relieved.

"Detective Oberlin." I nodded my hello.

"Ms. Inwood." When Gus nodded, it reminded me of one of those National Geographic videos of a glacier inching its way toward the ocean. "I just wanted to . . ."

Whatever he wanted to do, he didn't want to tell me in front of the crowd. Gus motioned me toward the office and we edged out of the pack and made our way over there. Before I shut the door behind us I noticed some of the reporters had already sat back down. A few others went outside, no doubt to lay a trap for Gus the moment he walked out the door.

"Just need to go over things again," the detective said.

"Sure." I motioned him toward Sophie's one and only guest chair, then realized it was piled with papers. I gathered them up and set them on the floor, then invited Gus to sit.

"Not staying," he said. "Just wanted to ask about that umbrella stand."

The office was tiny and Gus took up most of it. Since he didn't sit down, I didn't, either, and we stood toe-to-toe. Or more precisely toes of his scuffed black loafers to toes of my snakeskin flats.

"Somebody could have put it there after the murder," Gus said.

It wasn't like I was wedded to the theory, so I admitted he was right.

Gus made note of this.

"Except . . ."

He froze, pen to notebook.

"Well, if you saw the ring of dust around the base of the umbrella stand . . ." I assumed Gus already had when he'd stopped in the day before to look things over, but just in case, I led him out of the office. We ignored the surge of reporters who darted toward us and stepped into the kitchen.

"See." I pointed to the umbrella stand and the floor around it. "Those scuff marks are from where I moved the stand. If someone else had—"

"They could have moved it exactly like you did."

In the great scheme of things, he was right, but even Gus

knew it was well nigh impossible. He scratched behind his
ear with his pen.

"I just wanted to make sure," Gus said. "We got pictures yesterday, so now if you want to move the thing,
you can."

I saw no reason for it, but I did notice that out the window
where George passed food through to the waitresses, the
gaggle of reporters waited for Gus with bated breath.

"You want to escape through the back door?" I asked him.

Gus considered it, but gave up the idea with a grumble.
"I'd still have to get through that pack of hyenas out front,"
he said, and massive shoulders squared, he marched toward
the swinging door that led into the restaurant. He punched
it open, then looked over his shoulder toward the grill—and
George. "We need to talk, Porter," he said.

George flipped a burger, his back to Gus. "You know
where to find me."

THE REST OF the day was much the same.

Few customers who wanted to order, and those who did
weren't interested in either quinoa salad or salmon.

Reporters who hung around looking for quotes or gossip
or any hint of anything that would feed the frenzy that was
the media's response to Jack Lancer's murder.

By the time five o'clock rolled around and it was time to
close up for the day, I couldn't have been more relieved.

I told my staff I'd see them in the morning, and rather
than stick around and work on the day's books, I packed the
receipts (there weren't many of them) in my purse so I could
enter them into the accounting program on the computer
at Sophie's. When I turned out the lights, locked the door

behind me, and was outside on the sidewalk, I drew in a breath of chilly evening air and worked a kink out of my neck.

In the distance, I heard a motorcycle engine roar to life, but I didn't pay any attention to it. At least not until I was in the parking lot and a sleek cycle rounded the corner and purred to a stop beside me.

It was vintage, and beautifully restored, too. The painted fenders and center panel that said *Harley-Davidson* were a yellowish olive green outlined with maroon and highlighted with black and gold. The chrome shone. The headlights gleamed.

Somehow, I wasn't surprised when I looked up and saw that Declan was driving.

"It's Wednesday," he said, above the birr of the engine.

"And thank goodness it's over."

He sat back on the leather seat. He'd probably come from right across the street, but already the wind had tangled his dark hair and he scraped a hand through it. "So now . . . ?"

I stepped toward my car. "It's been a long day. I'm thinking a bubble bath and early to bed."

"Actually, it was what I was thinking about, too, except we only just met. I guess I'm old-fashioned, but it's probably a little early in our relationship for that."

When my mouth fell open, he laughed. "Just kidding. Except not about how it's Wednesday. Did you forget? We've got a date."

My mind flashed back to the day before and Declan's dinner invitation. My head snapped up. "You weren't serious."

His smile was in direct contrast to his words. "I'm always serious."

"But I . . ." I looked down at my black pants and the pink and white silk mock-wrap blouse that was a little wrinkled thanks to the fact that I'd worn an apron over it much of the day.

"I'm in no shape to go to dinner."

His smile inched up. "You're in great shape."

I ignored the smile and the heat it caused to spread through me like a California wildfire. "I can . . ." I took another step toward my car. "I can meet you somewhere. Say, in an hour or so."

"Oh no! Because then you'll call me and tell me you've changed your mind." He patted the way-too-small patch of seat behind him. "Come on, you don't want to miss the opportunity to ride on this baby, do you? This is a 1926 JD classic, and there aren't many others like it still on the road and none, I bet, that have been as lovingly restored. Seventy-four-cubic-inch engine, three-speed transmission, electrical lighting. Might not sound like much these days, but back when it was built, this was the crème de la crème."

"It's nice," I admitted, because it was, and talking about the motorcycle meant I didn't have to think about that picture that flashed through my mind and refused to budge. Bubble bath and early to bed.

"Hop on."

This time the image I shook from my head made my cheeks heat.

"Hop on," he said again. "Time's a-wastin' and we've got a reservation."

I'd been on a motorcycle before. In fact, I'd driven a few in my day. I could take a corner like a pro and I wasn't afraid to rev the engine and crank up the speed even in France, where the back roads were often twisting and dangerous.

That didn't stop me from eyeing the seat where Declan kept his hand. "There's not much room there for a passenger."

"You're small. You'll fit." He patted again. "Besides, we don't have far to go. Unless you're chicken, of course."

I hitched my purse up on my shoulder and climbed aboard.

Chapter 9

Tired, disappointed with life, and disgusted with fate or not, there was something about looping my arms around the waist of a handsome man, holding on tight, and feeling the wind in my face that went a long way toward cheering me up.

For exactly forty seconds.

That's when Declan stopped the motorcycle and cut the engine.

Right in front of Caf-Fiends.

"You're kidding me, right?" I sat back on the leather seat, my fists propped on my hips. "This is where we're having dinner? These guys are the enemy."

When Declan looked over his shoulder at me, his gray eyes gleamed. "Exactly!" He dismounted and offered me a hand and we stood side by side in front of the coffee shop. "You can't know what you're up against if you don't check them out," he said in a stage whisper that was totally for show since there was no one on the sidewalk but us. "I thought we could do a little reconnoitering."

"Reconnoitering."

"It's not exactly dishonest and besides, it's for a good cause. It's all in the name of saving the Terminal."

Just because I thought the Terminal was . . . well, terminal . . . didn't mean I was happy that it was public knowledge.

My shoulders shot back. "What makes you think the Terminal needs saving?"

Declan's steady gaze moved beyond the brightly lit front window of Caf-Fiends, where a gigantic yellow coffeepot shared space with oversized paper flowers, a couple kites shaped like butterflies, and a half-dozen Beanie Baby stuffed bees that hung from the ceiling on fishing line to make them look as if they were buzzing through the scene.

He leaned closer and, like it was some big secret, he said out of the corner of his mouth, "They have customers."

I responded with a grunt. "We had customers today."

"How many?"

I raised my chin. "I didn't count. But look"—I dug in my purse—"receipts I need to enter into the accounting program. That proves we had customers."

He made a move to grab the receipts and I had no doubt he would look them over and comment on the orders: coffee, pie, one lentil quinoa salad, some of our usual daily fare—and nothing else.

Before he could get ahold of them, I stuffed the receipts back in my purse. "We don't need a trendy cutesy display window to bring in customers."

His dark eyebrows rose a fraction of an inch. "We?"

I twitched away the implication of that single, loaded word. "You know I was referring to the Terminal."

"Your restaurant."

"Sophie's restaurant, and not a smoothies-and-wraps kind of place. I have plans to make it a little more upscale than that. Fresh food from local growers. Dishes that push the limits beyond smoothies, if you know what I mean. This place . . ." I looked over Caf-Fiends. Like the Terminal, it was housed in a building that had been here long before smoothies were invented. It had a redbrick facade and what looked to be apartments on the second floor with flower boxes outside each of the four windows that faced the street. At this time of the year those flower boxes were empty, but in another month or so, no doubt they'd be bursting with pansies and brightly colored marigolds.

"It's cute," I admitted, and then to make it perfectly clear that this was not necessarily a good thing, I was sure to add, "In a cloying sort of way. I guess that draws a certain kind of crowd." I tipped my head and gave the front window another look. "What they really need is a few teddy bears."

"You could loan them a couple."

My stiff smile told Declan I was only kidding.

"Come on. It can't hurt to see why people are attracted to the place." He tugged my arm. "Besides, I hear they've got pastrami today."

Pastrami is too fatty, too high in calories, and altogether too salty. I happen to love it.

Together, we stepped up to the door and Declan paused there, his hand on the knob. "With any luck, they won't know who you are. You can ask about the food and the service. You know, like a spy."

I laughed. It was actually not a bad idea.

At least it wouldn't have been if the moment we stepped inside, the welcoming smile didn't vanish from the face of the middle-aged woman behind the cash register. "Oh, it's you."

She wasn't talking to Declan.

My cover—such as it was—blown, I extended a hand, introduced myself to the woman who said she was Barb, and threw out a few compliments on the decor that was (truth be told) what we in Hollywood would have described as positively ho-hum.

Faux hardwood floors, and not the good kind.

Aquamarine walls that didn't even come close to matching the touches of color in the fabric curtain in the doorway below the RESTROOMS sign and the cloth napkins piled on a nearby buffet.

Framed prints lined like soldiers on either side of the long, narrow room, each picture featuring coffee in some way, shape, or form. Coffee beans. Coffeepots. Coffee drinkers.

Barb showed us to a table and I tried (not very successfully) not to notice that despite the ambience, there were more patrons in Caf-Fiends than we'd had at the Terminal all day. A couple in the corner munched decent-looking salads. Other patrons were scattered here and there among the twenty tables, sipping coffee, eating wraps, enjoying brownies that looked both decadent and delicious.

"Two pastrami sandwiches," Declan said the moment we sat down. "And I'll have an espresso. My date . . ." He grinned at me across the table. "Something tells me she's the iced green tea type."

"Iced green tea will be fine," I told Barb, and when she walked away, I added, "though I could have ordered for myself."

"Just being the perfect escort." Declan sat back and looked around. "So, what do you think?"

"Does it matter? What do you know about restaurant operations, anyway?"

"I know what I like. And I know where I like to spend my money."

"Fair enough." I nodded. "Here or at the Terminal?"

Lucky for him, I may have put him on the spot but he didn't have to answer right away. Another woman hurried over. She set a tall plastic cup with my green tea in it on the table in front of me but she never looked at me once. She was too busy staring, dewy-eyed and practically drooling, at Declan.

"Nice to see you again, Declan." The name tag that was handwritten in pink Sharpie and pinned to her blue and white blouse said she was Myra, and Myra twinkled down at my dinner date for all she was worth. "You haven't been here in a while."

"I've been kind of busy."

Myra's hair was the color of a chestnut and pulled back into a ponytail and she wore blusher that was a little too plummy for her olive complexion. Even so, I watched her pale. "You mean on account of the murder. Isn't it awful?" In a better, more perfect world—one that was not running strictly on the hormonal overdrive that had clearly taken over Myra's senses the minute she laid eyes on Declan—she actually might have asked the question of me, seeing as how I was the proprietor (temporary or not) of the place where the murder had taken place. But Myra had eyes only for Declan.

She put a hand on his arm and—I swear this is true—batted her eyelashes. "It must be horrible for you. I mean, your store being so close to where the murder happened."

"It's worse for Laurel."

When Declan looked my way, Myra's smile wilted. He

brought it back to life when he leaned just a little closer to her. "She found the body."

"Oh. My. God." As if there were cooties associated with the discovery and I was still carrying them around, Myra stepped back and away from me. Which, coincidentally, put her just a little closer to Declan. "You must be, like, grossed out! We've got hand wipes," she announced, because I either looked like I needed them or she thought that the remnants of Jack's murder could be so easily cleaned away. "I'll go get you some."

Big points for Declan: he waited until Myra was gone before he broke into a grin.

"She likes you," I said.

Barb brought over his espresso and Declan added sugar and stirred. "Myra's not my type."

I couldn't possibly pass up an opening like that. "So what is your type?"

"Irish," he said quite simply. "If I ever dated a woman who wasn't Irish, my family would disown me."

Let's face it, he had to be kidding so it was perfectly all right for me to laugh.

At least until he said, "Are you Irish?"

I sipped my green tea. A little sweet, but not half-bad. "I have no idea," I admitted. "I don't know anything about my biological family."

He considered this for a moment. "I can't imagine what it's like to not be clued in on a couple hundred years of family history."

"Is that a good thing or a bad thing?"

"It's"—he lifted a shoulder—"it's just the way things are in my family. A lot of us live close together and even the ones that don't are always passing through. We visit. We talk. Constantly. There's never a moment in a day when somebody's not talking to somebody in the family. Everybody knows everybody else's business. My cousins and I, we grew up together. We went to school together. We got in trouble together!" There was that easy smile again. A second later, it faded. "Do you ever feel . . ."

I wasn't sure if he was searching for the right word or wondering if he'd gotten himself into a conversation he didn't know how to get out of, so I finished the sentence for him. "Alone? No." It was a lie, but rather than give him time to notice, I was quick to ask, "Don't you ever wish you could have some time without your family smothering you?"

"It's not so much smothering as it is intense interest. In everything each of us does. I think it's true of the Irish in general—the importance of family loyalty, the need to communicate and share. But it's more so with us. We're Travellers."

I guess my blank stare said it all. Smiling, Declan leaned forward, his elbows on the table. "Some people say that Travellers are Irish Gypsies, but that's not technically right. We're not related to the Romany people in any way. We're Irish, through and through. The Travellers are an itinerant people; we have been for as long as anyone can remember. In fact, there are those who claim we've been separated from the settled community for more than a thousand years."

"So you . . ." The concept was new to me, and I turned it over in my head. "Travel?"

"Well, some of us do. My immediate family—my parents, Uncle Pat, and his family— we've been settled here in Hubbard for going on sixty years now. There are whole communities of Travellers in the U.S., some in Texas, some in South Carolina."

"Where Owen is from."

He nodded. "A lot of the Travellers keep to the old lifestyle, even in this country. They settle down for the winter, then go on the road in the warmer months doing any work they can find. A lot of them do home repairs, yard work, maintenance. That sort of thing."

"But not your family."

"Not my *immediate* family. They're all my family."

"And the Travellers, they've been doing this forever?"

"Well, it depends which legend you believe. Some say that the first Travellers were the tinsmiths who made Christ's cross. They were cursed to travel the world until Judgment Day. Another theory is that the Travellers are the descendants of the people who were made homeless by Oliver Cromwell's military campaign in Ireland in the 1650s. I'm more inclined to believe that we can trace our roots back to the poets and minstrels of the Middle Ages. They traveled the country telling stories and singing songs and they were much admired."

A gene pool that included the entertainment industry. It explained his glib tongue and maybe even the smile that never failed to make me feel as if Declan and I were the only two people in the world.

He used it on Myra when she brought over our sandwiches and I practically saw her melt beneath the heat of it. I was appalled to think I looked as starry-eyed when Declan looked at me that way, and vowed that I'd never let it happen.

I couldn't help but notice that his sandwich was considerably bigger than mine.

"I love my family to pieces," he admitted, unrolling his silverware from a not-quite-aquamarine napkin. "There's no use even trying to fight being in the middle of them. They'll never back off!"

Myra had yet to walk away, and seeing that Declan was

ready to eat, she set the wipes down on the table near my plate. "If you need anything else"—she smiled down at Declan—"you know where to find me."

"You know where to find me."

It was exactly what George had told Gus Oberlin, and, thinking about it and the murder, I pushed my plate away.

"Oh no." Declan already had his sandwich in one hand, but he shoved my plate closer to me with the other. "This is quality stuff, and you're not going to waste it." His wink would have been comical if not for the fact that his smoky gaze had a way of drawing me in and making me feel as if my feet didn't touch the floor.

I shook away the thought and grabbed my sandwich.

He bowed his head for a moment before he took a bite and chewed. "So?" he asked between bites. "How does it compare? To Terminal food, I mean."

"Oh no. You're not going to get off that easy." I took a bite, chewed, and sat back. "You never answered the question I asked you before. Where would you rather spend your money, here or at the Terminal?"

He'd just chomped into his sandwich and he held up one finger to tell me I'd have to wait for his answer.

Yeah, like a stall tactic like that was going to distract me.

"Well," I said, the second he'd swallowed, "which is it? This place? Or Sophie's?"

"Depends what's on the menu," was his answer.

"Comfort food or trendy wraps?"

"Depends on what I'm in the mood for."

I refused to let him get to me. "But if you were just walking in off the street, if you didn't know anything about the restaurants or the owners or anything else, which would you choose?"

"It's awfully good pastrami," he said, then because he

apparently saw the flare of anger in my eyes, he added, "but the espresso's nothing to write home about."

"We don't serve espresso at the Terminal."

"Maybe you should."

I twitched away the thought. "I tried to switch up the menu today. No one was especially impressed."

"Too soon after the murder." What one had to do with the other, I didn't know, but Declan was apparently convinced. He nodded. "Speaking of which, I've been watching the TV coverage. You know, *The Life and Times of the Lance of Justice*, that sort of thing. The local stations are all over it, just like you'd expect them to be, and now the national news has picked up the story."

It was hard to swallow the bite of sandwich I'd just taken, what with the fact that my mouth felt as if it were suddenly as dry as the Sahara, where I'd once spent two months with Meghan when she was filming an epic about a legendary queen of the desert. I washed away the sensation with a sip of tea and though I wasn't sure I wanted to know the answer, I had to ask. "The story's made the national news?"

"It was just a mention," he said. "On one of the cable stations, I think. But I wouldn't be surprised if the story doesn't pick up some traction. Crusading reporter. Mysterious murder. You know how the media loves anything and everything sensational."

Boy, did I ever.

A thought for another time, so I set it aside. "The story will lose its appeal if it turns out Jack was just in the wrong place at the wrong time. If your cousin Owen is the killer—"

"He's not." I got one pickle, Declan got two. He finished the first and crunched into his second one. "Check out the news tonight. You'll see. Owen was released this afternoon."

So Gus Oberlin did believe me.

Or he realized he didn't have enough evidence against Owen in the first place.

"That doesn't mean Owen didn't do it," I said for argument's sake.

"They're free to bring charges if they ever find enough evidence." Apparently, Declan didn't think they would, because he didn't sound the least bit upset by the prospect. "For now, I think it's more important to concentrate on the other suspects, don't you?"

It was pretty much what I'd told Kim Kline. No doubt, her reports were among those Declan had been watching. "So, what are the theories?" I asked him. "Who are the other suspects?"

"Your cook, for one."

This was not news, and the way I waved away the information told Declan that. "He has an alibi."

"Good. I'd hate to see George locked up for twenty years. You'd have to teach someone else to fry bologna."

I hoped my pasted-on smile conveyed my opinion of that plan.

"I was thinking about suspects when I watched the retrospective of Jack's career last night," Declan went on. "They featured his most sensational reports."

"Do you think there's something there that explains why he was killed?"

"I don't know. The old stories, that's all water under the bridge, so to speak. The people he exposed in them—people like your George—have already been shown to be dishonest. So it's not like any of those people would have anything to gain by silencing Jack. I guess one of them could still be angry, though. Is George angry?"

"Don't you think he has the right to be?"

"They showed a couple minutes of footage from that story last night. And some others, too. George claims he was framed, right? That Jack Lancer trumped up that whole story about how his place was filthy and rat infested? If that's true, then maybe Jack did it to someone else, too. That could explain why someone might have a grudge against the Lance of Justice."

"Or somebody could have been trying to keep him quiet and not report some new story." This was not a new thought. After all, I'd asked Kim what kinds of stories Jack had been working on at the time of his death.

Declan nodded. "Good point. The stories he was working on currently, well, those would be stories about people he hadn't exposed yet. Those people might have more invested in making sure Jack kept his mouth shut."

Again, my mind flashed to Kim. "It might be possible to find out what Jack was working on," I said.

Admiration gleamed in Declan's eyes. "That's why you let that reporter in the restaurant yesterday."

"I didn't exactly pump her for information," I lied.

His sandwich finished, Declan sat back. "What did you find out?"

"Not much." I hated to admit it. "She thinks there might be a personal motive. It seems Jack Lancer was something of a ladies' man."

"I'm not surprised. It's the whole TV thing. Some people are powerless to resist the pull of stardom."

Apparently roguish gift shop owners also made the list. Myra showed up, her blusher touched up since last she was at the table, and she had a fresh coating of lipstick.

"Can I get you anything else?" she asked Declan and not me.

He tipped back in his chair, the better to see the

refrigerated case near the cash register. "Peanut butter pie for me," he said. "Laurel will have—"

"Nothing, really." I'd already decided to take the second half of my sandwich home. "I'm stuffed."

"She'll try the key lime pie," he said.

I waited until Myra was gone. "Are you always so bossy?" I asked him.

"It's one of my most endearing qualities."

"What if I don't want to try the key lime pie?"

"Then you wouldn't be able to be objective about it when you find out it's Caf-Fiends' biggest seller."

"And you know this how?"

He jiggled his eyebrows. "Myra. She'd do anything for me."

"Like tell you which menu items sell and which don't."

"That, and other things. Like the fact that the night Jack was killed, she saw a car parked out front of the Terminal."

"Really?" I thought this through. "But Myra said she hadn't seen you in a while."

"To Myra, a day without seeing me is a while."

"So, yesterday you were here asking what she might have seen the night of the murder."

"I thought it was worth a try."

"Why?"

"My cousin was in jail, remember."

"And you decided to get him out."

"It's what I do."

"And this car, did Myra catch a license plate number? A color? A make?"

"You sound like Gus Oberlin." The way Declan said this, I knew it wasn't a compliment. I also knew that though Myra may have claimed to see that car, she didn't have the particulars to back up her story.

"It might have been my car," I said.

"No. She saw it earlier. Before you got here."

"Then it could have been Owen's."

"Owen doesn't have a car."

"You think it was the killer's?"

Declan's shoulders rose and fell. "If we knew, we'd have this case wrapped up."

"So that's why you've been buttering up poor Myra."

"Have I? Been buttering her up?" This was a new thought for him. "I thought I was just being friendly."

"She's hoping for more than friendly."

"And you?"

Lucky for my equilibrium, Myra showed up at that very moment with our desserts. When she set mine in front of me, I smiled across the table at Declan. Two could play the same game. If he was determined to throw out titillating innuendos, I could be just as determined to pretend they didn't bother me in the least. Or send my imagination soaring in directions it shouldn't.

"What am I hoping for?" I swapped him smile for smile. "After that sandwich, I hope I have enough room left to finish this pie. It looks fabulous."

Chapter 10

All right, I admit it—I completely got why the key lime
pie at Caf-Fiends was their bestselling menu item. It
was the most scrumptious thing I'd eaten in as long as I
could remember. Then again, ever since Meghan tossed me
out of her kitchen, her Beverly Hills mansion, and her life,
I'd been conserving the money I stockpiled while I worked
for her. Gone were the days of lobster salad and Japanese
flower mushrooms, truffles and sea cucumbers, and all the
other rare, wonderful, and expensive ingredients that made
cooking for Meghan the best gig in the culinary world.

These days, salads were more like it.

Salads and leftover pastrami sandwiches.

Back at Sophie's neat little bungalow, I tucked my to-go
container with half my sandwich in it in the fridge and
checked Muffin's food bowl. Empty. Again. In the three
days I'd been there, I'd yet to actually see Sophie's cat, who
apparently came out of hiding to eat only when I wasn't

around. I refilled the food bowl, called out the requisite, "Here, kitty, kitty," and when I was ignored as I'd been ignored before, I grabbed a bottle of water and headed into the living room, where I kicked off my shoes and sank onto the sofa.

I didn't mean to fall asleep, and believe me, I had no intention of dreaming about Declan when I did, but I guess my subconscious has a mind of its own. In my dream, he leaned over the table at Caf-Fiends, took my hand in his, and asked, "Are you Irish?" in that as-smooth-as-brandy voice of his. I tensed. I held my breath. Even dreaming, I was aware enough to know I wasn't sure I did—or didn't—want to know what was going to happen next.

Thankfully, I never had a chance to find out; I was jolted awake by a noise from out in the kitchen.

I sat up like a shot and, still half-asleep, looked around at a room both familiar and foreign.

Yellow walls, white woodwork, worn blue carpet.

"Sophie's," I told myself, relieved now that I felt as if I was back on solid ground. I glanced at the clock on a nearby table. I had been asleep for only twenty minutes and still, my head felt as if it were stuffed with cotton.

I shook it and heard another sound from the kitchen.

Scratching.

Curious, I pushed off the couch and headed that way. When I flicked on the kitchen light, I was just in time to see a black-and-white blur race away from the back door and duck under the kitchen table.

Muffin.

"Here, kitty, kitty." I tried for a voice both kindhearted and gentle—two things I generally am not—and bent down so the cat could sniff my hand.

Muffin had other plans. She swiped her claws across my

knuckles with enough oomph to draw blood, and I cried out and stood back up in a flash. "You little creep!"

I shook out my hand and, never one to easily give up, I closed in on the critter.

This time, my toes took the brunt of Muffin's displeasure.

Except to admit I was grumbling when I grabbed a paper towel, wet it, and limped back into the living room, I will not report what I said in response to that last attack.

Instead, I sat back down on the couch, propped my foot on the coffee table, and applied the wet paper towel. It stung like the dickens and, okay, I was probably being a little too overimaginative, but I had the distinct feeling that when Muffin sauntered into the room, she was grinning.

I made a face at the cat.

Other than emitting a throaty sound that was definitely not a purr, the cat pretended I didn't exist.

"Be that way. If you're not going to be nice, I can ignore you just like you're ignoring me," I grumbled, grabbed the remote, and turned on the TV.

A sitcom that starred one of Meghan's former lovers (as lousy an actor as he was a boyfriend) came on, but even before I could change the channel, the show cut for a commercial and Kim Kline's face and glossy curls filled the screen.

"Tune in at eleven for continuing developments in the Jack Lancer murder investigation," she said. "We've got the latest updates, including the release of Owen Quilligan, the prime suspect in the case."

They rolled tape of Owen being led out of the local police station by a handsome guy in a snazzy charcoal gray suit.

A handsome guy who looked awfully familiar.

But then, he should. I'd just had dinner with him.

I sat up and turned up the volume on the TV, the better

to hear it over the rumble coming out of Muffin that intensified the moment I moved.

"Obviously, the police have determined that they don't have enough evidence to hold my client," Declan told the nearest reporter at the same time the subtitle under his picture identified him as *Declan Fury, defense attorney*.

The screen flashed back to Kim. "Owen Quilligan," she said, "was the only suspect in Jack Lancer's horrible murder. What will the police do now? How long will the Lance of Justice have to wait . . . for justice?"

A car commercial followed, but I'd already switched off the TV before the spokesperson got two words out.

Declan was an attorney?

Funny, he'd never bothered to mention that to me.

Just like he'd never bothered to mention that he was representing his wayward cousin in the murder case.

Thinking this over, I drummed my fingers against my water bottle. No wonder Declan was so interested in that car Myra from Caf-Fiends may or may not have seen in front of the Terminal the night of the murder. No wonder he'd been anxious to look around the restaurant the morning after I found Jack's body.

He was looking for evidence, or maybe even more important, for exactly the opposite. Without concrete evidence, the cops couldn't charge Declan's client with Jack's murder.

Another thought hit.

No wonder Declan invited me to dinner! It was his opportunity to pump me for information.

Knowing Declan had an ulterior motive and that he wasn't looking for a relationship should have cheered me right up.

It did cheer me right up.

Well, except for the sourness that suddenly filled my
stomach.

Hey, blame it on the pastrami.

I know I did.

BY THE NEXT morning, I'd decided that two could play the
same game. Declan was out to charm his way to information?
Well, even on my best days, I'd never been accused of being
charming. But I sure as heck could be proactive and clever.

As soon as ten o'clock rolled around and I knew George,
Denice, and Inez didn't need any help at the Terminal (why
would we when our parking lot was empty and the parking
spaces in front of Caf-Fiends were full?), I headed over to
Artisans All, the gallery across the street that was wedged
between the beauty shop and the empty storefront.

Like Caf-Fiends, Artisans All was housed in a redbrick
building that had seen better days. Still, somehow the faded
bricks looked just right with the tasteful robin's-egg blue
front door and the wreath of bright spring flowers that hung
there along with the OPEN sign. Like Caf-Fiends, the front
window was decorated to the hilt. This time, there were no
stuffed bees or paper flowers. Instead, the gallery window
held a tasteful array of handmade jewelry, a hand-painted
silk kimono, ceramic pots, and hand-dipped candles.

I had never been a fan of artsy-craftsy and what I saw
sure wasn't worthy of Rodeo Drive, but most of it was
interesting and some of it was downright impressive.

I pushed open the door and was greeted by a woman of
sixty-some years with frizzy red hair piled loosely at the top
of her head. Her orange caftan and bead-encrusted sandals
seemed more suited to Key West than they did to Hubbard.

"You're Laurel." She held out a hand and, before I had a

chance to shake it, she introduced herself as Carrie Farmer and added, "You know, we've all been talking, everyone in the neighborhood. We knew you were coming. Sophie told us. But no one imagined you'd bring so much excitement along with you."

"The excitement has nothing to do with me," I was sure to tell her.

Carrie smiled. She wore a thick gold hoop in one ear, a thinner, bigger hoop in the other, and three rings on each hand. "I've got coffee," she said, and turned to glide to the back of the store. "Cream and sugar?" she called from a back room.

I asked for sweetener and took a minute to look around. As I suspected from the display in the front window, the gallery was filled with pretty things: framed photographs of wildflowers, handmade soaps from a place called A Goat in Bubbles, beaded jewelry, knitted scarves. It was all displayed with style, and the prices . . .

I checked out a pair of earrings—dangling purple stone balls—displayed near where I stood.

I was in the Midwest; the price was a steal. Back in the day when I had a job—I mean a real job—I wouldn't have thought twice. These days . . .

I set down the earrings, and when Carrie returned to the front of the gallery I took the cup of coffee she handed me.

"So . . ." She looked me over. "I guess everything they say about you is true."

I sipped my coffee. "That depends on who they are and what they say."

When she laughed, she opened her mouth wide and threw back her head. "Alexander McQueen shoes, and that green-and-black-striped jersey top is from the spring collection at Saks, if I'm not mistaken. The jeans . . ." She gave them another look. "Maybe not top-of-the-line, but very close to it. You were some hot shot out in Hollywood, weren't you? Just like Sophie told us."

"Sophie tends to exaggerate. I was a personal chef, that's all."

"Well, you were a personal chef with very good taste." Carrie set her china coffee mug down on the glass-topped display counter and folded her hands together at her waist. Her fingernails were very long and painted a blue that matched the front door. "And now you've got a murder mystery on your hands."

I was grateful she'd brought up the subject. It saved me from doing it. "The police have released their only suspect."

Carrie wore lipstick that was nearly the same shade as her flowing caftan. When her top lip curled, it left a smudge of orange under her nose. "Those people!" She snorted. "You can't tell me that little twerp didn't do it."

"You know Owen Quilligan?"

She tsked. "I don't have to know him. I know *them*."

I wasn't sure what she was getting at. I was sure from the tone of her voice that whatever she was talking about, it was sure to piss me off. "Them? You mean the Quilligan family?"

"Like I said, never met the kid. Or his family, as far as I know. But the Sheedy family, the Fury family . . . all those types who call themselves Travellers. That's who I mean. I wouldn't put it past any one of them to kill somebody and not blink twice."

Her assessment didn't jibe with what Declan had told me about family and loyalty. "What can you tell me?" I asked Carrie.

"Gypsies. Crooks. Every one of them."

Oh, don't think I'd forgotten that Declan was only out to charm the socks off me so that he could help his cousin out of a bind. But that didn't make him dishonest. Did it?

"They've got records?" I asked Carrie.

She gave an unladylike snort. "They should. You know what they do, don't you?" she asked, then without waiting for me to answer, she told me. "They live by some old-time, old-fashioned, outmoded set of rules and they keep to themselves because they have plenty of secrets and they don't want anyone on the outside to find them out. I wouldn't be surprised if some of them spend their days gazing into crystal balls and reading tarot cards! The rest of them? They travel through the area, mostly in the summer. They go around and offer to do maintenance work on people's houses. You know, new roofs, new driveways. Then they do a half-baked job. Or they use crappy materials. Or they take a person's money, start the work, then never come back to finish it. Travellers!" Another snort emphasized her opinion. "Around here, we know better than to trust any of them."

"Declan doesn't seem to be like that."

"He doesn't have to be, does he? All right, I admit it, the man deserves one of those Sexiest Man of the Year awards. No doubt you've noticed. But, you know, him being over at that gift shop, that's just a front of sorts."

I guess I was not as immune to charm and a handsome face as I'd hoped because the very thought made it hard for me to get the words out. "A front for something dishonest?"

"For his law practice!" From the way she said it, I wasn't sure Carrie thought that made it dishonest or not. "The man's job is to *keep* his relatives out of trouble and when that's not possible—and believe me, it's not usually possible—his job is to *get* his relatives out of trouble. You know that, don't you? He's an attorney, all right, but he only has one client, his own family. You can see why they'd need him, all those Traveller types showing up here from down south and pulling their scams. And that uncle Pat of his . . ." Carrie leaned closer and lowered her voice at the same time she slid a look in the direction of the beauty shop next door. "They say he used to run the Irish mob in this part of the state, you know."

"Used to?"

"Not what it used to be." I couldn't tell if she approved or if she thought less of Uncle Pat because he hadn't made it to Al Capone status. "Not nearly as influential or as violent as they were back in the day. But that doesn't mean they still don't get in trouble. The whole lot of them! Oh yeah, Declan, that's his job. He runs interference between his family and the law."

Another thing he'd forgotten to mention.

I made a mental note of it, but rather than get distracted, I got down to business, and since Carrie apparently had something against Declan and his family, I decided to leave him out of it. "Myra over at the coffee shop told me that on the night of the murder, she saw something outside the Terminal. A car. Parked there sometime before Sophie and I showed up around nine o'clock. I don't know if you were open late that night, but—"

"Monday nights, I close at five."

I guess Carrie saw the way my shoulders drooped because her plucked-to-a-hair-breadth eyebrows rose and she was quick to add, "But I was here late that particular night, going over the books."

My head came up. "Did you see the car?"

"A car?" As if it might kick-start her memory, she strolled toward the front window and looked across the street at the Terminal. For a long time, she stood lost in thought before she said, "You know Jack Lancer spent a lot of time over there these last few weeks."

"So I've heard." I joined her. From this vantage point— with that pink and white kimono, a flowered teapot, and a row of silky scarves framing the scene—the Terminal looked more dreary than ever. "Do you know what he was doing there?"

"I know what he wasn't doing!" Carrie tossed back her head. "Man sure wasn't looking for a story idea. First day he showed up, see, it was all anybody around here could talk about. Then the next day, he was back again. I heard about it from Denice when she came outside for a smoke. Hey, I know how these TV types are. They're always looking for something new and interesting. So I figured, what the heck, nothing ventured, nothing gained, and I put this on." She pointed to our right and a display of chunky stone jewelry and touched a finger to a necklace made of sterling beads and lapis drops polished to a velvety finish.

"Wore that, and took a walk over to Sophie's place."

The why wasn't a mystery. Hollywood had taught me a lot about self-promotion.

"You were hoping he'd realize that you sell wonderful art and do a story about the gallery. What did Jack Lancer say?"

"The son of a gun didn't even notice my jewelry. He did"— Carrie elbowed me in the ribs—"he did notice me, though. Not only did he ask me to join him for coffee, he wondered what I was up to that night and just about came right out and propositioned me."

Kim did say Jack was something of a ladies' man. "And you told him?"

Carrie hooted. "I told him that I sell art, not myself. And I didn't have coffee with him, either, in case you're wondering. He might have been a TV star, but Jack Lancer was not my type. Too loud. Too pushy. You know what I mean?"

"But even after that day, Jack kept coming back to the Terminal."

"So I hear. I never saw him again. I never bothered."

"And the night of the murder, when you were here late doing the books?"

Carrie turned around and went to retrieve her coffee cup. "There was someone there, all right," she said, glancing across the street over the rim of her cup. "About seven o'clock."

I didn't want to look too eager so I stopped myself just as I was about to close in on Carrie. "Who?"

When she shrugged, her caftan rippled in orange waves. "Long shadows on that side of the street at that time of the evening. I couldn't really see who it was. But I did see the person go in through the front door."

"But the back door was broken into. That's how Jack and the killer got inside!" I didn't want to say too much, but it really didn't matter. Like the rest of Hubbard, Carrie had obviously been glued to TV coverage of the Lance of Justice's death.

"The killer got in through the back door. Yeah, that's what they said on the news. But I didn't see anyone go around back. Like I said, I couldn't tell who it was, but I saw a person walk up to the front door and open it with a key."

WHATEVER I HAD expected to hear from Carrie, it wasn't this. I pretended I wasn't knocked for a loop, told her I'd be back on a day when I had more time to look around her shop, and made a beeline across the street and into the Terminal kitchen.

Since there were no customers out front, George, Denice, and Inez were taking a break.

"Who has a key?" I asked.

They looked at me in wonder.

"To the restaurant. Who has a key to the restaurant?"

George grunted. "You."

"And?" I turned to Denice and Inez.

Denice had been checking her messages and she tucked her phone in her pocket. "Nobody," she said. "Nobody but Sophie and now, you."

"But . . ." I paced a pattern between the food pickup window and the grill. "What happens when Sophie's sick?"

"Sophie's never been sick," Inez said.

"Well, what about if she takes a day off?"

"That's never happened," George said.

"When her sister died out in California a few years ago, Sophie closed the restaurant for a week or more." Denice rose from the chair where she'd been sitting. "Besides, she always said if something like that would happen . . . you know, if she would get sick or something . . . then she'd call one of us and we could stop over at her house for the key."

We heard the front door of the Terminal open and Inez popped out of her chair and hurried out of the kitchen. "She was always the first one here in the morning," she called over her shoulder. "And she was always the last one to leave at night. Nobody ever needed a key but Sophie."

Sophie, and whoever had let themselves into the Terminal on the night Jack Lancer was murdered.

The thought burned through my brain along with the fact that if that was true—if someone came in through the front

door—then that broken window on the back door that led
directly into the kitchen was just for show so the cops would
think the person got in that way. I kicked this around while
I went out to the restaurant to see who'd just come in. Stan,
Dale, Phil, and Ruben. Early that day, and no doubt anxious
for the day's special, chicken fried steak.

I greeted the men, then hurried to the office, the better
to have a few minutes to think over everything I'd learned
that morning.

Jack had been a Terminal regular as of late.

I'd heard that much from any number of people, so that
wasn't a surprise.

The question of course was why he was suddenly
interested in the Terminal.

But that wasn't my only question. Now that I knew
Sophie was the only one Carrie could have seen earlier that
evening, the only one with a key, I had to wonder why she'd
made an after-hours visit to the Terminal and why she hadn't
mentioned—to either me or to the police—that she'd been
there earlier that evening.

Even those questions weren't as disturbing as the final
one that pounded through my brain.

What was Sophie trying to hide?

Chapter 11

"How was the chicken fried steak?"

"No hello?" When I got to the hospital that Thursday evening, Sophie was sitting up in the green vinyl-covered chair in the corner of her room, so I perched on the edge of her bed. "The first thing you ask about is today's special?"

"Today's special, tomorrow's special." She shifted in her seat and for a moment, her face contorted into a mask of pain. Settled, she took a deep breath. "Better I should think about the Terminal than about what those doctors did to me."

I didn't even have to ask. From this angle, I couldn't help but see that both above and below the bandage that swathed her knee, Sophie's right leg was swollen. There was an IV in her arm that slowly dripped what I hoped was enough painkiller to alleviate what must have been terrible discomfort.

"No problems at the Terminal," I told her without

bothering to add, *no customers, either.* "Everything's as right as rain."

"George is behaving?"

I assured her he was.

"Denice is still as on top of things as ever?"

This, too, I had no problem telling her was true.

"And how about Inez?" Sophie frowned. "Nice girl. And she needs the job to help support that kid of hers because that no-good lowlife of a husband walked out on her. But she's not always as conscientious as I would like. She hasn't been late, has she?"

Since I didn't want Sophie to worry, I lied.

"So . . ." I slipped off the bed. "You've probably been watching a lot of TV."

"You mean about the Lance of Justice's murder." Sophie nodded. "It's all anybody can talk about. My roommate . . ." She poked her chin in the direction of the second bed in the room, but that bed was empty. "Before she went home today, my roommate said I should be sure to give her a call. You know, when the police solve the mystery. She was mighty impressed about how Jack was found at the Terminal, I can tell you that much. She acted like she was sharing the room with a celebrity."

"There's certainly been a lot of talk about the murder," I told Sophie and this time, it wasn't a lie. "Everyone has their own theories about what happened and why."

"I sure do." Sophie shifted in her seat again and when she reached for the pillow propped at her back and couldn't quite get it the way she wanted, I went over to help. "It had to be someone he was investigating," she told me, keeping her voice low as if she were the only one clued in to the possibility. "Someone wanted to keep the Lance of Justice from blabbing about something."

Something he was investigating. Like a certain restaurant where he'd been spending an unusual amount of time?

I didn't dare come right out and ask. Not if I expected any kind of answer that actually might help.

Instead, I went over to the bedside table, poured a glass of water, and handed it to Sophie. "You need plenty of water when you're recovering from surgery," I told her. "And plenty of time to rest and relax and let all your cares fade away. Maybe if there was something you were worried about . . ." I gave her a knowing look.

She returned it with a blank stare.

I drew in a breath, then let it out slowly. "I've been talking to the other merchants in the neighborhood," I told her.

"That's good. That's just the kind of thing I was hoping you'd do. It's a great way to build morale, don't you think?"

"It might be if we were talking about business."

As if I'd never dropped that not-so-subtle remark, Sophie's eyes twinkled. "I hope Declan is one of the people you've been talking to. He likes you."

"He doesn't know me."

"Not well. Not yet. But when he does, he'll like you even more."

Chances were, once he really got to know me, he wouldn't. Especially since I wasn't Irish. And he, apparently, wasn't totally on the up-and-up.

"I'm not talking about Declan," I said.

"The others. Sure. You mean like Carrie at the art gallery. And Myra and Bill and Barb over at Caf-Fiends. Oh, don't look so embarrassed."

I was pretty sure I didn't, but that didn't matter, because Sophie went right on. "It makes sense that you'd talk to them. They're our biggest competition. It's just too bad, that's what it is. They seem like nice enough people. It's too bad their coffee shop will never be able to compete with the Terminal."

"It wasn't business we were talking about," I mentioned again. "It was the murder."

"Well, I imagine it was. It's the biggest thing that's happened in the old Traintown neighborhood in as long as anyone can remember. Well, at least since back in the 1930s. You know there was a serial killer working along the railroad lines then. All the way from Cleveland to Pittsburgh. And there are people who say—"

"Someone saw you." I didn't mean to be impolite, but if I just sat there and listened to Sophie avoid the subject and if I held my tongue and didn't get to the bottom of what was going on, I was going to pop like a champagne cork. "The night of the murder. Someone saw you at the Terminal, Sophie. Before you and I showed up and found the body."

Except for her right hand picking at her blue and white hospital gown, Sophie went perfectly still for so long, I was able to tune into the *click, click, click* of the second hand as it swept around the clock on the wall.

She cleared her throat and looked up at the ceiling. "Who says?" she asked.

"What difference does it make? Someone said you were there."

She blinked. "They're wrong."

"You let yourself in through the front door."

"That's not possible and you know it. I was home when you stopped by to collect me."

"That doesn't mean you weren't out earlier."

"I was out earlier. To the pet store for food for Muffin. And to the grocery store so I could make sure the refrigerator was stocked for you. I stopped at church, too. You know, just in case. The night before surgery, I figured it couldn't hurt to light a candle."

"Then you weren't at the Terminal?"

When she shifted her gaze to me, her eyes were wide. "Why would I be?"

"I was hoping that's what you'd tell me."

"Well, of course I would tell you." Sophie offered me a smile that could have melted butter. "If there was anything to tell."

"So you weren't at the Terminal?"

"I was. With you."

"But not before that."

"My goodness, Laurel!" Her laugh sounded as fatigued as Sophie looked. "I don't know why you're going on about this and I don't know . . ." She winced and grabbed her right leg and when I hurried over to see what was wrong, she put out a hand to tell me to keep my distance. "I'm fine," she assured me after a moment. "I'm just a little tired."

I offered to call the nurse but Sophie refused. "I just need to put my mind to feeling better," she told me. "I just need to concentrate on getting well again. Once I'm out of this place and in Serenity Oaks, I'll be right as rain in no time at all."

We'd had this conversation more than once before I ever agreed to come to Hubbard. "You don't have to go to a long-term care facility to recuperate," I told her. "You can come home as soon as you're discharged on Saturday. I can help take care of you and—"

"And who will take care of the Terminal if you're home fussing over me?" Her lips pressed together, she shook her head in a way that told me the subject was closed for discussion. "Besides," she added, "Vi and Margaret are over at Serenity Oaks. They're my old bowling buddies. Not to worry." She gave me a wink. "Me and Vi and Margaret, we're planning to get in all sorts of trouble once I get there."

I had no doubt of it. Just like I had no doubts that I was getting nowhere with my questions. That didn't stop me from asking another one.

"Do you know why Jack Lancer had been hanging around the Terminal?"

Sophie's eyes twinkled. "The food is mighty good."

"But that doesn't explain why he'd come in every day."

"Dale and Phil and Ruben and Stan do."

"Dale and Phil and Ruben and Stan . . . they're not investigative reporters with jobs at a TV station. They stop in to pass the time. I think . . ." There was no use holding back, not now that I'd committed myself, so I forged on. "I think maybe Jack Lancer was there because he was doing a story and the Terminal was the only place he could find the information he wanted."

Sophie's laugh would have been a good sign that she was feeling better if it were even half-convincing. "What kind of information could he possibly find at the Terminal?"

"I was hoping you'd tell me that."

"Well . . ." She picked at her hospital gown again. "There's certainly nothing going on at the restaurant that the Lance of Justice would have been investigating."

"So, maybe he was trying to pull what he pulled with George. George, he says that the Lance wanted free meals and when George wouldn't provide them, that's when the Lance of Justice trashed his restaurant on TV." Just thinking about it made me choke on my words. "He wasn't trying to pull something like that on you, was he? Because if that was the case—"

"It wasn't." Sophie reached over and patted my hand. "But thank you for caring."

Caring wasn't part of my makeup, but before I could remind Sophie, she leaned back in her chair and sighed. "I think I'll take a bit of a nap."

"Of course." I gathered my things and resigned myself to the fact that though I'd satisfied myself in terms of Sophie's recovery, I was still left with plenty of questions and the suspicions that went along with them.

I stopped at the door. "Does anyone else but you have a key to the Terminal?" I asked.

"Nina had one."

"In California?"

"Well, yes. I thought if I ever lost mine . . ." I guess even Sophie realized how crazy this sounded, because she grinned. "Well, I guess it wasn't the best plan, but it made me feel more comfortable knowing I had a backup. I suppose if I ever did lose my key, Nina could have sent the duplicate in the overnight mail."

Apparently, the smile I gave her in response to this convoluted plan was not as wide or as convincing as I hoped, because she said, "Don't worry. Nothing's wrong. Not with me. Not with the Terminal. The police, they'll find out what happened, and then everything will go back to being normal. Now, tell me, how's my sweet little Muffin doing?"

My smile was as painful as the still-red scratches on my hand and foot. "She's eating every bite I give her."

"Good. She's such a sweet little thing. Always so quiet and pleasant and wonderful."

What else could I do besides get out of there before the words *cat from hell* escaped my lips?

Muffin was sweet and pleasant, huh?

It wasn't the first thing Sophie said that night that I didn't believe for one instant.

* * *

I WAS ALREADY in the Terminal kitchen Friday morning making the day's first pot of coffee when I heard George call out from the front door, "You'd better get back to the parking lot!"

I was just about to loop an apron over my head, and I set it on the counter and trailed outside. I'd parked my car at the side of the building, but I found George all the way around back, standing about four feet from our Dumpster and surrounded with what looked like everything we'd thrown away in the last week.

"What on earth?" My gaze roamed over used paper napkins, coffee stirrers, crumpled wax paper, and empty cans of everything from diced tomatoes (the meat loaf special) to bread crumbs (that would be on account of the chicken fried steak). "What happened?"

George scraped a hand along the back of his neck. "Darned if I know, but it sure is a mess. If you get me the push broom from in the kitchen . . ."

I not only got the broom, but since Denice and Inez were just on their way in, I told them what was up and headed out to help.

"Dumpster's practically empty." George peered down into it. "What crazy fool would tear through the garbage like that?"

"Cats?" Since my only experience with cats was sweet and wonderful Muffin, I can be excused from having less than a good opinion of felines. "Dogs?"

"Dogs and cats don't get down into the Dumpster and toss things out left and right. And they might lick out a can of green beans, but they sure don't finish up and haul the empty can out and drag it halfway across the parking lot." To emphasize his point, George kicked one of the cans and it skittered across the blacktop. "And they sure as heck don't take every garbage bag out of the Dumpster, rip them open, and scoop every last little thing out. Look at this mess. It had to be done by people."

I couldn't help but slide a look toward the front of the restaurant. This morning, like every morning since we found Jack Lancer's cold and lifeless body, the street was filled with news vans and reporters, eager to dig up the latest on the murder. "You don't suppose . . ."

George must have been thinking what I was thinking. His eyes narrowed, he tossed a look out front, and grumbled a single word under his breath. "They're all alike. Bottom-feeders. Looking for something sensational, I bet."

"In our garbage?" It shouldn't have surprised me. Back when I worked for Meghan, we'd had more than one incident of too-enthusiastic paparazzi who'd been found going through the trash. At least in their case, I could understand. Sort of. Anything they found was fair game since they'd take the information and sell it to the tabloids. In fact, I was convinced that something Meghan had tossed away without thinking was what led to the media finding out about her teenage son's drug addiction.

My mouth soured.

But maybe that had more to do with the odor rising off the sea of trash than it did my memories of my last days in Meghan's employment.

Maybe.

"Well, they sure didn't find anything here," I told George and reminded myself. "Not unless one of them has psychic powers and can figure out what happened to Jack Lancer from the vibes coming off used coffee grounds." I looked at where they were scattered across the parking lot in gritty little mounds and groaned.

"I'll start sweeping," I told George. "You go inside and get some garbage bags."

"And if you bring out a couple of cups of coffee, too, we'd appreciate it."

I tossed a look over my shoulder just in time to see George go inside and Declan close in on me. "Somebody's idea of a joke," I said.

Since it was warm, he was wearing a gray T-shirt with the words *Property of CWRU Law School* printed on the front, and when he crossed his arms over his chest, the muscles in his arms bunched. "Maybe, but it's not exactly funny," he said.

The look I gave him should have told him this wasn't news to me.

His nose wrinkled, Declan glanced around. "Is it all from your Dumpster?"

"Every last crumb."

"What do you suppose someone was looking for?"

"Trouble?" I hoped he caught the edge of sarcasm in my voice, but something told me he didn't even notice. George showed up with the garbage bags and the coffee and Declan grabbed one cup, handed it to me, and kept the other for himself. Since he kept his voice down, I don't know what he said to George, but George nodded in response, left the roll of garbage bags on the ground, and went back inside.

"Hey, you might get busy and you'll need your cook in there, not out here," Declan said in response to my quizzical look. "So finish your coffee." He encouraged me with a lift of his own cup. "And let's get to work."

I did, and we did. I swept up mounds of garbage and Declan shook out bag after bag and held them open so I push the garbage into them. He tied each bag and tossed them back into the Dumpster they'd come out of.

After fifteen minutes, we could actually see the blacktop again.

After thirty, my arm muscles protested.

"My turn to sweep." Declan grabbed the broom and we traded tasks.

I watched him cover a wide swath of parking lot in four efficient swipes. "I saw you on the news," I told him.

It should be illegal to smile when you're standing ankle-deep in garbage. "I hope they showed my good side."

I refused to let him know that I thought every side was his good side because number one, it would make me look as pathetic as Myra, and number two, something told me he already knew that. It would explain the attitude. And his cocky self-assurance. And maybe the fact that he thought that smile that had a way of tickling its way inside me and igniting all sorts of fantasies I hadn't had the time or the energy for of late was his ticket to information.

"Why didn't you tell me you were representing Owen?" I asked him.

As if he actually had to think about it, he pursed his lips. "You never asked." He moved effortlessly and swept up another long, straggling line of paper napkins and paper towels toward the bag I held open.

"I thought you were a gift shop manager."

"I am a gift shop manager."

"And you practice law on the side."

"Actually, the gift shop is my side job."

"Because keeping your family out of trouble is your full-time job."

His eyebrows rose. "You've been talking to Carrie over at the art gallery."

"She doesn't like your family."

"Believe me, she's made that perfectly clear. She thinks

we're some kind of Irish version of the Mafia, who travel from hit to hit in Gypsy wagons and tell fortunes on the side."

"She says your uncle Pat—"

"Oh, come on!" Declan's groan was overdramatic. "You don't actually believe that kind of nonsense, do you?"

"I'm new in town. I don't know what to believe."

"Then believe me when I tell you not to believe everything you hear."

"Even everything I hear from you?"

He had the good grace to smile and keep on sweeping.

When he was done with that particular mound of gunk, I scooped, tapped, and tied the bag, and when I was done, I realized he was watching me carefully. "What?"

"I didn't expect you to be the type who'd get down and dirty."

"I didn't expect you to try and bribe me with pastrami."

"Because I bought you dinner? You think it was a bribe?"

Could I still smile now that my shoulders ached and the stench of garbage had settled into my pores? I tried. "I think you want to find out what I know so you can help your cousin get out of trouble."

"What's wrong with that? It's my job. He's my client."

"And you never mentioned it." He opened his mouth but I beat him to the line. "Because I never asked."

"Exactly." He started in on the last of the scraps, sweeping across the parking lot and closer to where I waited, bag in hand. "What we really need to figure out was what Jack was doing here," he said once he'd closed in.

I couldn't agree more, but I didn't bother to mention it. If we did find out why the Lance of Justice had been hanging around and that discovery somehow led back to Sophie . . .

I swallowed the sudden panic that filled my throat.

"Maybe it would help if you let me talk to your cousin."

He stopped midsweep. "Why?"

"Why not? He might be able to tell us something that will help."

He gave the broom two quick pokes forward. "He says he doesn't know anything about the murder and I believe him."

"Come on!" I threw my hands in the air. "I'm the one who figured out that Owen couldn't have come upstairs from the basement. The least you can do is let me talk to the kid."

"Just to satisfy your curiosity about who killed Jack Lancer."

"Absolutely." I didn't bother to add that whatever Owen had to say, there was an off-chance that it might also shed light on what Sophie was up to and what she was trying to hide.

I wasn't exactly lying, just telling a half-truth.

But I wasn't about to take chances.

Under the folds of the black garbage bag, my fingers were crossed.

Chapter 12

Since it was a little early in the morning for a motorcycle ride and in lizard-patterned leggings and a silk chiffon henley, I wasn't dressed for it anyway, I drove. On the way across town Declan explained that because Owen was from out of town, he needed someone to vouch for him while he was awaiting a hearing on breaking and entering charges. No one—and Declan emphasized this point—was more well respected in these parts than his parents, Malachi and Ellen Fury, so Owen was staying with them.

After what Carrie at the art gallery told me, I was expecting brightly painted Gypsy wagons and a booth out front where various and sundry Fury and Sheedy relations told fortunes. What I found instead was a tasteful blue colonial with understated cream trim. The lawn was neat and as green as the shamrocks that decorated the mugs over at the Irish store, and tulips in every color of the rainbow lined the walk to the front door.

"Party tomorrow," Declan said when he saw that I was checking out the three cars parked in the driveway and the people—women, men, and children—who scurried from those cars to the front door and back again, their arms filled with serving bowls and chafing dishes, loaves of bread and fifty-pound bags of potatoes. "My niece Caitlin is making her first holy communion."

"You have siblings." I don't know why it surprised me; Declan had talked about the importance of family in his life.

"Four brothers, two sisters, eleven nieces and nephews. So far." He flashed a smile and pushed open the car door. "My parents would like more grandchildren than that. Come on. You are about to meet some of them."

I did.

Rusty-haired James—whom everyone called Seamus— was older than Declan and married to a woman named Kate, who was in the kitchen and elbow-deep in peeling potatoes.

Broad-shouldered Aiden was closest in age to Declan and looked the most like him. It was his little girl who was being honored the next day. He was busy wrapping knives and forks in napkins and he told me his wife, Fiona, would be by later after she got off work.

Sisters Bridget and Claire weren't there, either, because both were RNs and both were at work at the hospital in Youngstown that morning. Truth be told, I was grateful. By the time I'd also met brother Brian and his wife, Nora, and heard about the oldest in the family, Riordan, who was in the air force and stationed in South Korea, my head was in a spin.

It was a wonder I was coherent by the time a woman of sixty or so stepped out of the family room. Ellen Fury was petite and once upon a time, she must have had the same flaming red hair I saw on any number of her grandchildren. These days, the color was faded to that of a well-thumbed penny, but no less spectacular against her porcelain skin. She had small, fine features and bright eyes the same shade as the blue T-shirt she wore with jeans. She also had a generous smile. Big points for her: it didn't wilt around the edges—at least not too much—when she realized her youngest had brought an unfamiliar woman into the house.

Ellen shook my hand and offered a smile at the same time she slid a look at her son. "Declan didn't tell me he had a new friend."

I wasn't sure how I was supposed to respond to this so I left it up to Declan to handle his mother.

"She's not exactly a friend," he said as if he were sharing a confidence, but loud enough so everyone was sure to hear. "She's more like a new neighbor over in Traintown. And she's poking her nose into the murder."

"You mean the Lance of Justice?" Kate set down her potato peeler long enough to squeal with delight. "It's all anybody can talk about."

"And Laurel"—Declan made a ta-da sort of gesture in my direction—"she found the body."

This caused a flurry of excitement. Before I knew it, Ellen grabbed my left hand, Kate grabbed my right, and with the rest of the crowd following, they dragged me into the dining room, where they deposited me in a chair and gathered around.

"The kettle's about to boil," Ellen told Declan, and settled herself. "You can make us tea while Laurel tells us more."

"There's really not much to tell," I assured her. "I don't know much of anything besides what you've heard on the news already."

"They say it was a mob hit." Kate was breathless.

"Because of something the Lance of Justice was investigating," Nora added.

"Hey, maybe it's the food pantry down at church!" Aiden barked out a laugh and raised his voice so Declan could hear him. "Wasn't that Lance guy down there once poking around?"

Declan stuck his head out of the kitchen door. "He was doing a piece on hunger in the county," he said. "Not looking into what we do down at the pantry."

"We?" Since Declan ducked back into the kitchen, I shifted my gaze to his mother. "You all work down at the food pantry?"

"Declan does." Ellen's smile told me she approved. "He has for years. So has your aunt Sophie."

"She's not really my aunt," I was sure to add, even though I doubted anyone was listening.

Ellen leaned forward, her gaze pinned to me. "So . . . ?"

I reminded myself what we'd been talking about and shrugged. "So, if the police know anything more than what's being reported on the news, they aren't sharing the information with me. That's why we . . ." I slid a glance toward the doorway between the kitchen and the dining room. "We thought maybe if we talked to Owen—"

Ellen tsked.

Kate frowned.

Nora's lips thinned.

Seamus grumbled a curse and at that, the various kids collected around the table giggled and whispered.

Honestly, I wasn't sure if their reactions were a criticism of my plan or of Owen.

I found out soon enough when Ellen shooed the kids away. Once they were out of the room she said, "That Owen

Quilligan's got cabbage for brains. It's why we invited him
to spend some time with us in the first place. We thought a
change of scenery would be good for him. He got in some
trouble back home, you see. A stolen car."

"And that pizza place where he was working was missing
some cash," Nora added.

Ellen shot her a look that clearly said that it wasn't right
to air all the family's dirty laundry in front of strangers. She
folded her hands on the oak table in front of her. "We
thought the family here would set a good example."

"We thought," Kate added, "that we might be able to
change his sneaky, thieving ways."

"Or at least if he kept them up, Declan would be able to
spring him from jail," Nora put in.

"Which he did," her mother-in-law reminded her. "But
that doesn't change the fact that the boy betrayed our trust.
Imagine, him stealing copper like a street thug!"

"I told you he was no good." Aiden shook his head in
disgust. "I wouldn't be surprised if he was involved in the
murder, too."

His mother shot him a look. "You know that's not
possible. He might be stupid, but he's not evil."

"Or he is and he's never been caught," Aiden said.

"Which is why—" Declan returned with a teapot and
cups on a tray and I waited to say anything else until he set
it down and passed the cups around. I waved off the offer
of a cup of tea. "If I could just talk to Owen . . ."

Ellen looked up at Declan.

"I don't see what it would hurt," he told her.

Ellen nodded, and Declan offered me a hand and led me
through the living room with its beige carpet and soft green
upholstered couch and easy chairs and up the stairs where
the walls were lined with framed pictures of children and

grandchildren and Ellen herself with a broad man with a beard, both of them smiling and Blarney Castle in the background. We stopped outside a closed door at the top of the steps.

Declan knocked and identified himself before he pushed open the door.

Owen sat on the edge of one of the two double beds in a room I didn't even have to ask about; I knew it had once been shared by Bridget and Claire. The walls were pink, the woodwork was white, and there were framed photographs hung over each bed. A red-haired girl gymnast; a blonde posed with her swimming team.

Owen glanced up when we walked in and shut the door behind us and when he looked at me, his eyes narrowed and his lips thinned.

"If she's a cop," he grumbled, "I'm not saying nothing."

Declan pulled over a chair from the desk that sat along the far wall and waved me into it. "She's not a cop, she's a friend."

"And a gorger. You told me not to talk to any of them."

Declan glanced my way. "A gorger is an outsider, a person who's not a Traveller," he explained before he turned back to Owen. "You haven't been paying attention to a word I've said to you since you came here. We don't live in a bubble anymore, Owen. Not any of us. You have to start dealing with those in the outside world. When I told you not to talk to them, I was referring to the media. Not to someone who might be able to help you."

The kid folded his arms across his chest and looked at me through the shock of carroty hair that fell across his forehead and into his eyes. "How's a girl going to help me?"

"First of all, Laurel's not just some girl. She's a businesswoman and a smart one at that. Which means you'll be polite when you're addressing her and you'll call her Ms. Inwood. You got that?"

Whether he did or not, Owen gave a brief nod.

"As for how she's going to help . . ." Declan drew in a breath and let it out slowly. "We don't know yet. We thought if we talked—"

"You mean if I talked. You want me to admit I was there in the building the night that guy was killed."

"You were there in the building." Declan's voice rang with authority. He sounded so different from the man who'd ordered pastrami and key lime pie for me, my head snapped up and I found him standing opposite Owen, his fists on his hips, his feet slightly apart. There was steel in his stance and fire in his eyes. "I'm not going to put up with your crap, Owen, and I'm not going to lie for you. Not to the cops and not to any judge. We know you were in the basement. Your fingerprints were all over down there, and all over that door that led from outside to the basement steps, the door you broke into to get inside. We know what you were doing there. It's time to pay the piper, lad. Do the crime, do the time."

Owen's pale skin went ashy. "You think I'll actually go to jail?"

Some of the rigidness went out of Declan's shoulders. "Not if you're honest."

"Okay, all right." Owen pushed off the bed and stomped to the other side of the room. There were two windows there that looked out over the spreading branches of a maple tree, and Owen watched a brown squirrel scamper out on a limb. "I was going to take the copper. I admit it. I'll admit it in court if I have to. But there's no way I had anything to do with killing that guy." He spun toward his cousin. "You know that, Declan. You know I'd never do a thing like that."

"I do know it. And we've got the evidence to back it up. Your fingerprints are downstairs, but not upstairs, not even on that back door upstairs that was broken into. We've got to keep that in mind. We've got to make sure we have all the facts and we've got to figure out what they mean. And Laurel here, she's trying to help. She's the one who proved to the cops that you never came upstairs.

Owen scrubbed a finger under his nose. "I was just sort of, you know, hanging around. After I left Bronntanas. I figured I'd walk around the neighborhood and see what was happening. Only there's not much happening there at all, is there?" He made a face. "Then I saw that there were no lights on in that dumpy restaurant and—"

"Hey!" Declan's voice snapped the kid to attention. He pointed at me and Owen paled even more.

"Sorry," he said. "I didn't mean dumpy. I meant . . ." Since he obviously did mean dumpy, he shook off the rest of his apology and went right on. "There weren't any lights on and there was nobody around so I figured I'd just go in and see what I could see."

"And take what you could take." It was the first I'd said since we walked into the room, and I made sure to keep my voice even and neutral. We all knew Owen was a thief; there was no use hitting him over the head with my opinion.

"I wasn't planning on touching the cash register or anything," the kid told me. "I just thought . . . well, you know what I thought. I figured I could make a few fast bucks. It wasn't like I had a truck or anything to load the copper into. So it's not like I was gonna take out all the plumbing or anything. I figured just a couple pieces. Just so I could sell it and get some pocket money. I found a wrench and a pair of pliers and these big scissors sort of things down on one of the shelves and I figured with that stuff, I could pull out some of the copper. I got a couple small pieces, and that's when I heard noise from upstairs."

"What kind of noise?" I asked.

"People walking around. Voices."

I glanced at Declan but since he didn't say a thing, I took the lead. "Men's voices?"

The kid shrugged.

"Women's?"

Another shrug. "Just voices, and I wasn't paying a whole lot of attention because I thought . . . well, I figured I was screwed for sure. That somebody who worked there came in for something and that they were going to find me if I didn't haul my butt out of there."

"And that's when you dropped what little copper you'd already cut and ran?"

He nodded in answer to my question. "Only I didn't get very far. I just got over to the steps that led up to that door I came in when I heard a guy say something pretty loud. Then there was another sound, like chairs falling over."

I could picture the scene. "And then?" I asked him.

"Then things got really quiet." As if he were reliving the scene, Owen froze at the center of the room, his arms tight against his sides, his breath suspended. "I waited," he said, glancing up at the ceiling just like he must have glanced up when he was down in the Terminal's basement. "I dunno how long. I thought"—he swallowed hard—"I thought if I ducked out the door I came in, somebody might see me. So I just stood there. And then, that's when I heard the glass break."

I glanced at Declan. "The back door? Upstairs? The door that leads right outside?"

He looked at Owen. "You're sure it was after you heard

the commotion? Not before? Because both the killer and the victim had to get in the restaurant, and that broken back door was the only way in."

Not the only way.

It wasn't like I thought Declan could read my mind, but I looked away, anyway. Just so there was no chance he'd pick up on the fact that I was thinking about Sophie. Sophie, and her front door key.

"It was after," Owen said. "I'm sure. I think."

"It's important, Owen," Declan reminded him.

The kid squeezed his eyes shut. His hair was blunt cut and hung to his collar and he tugged at one red lock. "Maybe it was before," he said, and turned pleading eyes toward his cousin. "I dunno. I was scared, Declan. That proves I couldn't have killed that guy, right? I was scared that somebody would find me and that means I'd never have the nerve to do something like kill somebody. I sneaked back up the steps and I couldn't risk walking out of the building and going around front and over to Uncle Pat and Aunt Kitty's because I figured whoever was in the restaurant, they might see me and figure out what I was doing. So I hid behind the Dumpster."

"For how long?" I asked.

The kid shrugged. "Don't tell nobody." He slid Declan a look. "If Jamie or Connor or Brendan find out—"

"What your cousins think of you is the least of your worries," Declan told him. "You realized you'd done something wrong, you were afraid of being caught. They'd understand why you were hiding."

"I should have took some of that copper with me," Owen grumbled, then swallowed his words at a fierce look from Declan.

I ignored their sparring. "Well, you couldn't have been

there for hours and hours," I said, thinking over everything Owen told us. "So when Sophie and I arrived, that must have been soon after whoever killed Jack left."

"I just got up the nerve to slip out from behind the Dumpster and run. That's when I heard your car," Owen said. "After that, well, I heard you talking from out front." He looked toward Declan. "And then the lights came on. And then . . ." Owen ran his tongue over his lips. "Then the police cars showed up and the ambulances and all those reporters. If I ran, it would look really bad. So I went back behind the Dumpster and stayed there."

"And that looked really bad, too," Declan reminded him.

One hand out, Owen took a step toward his cousin, then realized that he looked too needy and pulled back. "What's going to happen to me?" he asked.

"Well, you're not going to prison for a murder you didn't commit," Declan told him. "I can guarantee that. As for the copper . . ."

He left the words hanging in the air, and Owen to think about them.

Outside in the hallway, Declan shut the bedroom door and turned to me. "So the back door was broken in either before or after the murder. What does that tell us?"

"I can't imagine." I could, of course, but since what I imagined was Sophie using her key to go into the restaurant for some unknown reason, killing Jack for some other unknown reason, and then breaking the window in the back door to make it look like the Terminal had been broken into, I decided I was better off playing dumb.

Playing dumb and changing the subject.

As it turned out, that was easy enough to do when we walked back down into the living room and I caught a whiff of the scent wafting from the kitchen.

I drew in a deep breath. "Cayenne pepper," I said. "Just a little. And garlic and thyme. And beer. Something dark and strong."

Declan confirmed this with a nod. "Mom's cooking for tomorrow. I have no doubt you smell Guinness and some red wine, too, I bet. She likes to replace some of the water in her grandmother's recipe with a little of each."

The scent was a siren's song, and I followed it, my nose in the air. "There's Worcestershire, too," I said before we arrived in the kitchen. "And bay leaves and onion."

"You've got another convert, Ma," Declan announced when we stepped into the bustling kitchen. "Laurel's come about the Irish stew."

Ellen wiped her hands on her apron. "It's not ready yet, I'm afraid. If you'd like to come back tomorrow for the party—"

"I've got to work tomorrow." Was that my voice, so high-pitched and eager to distance myself from the swirl of Declan's family life? I consoled myself with the fact that no one could blame me. I'd never had a family of my own and this . . .

Three little kids barreled through the back door and their grandmother reminded them to walk inside the house. They listened, at least until they got as far as the dining room, where they checked over their shoulders to make sure she was busy and broke into a trot.

This was overwhelming.

"Well, if you can't come back tomorrow, maybe Declan can bring you a container of stew," Ellen said. "That is . . ." She looked up at her son, all sweetness and innocence. "If you'll be seeing Laurel again, that is."

"She works across the street, Ma," he reminded her.

"Of course." Ellen scurried over a desk built into the

countertop next to the refrigerator. She dug around and came back my way holding an index card.

"Here's the recipe," she said. "We say it's Grandma's but truth be told, I think it was her grandmother's and probably hers before that." She stopped just before she handed over the card. "We don't share this with just anyone."

"Then I'm grateful," I said when she handed over the recipe. "I can't wait to try it."

"She'll add sushi to it," Declan said. "Or tofu. Then Grandma will haunt her."

Thank goodness for the distraction! I elbowed him in the ribs.

After all, it was better than letting him know that I was worried.

About murder.

About lies.

And about why someone had unlocked the front door of the Terminal, then smashed in the back window to make it look like a break-in.

Chapter 13

The good news—when I got back to the Traintown neighborhood, the street in front of the restaurant was crammed with cars and news vans and reporters who were lounging around looking antsy and eager for a tip just like they'd been lounging around and looking antsy and eager for a tip since I'd discovered Jack's body.

The bad news—as far as I could see, just about all those reporters in all those cars and news vans had a Caf-Fiends bag or to-go coffee cup with them.

"Bad morning?" Inez was just refilling Lou's daily order of pancakes and she looked up when I stomped in and slammed the door behind me.

"No." I didn't want to give Lou—our one and only customer at the moment—the wrong idea, so I waved off her concern. "Just hard finding a parking place out there."

Inez leaned back so she could peer beyond the waiting area to the front door and the street outside. She didn't say a word. She didn't have to. She raised her eyebrows and shook her head.

I glanced around the quiet restaurant. "No Denice?"

"Not this early. Not on Friday." Inez scampered up front to cash in Lou's bill and I followed along. "We're open late Fridays and Saturdays, until nine. So I do the early shift and Denice comes in later and works until closing. And if we're busy . . ." The way she said it, I could tell that Inez didn't think this was actually a possibility. "We call Judy. She used to work here full-time. Back in the day. And she's always willing to work an extra shift if we need her."

Good to know.

If we were ever busy.

The thought settled in my head and my shoulders drooped. "I don't know how we're ever going to be busy unless we try something different. But people around here don't want to try menu items that are new and different, not unless it's pizza and wraps," I grumbled, more to myself than to Inez.

That didn't stop her from replying. "This is Hubbard. We're pretty ordinary people. We don't like things like salmon and leeks. Not in a restaurant like this, anyway. If we're looking for food like that, we get dressed up and find a linen-tablecloth kind of place. But when we just want good food, we come to a place like this, and we come to a place like this because it's homey. That means we're looking for comfort food."

"Then we should be packed! Fried bologna and onions, some people think that's homey, don't they?" The very thought made me shiver. "Or meatballs and rice."

"Or wraps and pizza."

The new comfort food.

"So people's idea of what comfort food is and isn't

changes," I commented. "Maybe we need to change, too. And not to a place that sells panini sandwiches and wraps. It wouldn't do us or Caf-Fiends any good to fight over the same customers."

"At our house . . ." Just thinking about it made Inez smile. "Comfort food is things like chicken and rice. What we call arroz con pollo. Or fried plantains, or bean and cheese burritos or menudo." She sighed. "That's tripe and hominy soup, and before you turn up your nose—"

"I've had menudo. I've cooked menudo," I assured her, thinking of the months I'd spent in Mexico with Meghan when she was shooting a movie there. Menudo's ability to cure hangovers is legendary and the way I remembered it, Meghan was feuding with a certain somebody who eventually became her ex. Those days, the tequila flowed like water. Meghan needed plenty of menudo. "You don't have to convince me how good it is."

"Well, that's just it, isn't it?" Inez scooped Lou's change out of the cash register, took it over to him, and headed back into the waiting area. "Everybody has their own idea of what comfort food is, and it changes, you know? The way cities change because the people who live in them changes. Some people think of comfort food as arroz con pollo, and some people think it's something like stuffed cabbage. Some people think of it as Italian food or Hungarian food or—"

"Irish food." I plucked Ellen Fury's recipe for Irish stew out of my purse and, thinking, tapped the index card against my chin. "What if we tried to cater to them?"

"All of them?" Inez laughed. "If we tried to pack our menu with Polish food and Japanese food and Indian food—"

"There's no way we could handle that. Not with our small

kitchen." I nodded. "But if we ran specials featuring one ethnic food at a time . . ."

"Like every day."

"Or every week or two. That would be more practical from a menu standpoint and as far as getting supplies and arranging advertising." The moment the words were out of my mouth, an unfamiliar feeling zipped through my bloodstream and thumped inside my rib cage. It caught me by surprise and it took me a moment to realize what it was.

Interest. Curiosity. Excitement.

Emotions I'd been too numb to feel since Meghan gave me the ol' heave-ho and pummeled my culinary dreams.

When I headed into the kitchen, recipe in hand, I found myself smiling.

"Ethnic foods," I crooned. "Different, interesting ethnic foods. Designed to appeal to the different and interesting people of Hubbard." I imagined the ad we'd put in the local paper, and practically skipped the last few steps and, yes, when I handed Ellen's recipe to George as if it were being presented on a silver platter, he did give me a funny look.

It didn't help when I added, "Take that, wraps and pizza!"

IT WAS NEARLY four, and I knew Dale, Phil, Ruben, and Stan would be hitting the road soon. They'd enjoyed the lunch special—Swiss steak—and I don't know how many cups of coffee, and even though we were open late, they'd disappear to wherever it was they disappeared to every day at this time.

Which was why I was surprised when instead of saying, "See you tomorrow, kiddo," like he always did on his way out the door, Dale waved me over to the table near the windows.

"What is it?" he asked.

Blank stares are so not a good look for me!

I snapped my mouth shut so I could ask, "What is . . ."

Phil breathed in deep. "That smell. What is it? It smells like—"

"Heaven!" Stan grinned.

And I couldn't help but grin back. "That is tonight's dinner special," I told them. "Irish stew."

"Irish!" Dale chuckled. "We've already got an Irish store around here. We don't need more Irish. We need Polish food."

"Or Latin food," Ruben put in.

"Or good ol' Southern home cookin'!" Stan rubbed his stomach with one hand. "My mother could cook up a pot of red beans and rice like nobody else. I'll bring you her recipe."

"I'd appreciate that. And I'll take your suggestions into consideration." I passed around the handwritten menus I'd gotten ready for the evening. In addition to our usual Friday-night fare—fish and chips, Swiss steak (hey, why waste anything left over from lunch?), and bean soup—I'd added Irish stew and even embellished the menu with a couple little hand-drawn shamrocks.

Declan would approve.

I shook the thought away. "For the next week, we're going to feature Irish food," I told the guys and prayed they didn't ask which dishes we'd be adding since I hadn't had a chance to research Irish recipes yet and I had no idea. "We're starting with a local family recipe."

"Well, if it tastes anything like it smells . . ." Stan drew in a deep breath right before he fished his phone out of his pocket. "I'm going to call Alice and tell her to meet me here for dinner."

"Good idea." Dale grabbed his phone, too. "I'll give Georgia a call. She's watching the grandkids today and it would be easier for her to come here for dinner than have her cooking for three extra people."

Smiling, I left them to it.

My smile didn't last long when I saw Kim Kline and a colleague come through the front door.

"Dinner, or are you looking for info?" I asked her.

"Dinner? Here?" She glanced around, a little uncertain, then realized that kind of charm would get her nowhere. "It's not like I haven't thought about ordering anything to eat here," Kim said, glossy curls swinging. "It's just that my schedule never allows it and it's never been convenient to stop in for a meal and—"

"Uh-huh." I backed up a step, the better to let her walk through the waiting area and to a table.

Like she was facing a firing squad, she squared her shoulders and looked at her companion. "Dustin? I'm game if you are."

Dustin was apparently game. I showed the duo to a table and wondered where the heck Denice was. It was after four and she should have been here, and now that we had something of a minirush (Okay, very mini) going, we'd be needing her.

As if just the thought conjured her up, Denice raced through the front door. Her son, Ronnie, was with her.

"Sorry." She zipped past me, her yellow Terminal polo shirt untucked. "Ronnie and I had some stuff to take care of at the bank and the lines were long and . . ." She waved her son over to a table. "I'll get you coffee, hon," she told him. "Just give me a minute."

Since she was getting herself settled, I grabbed a couple

of my new, handwritten menus and gave one to Dustin and one to Kim.

"Irish stew?" She crinkled her nose.

I darted a glance across the street toward the Irish store. "A neighborhood family recipe," I told her, and was sure to add, "though I've changed it up a bit, made a few modifications."

"The Fury family?" Kim sat up and looked across the street, too. "All right, I'm game. I'll give it a try. Denice . . ." When the waitress zipped by, Kim buttonholed her. "I'll try the stew and Dustin . . ." She looked his way and he nodded. "Make that two."

I am happy to report that the rest of the late afternoon went pretty much the same. Dale, Phil, Ruben, and Stan's significant others showed and brought along an assortment of friends and grandchildren. Once a couple of the reporters outside saw that Kim was inside at a table and talking to the staff, they obviously thought they were missing something; they came in and ordered, too. Marvin, the customer who a few days earlier had been worried that I'd scoop up Denice's $1.75 tip and leave town with it, showed up and sat down at a table close to where Ronnie sipped cup after cup of coffee and wolfed down the slice of apple pie I wasn't supposed to notice that Denice slipped him.

Inez—bless her!—arranged for her mom to watch her son and agreed to stay on a couple extra hours. I was headed into the waiting area to get the next batch of guests to seat, and met her near the table where Kim and Dustin were enjoying their stew.

"You're a genius," she said.

As much as I'd like to believe that, I wasn't convinced. "They're not all ordering the Irish stew."

She laughed. "They're not. Not all of them. But George said if you're keeping it on the menu for tomorrow, he'll have to make another batch in the morning."

"Hey, Inez! More coffee here!"

She glanced across the restaurant at Ronnie, who waved her over.

"Kid must have kidneys like nobody else in the world," she grumbled at the same time she held up a finger to tell him she'd be right there. "Drinks plenty of coffee and never budges from that table."

"And, let me guess, he never actually orders a meal. Not one he's going to pay for, anyway."

She rolled her dark eyes.

Apparently, that was enough to signal to Denice what— and who—we were talking about. "He's a good kid," she said when she zipped by with a tray on her shoulder. "And it's not like he's taking up a table where customers would be sitting. Well, not usually, anyway. Am I right, Marvin?" She raised her voice enough to be heard by Marvin, who was seated two tables away. "My Ronnie, he's a good kid, right?"

Marvin wiped a paper napkin over his mouth. "The best. He should be on TV!"

"Yeah!" Denice laughed. "Imagine him on the big screen. You know, one of those flat-screen TVs like they hang on the wall, forty-two inches wide."

"Forty-eight inches," Ronnie called out. "I'd look way better on a screen that was forty-eight inches wide."

"Forty-eight inches." Marvin chuckled. "Yeah, that sounds good."

It was all in good fun and we all laughed before we headed off to our duties. Denice and Inez waited on customers. I ducked into the kitchen to make sure George was handling the rush, and I wasn't surprised to see that he was. As long as I was in there, I talked him out of two pieces of chocolate cream pie and brought them out front with me. I set one piece down in front of Dustin and the other in front of Kim. That is, before I sat down in the seat across from hers.

"What's this? We didn't order pie."

"Compliments of the house," I told her. "If this is your first time eating here, we want to make sure you have a good experience."

Dustin—who was apparently a man of few words—dug in. Kim took a bite of pie and smiled her approval. "I wasn't lying," she said, her disposition sweetened by the combination of chocolate pudding and real cream whipped to peaks of perfection. "I have thought about eating here before, I've just never had the opportunity. Then when Jack's body was found here . . . well"—she set down her fork—"I have to admit that just the thought of eating a meal in a place where a murder happened . . ." She shivered and hugged her arms around herself.

I glanced at Kim's and Dustin's empty dinner plates. "Well, I'm glad you enjoyed your dinners in spite of all that. And I was wondering . . ." I waited until Kim lifted her fork again. With any luck, she'd keep her mind on George's rich and creamy pie and she wouldn't notice how eager I was for an answer. "Have you found out anything? You said you were looking into the Lance of Justice's old files. And I know it's none of my business," I was sure to add even though since the murder went down at the Terminal, I figured it kind of was. "But I just can't help but wondering if there's some connection to the restaurant."

And to the woman who owns it.

I clamped my lips shut and didn't dare let those last words

sneak past them. The last thing I needed was to let some nosy reporter find out that I had my suspicions about Sophie.

What I got in return from Kim was a smile that I wouldn't exactly call gracious. I had a feeling it was more like the kind of smile she would have given a cute—but naughty— puppy. Or someone she considered far below her in brainpower.

"The story of the Lance of Justice's murder has local Emmy written all over it," she crooned. "You know I can't give away the details. They're just too delicious."

I wasn't sure if this was good news or bad. That would explain why my heart started up a funny, stuttering rhythm inside my chest. "Then, you do know something?"

She gobbled down the last bite of chocolate pie and her timing was perfect; Denice came over to collect the dishes just as Kim said, "Not only do I know something, but I have a line on who killed the Lance of Justice, and why."

I caught my breath, almost afraid to ask, "Shouldn't you tell the police?"

Kim sat back so Denice could reach across the table and grab Dustin's plate. "Not yet," she purred. "I'm not quite ready yet to reveal all. I will tell you . . ." She looked left and right and, sure that none of the other reporters were anywhere near, she leaned closer and lowered her voice. "I will tell you something curious and maybe you can explain it to me."

I swallowed hard and prayed that Sophie's name wasn't about to come up. "I'll try."

"I went through Jack's files. You know, as part of digging into his life and his final days. He had receipts from here at the Terminal. He was here just about every day."

This wasn't news and I told her so.

"But here's the thing I think is weird." She scooted her

chair closer to mine and it scraped across the weathered floor like fingernails on a blackboard. "This is the most people I've ever seen in this place. I'm right, right?" She didn't wait for me to answer. "I mean, no offense, but every time I looked in the windows before today, this place was like a morgue. No customers. So, I'm thinking in the last few weeks when Jack was here, there weren't all that many customers, either. I'm guessing . . ." She looked around and then, because she was afraid she'd look too obvious and some of the other reporters at nearby tables might catch on, she sat back and stared down at the table in front of her. "He could have sat anywhere, right? I mean, if there were no customers, he would have just waltzed in and sat anywhere he wanted to."

"That's not exactly the way it works in restaurants," I told her. "When there are fewer customers . . ." Notice I did not use the words *no customers*. "We generally close off a section or two. Let's say it was a typical afternoon. We might have seated Jack over by the windows because people like to watch the trains go by and so that's the first section we fill. We'd leave the tables by the kitchen empty and the ones over there." I waved in the general area of the tables along the front of the restaurant where I'd found Jack's body. "There's no use having our waitresses running all over the place. If we keep our customers contained in one area, our waitstaff has less ground to cover."

"Well, that explains it, then." Kim nodded like she'd already thought of this theory on her own and just needed confirmation. "See, every receipt I have of his says Jack was seated at table number sixteen. Every time he came here. So I guess table number sixteen"—she gave the restaurant a sharp-eyed once-over—"that must be right over by the windows somewhere."

I managed a smile and, three cheers for me, I kept it in place, too. Right before I pointed toward the windows along the back of the Terminal and to a table that was definitely not table number sixteen.

"Right over there," I told Kim.

A lie?

Theoretically, I guess it was. But see, I had my reasons and they bounced around inside my head along with the question that burned through my brain.

Jack Lancer kept his receipts from the Terminal?

Before I got carried away, I reminded myself that there were any number of possible reasons.

He might have kept the receipts because he was simply careless and didn't clean out his files often enough.

Or it could have been because he was dishonest and had plans to scam the system.

But those receipts might mean something else, too. And my money was on that something else.

See, if Jack kept his Terminal receipts in with his business files, that told me he thought of the money he spent here at the restaurant as legitimate business expenses.

And that meant he was hanging around the Terminal because he was working on a story.

Ice formed in my stomach, but I kept my voice even when I managed to say, "Maybe Jack liked to watch the trains."

"Maybe." Kim gathered her purse and her receipt and went up front to the register with Dustin trailing behind, and because I knew Inez and Denice were both busy, I cashed them out. I counted to ten once Kim and Dustin were out the front door, and when I was done, I counted to ten again and I refused to budge. Just in case Kim happened to look back, I didn't want to look too eager.

With that in mind, I took my time when I strolled back into the restaurant to do a little verification of my own.

Table sixteen.

I skirted the jut-out that was the back wall of the waiting area and headed over to the tables at the front of the restaurant, where I'd found Jack's body.

That table, just for the record, was number fourteen.

And table number sixteen?

I got to that table—the one right next to the one at which Jack had spent his last moments on earth—and sat down where Jack must have sat all those days when he'd been here on business, all those days when he must have been working on a lead.

And a story.

And an investigation.

And I looked where he'd been looking all that time. And watched what he must have been watching.

My heart skipped a beat, then another one just for good measure.

Table number sixteen.

Table number sixteen gave Jack Lancer a bird's-eye view of the Irish store.

Chapter 14

"What, no line out the door yet?"

We'd been blessedly busy on Friday evening, that was for sure, but we were far from slammed, so I should have known Declan wasn't serious. That didn't keep me from stepping back, my weight against one foot, and giving him a long, hard look when he breezed into the Terminal bright and early on Saturday morning.

That is, right before I looked over his shoulder, out the window, and at the Irish store.

Curious?

Oh, I wasn't just curious about what the Lance of Justice had been up to every day with his butt in a chair and his eyes on Declan's business, I was downright dying to figure out what was going on.

And if it had anything to do with Sophie.

And Jack Lancer's death.

Hoping to make it look like I wasn't nearly as interested

as I really was, I kept my voice cool and level when I asked, "Don't you have a first communion party to go to?"

"You remembered." Declan was carrying a box, one of those white cardboard archive boxes with a lid, and he set it down on the rolltop desk. "You sure you don't want to come?"

"To your family party?" Because I couldn't explain how the very thought of being with that much family was not only unfamiliar, but terrifying, I didn't elaborate and I didn't answer. "What are you doing here at this time of the morning?" I asked him instead.

"The party doesn't start until this afternoon." As if he had every right, he moved toward the kitchen. "That means I have time for a cup of coffee. Have I told you that you make a really good cup of coffee?"

Flattery would get him nowhere, and he should have realized that by now. But I hadn't had my first cup of coffee yet, either, and I did want to dig a little deeper. Into Declan's business. Into Declan's motives. I pushed through the swinging kitchen door and behind me, he stopped, his fists on his hips, and breathed in deep.

"Mom's Irish stew! I'd know the smell that lingers in the air for days anywhere. So, what I heard yesterday isn't just a neighborhood rumor."

"Before you get the wrong idea—"

"Would I?" When he stepped nearer and looked down at me, his eyes gleamed. "Get the wrong idea, I mean. What about?"

"It is your mother's recipe." Since that index card from Ellen was out on the counter, there was no use denying it. "But I made some modifications."

As if he'd never seen the recipe before—and really, I didn't believe this; I think he'd seen it so many times, he knew it by heart—he picked up the card and read over the ingredients.

"I changed up the red wine for Bloody Mary mix to give it a little kick," I told him, pointing to the entry in his mother's neat handwriting. "I added a little bit of brown sugar and a dash of Irish whiskey, too."

"You didn't mess with the Guinness, did you?"

"Never!" I handed Declan a cup of coffee and poured one for myself.

"There's a tradition in my family," he told me. "About how stew is always better the day after it's prepared. Especially if you allow it to simmer on the stove nice and slow for a couple of hours before you serve it. But that doesn't mean a bowl of it couldn't be heated up in the microwave. I mean, if there was an emergency."

He was teasing.

And I was thinking it was the perfect opening I needed. To get him to hang around. To get him to talk.

With a smile I hoped didn't look too self-satisfied, I took a bowl to the cooler, loaded it with some of yesterday's stew, and stuck it in the microwave.

"Are you going to report back to your mother?" I asked him while it heated.

"No doubt she already knows what you're up to. Kitty and Pat would have made sure of that."

Kitty and Pat. I thought back to what I'd heard from Carrie at the art gallery the day she dished about the neighborhood and its denizens and threw caution to the wind. Hey, this was a murder investigation. And I needed answers.

"It is true?" I asked Declan, stopping the microwave and checking the temperature on the stew. It was just right, but when I took the bowl out, I held on to it for a while. The aroma that drifted off it was both tempting and tantalizing. Maybe that would work to my benefit.

"I heard your uncle is the head of the local Irish mob."

Declan's granite gaze snapped from the bowl in my hands to me. "Who says?"

"I heard it around."

"And you're wondering if Uncle Pat's . . . affiliation . . ." He pronounced the word exactly as I would expect an attorney to. Carefully. As if to say I could draw my own conclusions, but he sure as heck wasn't going to say anything specific. Or damning. "You think what Uncle Pat may or may not have been up to has something to do with Jack Lancer's murder?"

"I think Jack Lancer wasn't just hanging around here every day because he liked the pie, though I do have to say, we have really good pie."

"And really good Irish stew. So I've heard."

What is it they call it in lawyerspeak? Quid pro quo?

Clearly, if he was going to tell me anything, it would cost me a bowl of Irish stew.

Since it was warm, I set the bowl down on the counter rather than hand it to him, and I got him a spoon.

"Bon appétit," I told him.

"*Sláinte*," he said, and he pronounced the word *slantay*. That is, right before he bowed his head over the bowl of stew.

"For food in a world where many walk in hunger," Declan said softly. "For faith in a world where many walk in fear. For friends . . ." He glanced my way before he lowered his eyes again. "For friends in a world where many walk alone. We give you thanks, Lord."

He grabbed the spoon and dug in. He blew on the spoonful of beef, potatoes, and carrots, then popped it in his mouth and held it there before he chewed and swallowed. "Hmmmm."

"Hmmmm? Is that hmmmm good, or hmmmm bad?"

"Hmmmm."

He was teasing. Again. Rather than look too eager, I went to the cooler and got out the ingredients that George would need to start the day's batch of stew. Carrots, potatoes, parsnips, leeks.

It didn't hurt to look busy, and not too interested in what he might—or might not—be willing to share about his uncle Pat.

Unless Uncle Pat wasn't the one Jack Lancer was interested in.

It wasn't the first time I'd run the theory through my brain, because the night before when I tried to make friends with Muffin and got slashed knuckles again for my effort, I couldn't get it out of my head.

Jack Lancer was watching the Irish store.

And in addition to taking care of all his family's business, Declan ran the Irish store.

"So, what kinds of work do you do for your family?" I asked him.

He swallowed a mouthful of stew and don't think I didn't notice that the question didn't surprise him. "Like I told you before, I help them out. With legal questions and all."

"Was there any reason that might have interested Jack Lancer?"

He'd been blowing off a particularly hot chunk of parsnip and he paused, his lips pursed, and looked over at me. "You think he was here at the Terminal because of me?"

"I think he had a line on an idea for an investigation. And I wonder if that investigation had something to do with you."

"It didn't."

"You seem pretty sure."

His smile was nothing if not angelic. "My soul is as pure as the driven snow and my reputation is just as sparkly clean. In case you're wondering, so is Uncle Pat's."

"That's not what I heard."

"About me? Or about Uncle Pat?"

I threw my hands in the air. "Don't you want to get to the bottom of this?"

"This bowl of stew?" He scraped his spoon through the last of the thick gravy and finished it off. "Absolutely. And I'll be back later for more. But you know, if you're going to feature Irish food, you'll need to add another dish or two. I'm thinking colcannon would be perfect."

I hadn't asked for the recipe. How could I when I was so busy choking on the aggravation that stemmed from that oh so easy smile and the maddening way he had of blowing off every important question I asked him? Declan, though, had other ideas. He pulled a printed recipe out of his pocket and handed it to me.

"Mashed potatoes with plenty of butter," he said while I looked over the ingredients. "Steamed shredded cabbage and my own secret ingredient, a bit of steamed kale. You won't see that in most recipes, but it adds a nice dash of color. So do the chopped scallions you sprinkle on top before you serve it. Panache—it's what you California girls are all about, right?"

Right about then, I was all about feeling as if I wanted to wring his neck. I might have, too, if George hadn't tromped into the kitchen.

"Good morning," Declan called to him.

George grunted.

Frustrated and annoyed, I went out into the restaurant. I wasn't surprised when Declan followed.

"It's better than hers, you know," he said, stopping me in my tracks.

I turned to face him. "I assume we're talking about the stew because apparently, stew is all we can talk about, even when there's been a murder here and the murderer is still on the loose."

"Stew is what we're talking about. And yours is better than my mother's. I will say that to you here and now, but don't ever expect me to say it in front of her. Ellen Katherine Kane Fury has a reputation in these parts, and she takes it seriously. It would break her heart to know some fancy-schmancy chef could actually improve the old family recipe."

I bristled at the *fancy-schmancy*, but there was no use mentioning it. He wouldn't listen, anyway. "Your secret is safe with me."

"But still, you don't trust me."

"How can I?" I spun away from him and went to the waiting area. "I never get a straight answer out of you."

I knew he'd followed me, but I didn't realize just how closely. When I got to the rolltop desk and whirled around, my nose was practically pressed to the dark green T-shirt he wore with an unbuttoned green and white plaid shirt.

He crooked a finger under my chin and this time when he looked into my eyes, there was no sparkle of amusement in his. He was as serious as a heart attack. "I'm being as honest with you as I can be," he said.

Since my mouth was suddenly dry and my voice was breathy, it wasn't easy, but I managed to say, "Spoken like an attorney."

"Hey!" His mouth inched into a smile and he stroked his finger from beneath my chin to just under my bottom lip. "Now you're getting personal."

"I could say the same about you."

"Not as personal as I'd like to get."

"Really?" I batted his hand away and backed up as much as I was able. No easy task considering the corner of the rolltop desk poked me in the small of the back. "You think I can be so easily distracted?"

His pout wasn't all that convincing. "I've been told I'm pretty good at being distracting."

"Well, it's not going to work. Not with me. So, here's an idea: you can take your oversized ego and your lame pickup lines and your—"

"But I brought presents." Declan whisked the archive box off the desk and popped off the top. "The least you can do is not kick me out until I can give them to you."

I crossed my arms over my chest. "I don't want your presents."

"You don't know what they are." He reached into the box, brought out a dozen small orange, white, and green Irish flags on sticks and wiggled his eyebrows. "See? What do you say? Would these make great decorations, or what? If you're going to feature Irish food, you should have Irish flags, too. Everybody knows that."

"Everybody doesn't know anything."

"And a large Irish flag." He pulled that out of the box, too. "You can hang it . . ." He looked around the waiting area and his eyes lit up and he pointed to the front door. "I've got one of those flagpoles back at the shop. You know, the kind you can mount to a wall. I'll have it up outside your front door in a jiffy. What better way to advertise the fact that you're featuring the greatest cuisine in the world!"

"We don't need hokey gimmicks," I grumbled.

"Yeah, like adding Irish food to the menu to entice customers isn't a hokey gimmick?"

He didn't give me a chance to answer before he pulled a stuffed leprechaun out of the box.

"Paddy!" I remembered the leprechaun in his green suit from the visit I'd made to the Irish store. "You said he was your shop mascot."

"Well, he's good luck, and it's only fair to spread a little of that around the neighborhood." Declan plopped Paddy down on top of the cash register. "I've got other things in here, too," he said, tipping the box so I could see inside. "Green streamers, sparkling rainbows, a wreath made of wooden shamrocks. And check these out!" He took them out of the box so I could see them better. "Little pots of gold on sticks so you can put them in drinks or in pieces of cake."

I can't say if I was horrified by the over-the-top tackiness of it all or just speechless at the fact that Declan had decided—without even consulting me—that a change in decor was needed along with a change in the menu.

Before I had a chance to think it through, Inez came in. She took one look at the box of goodies in Declan's hands and a broad smile lit her face. "What a terrific idea!" Before I could tell her it wasn't, she grabbed the streamers and the rainbows and the wreath and skipped into the restaurant with them. "I know just where to put it all," she called back to me. "This is going to be terrific."

"See, terrific." Declan poked me in the ribs with one elbow. "Get with the program. Have a little fun."

"Fine. Good." I knew a losing cause when I saw one. "If it will help fill the tables . . ."

"Oh, the Irish food will do that." He gave me a wink before he went to the door. "You'll see. Paddy . . ." With one finger, he pointed at the grinning leprechaun perched on the cash register. "Paddy will take care of the rest."

With that, he walked outside whistling "When Irish Eyes Are Smiling," and before I even had a chance to catch my breath, George shuffled into the waiting area. "I've got it ready," he said. "You know, for tomorrow."

I shook my head to clear it. For reasons I didn't exactly understand and didn't want to think about, whenever Declan was around, it felt as if the earth had tipped a bit on its axis. In an effort to get my bearings I braced a hand against the desk, squared my shoulders, and faced George.

"What is it and what's happening tomorrow?"

He scrubbed a finger under his nose and looked down at his shoes. "Sorry. Forgot you haven't been here on a Sunday. The stuff for the food pantry at St. Colman's. I get it ready every Saturday. So Sophie can take it over on Sunday after she goes to church. This week we've got some canned tomatoes, a few bottles of apple juice, tuna. They always need tuna."

George showed me the spot in the kitchen where everything was boxed up and waiting, and even before he walked away I found myself thinking.

Food pantry.

Where Declan volunteered.

And so did Sophie.

And didn't Kim once mention that Jack Lancer had a slim file about the food pantry?

I set all this aside as thoughts for another time and gave George and Inez instructions about what they should do for the rest of the morning.

Me?

Like everyone else in Hubbard, I'd watched the news the night before and I knew that there was a memorial service scheduled that morning for Jack Lancer.

The least I could do was pay my respects.

Chapter 15

I was wearing black pants and a black-and-white-striped silk shirt, and I threw on a white linen blazer, a pair of Kate Spade lace and leather pumps, and a big dose of the attitude that I'd learned back in Hollywood when I found myself dealing with stylists, paparazzi, publicists, actors with egos the size of Texas, and the hangers-on (most of them pathetic wannabes) who flocked around them all like seagulls following in the wake of a ship.

Not to brag or anything, but when I arrived at the Worth Funeral Chapel, I got the distinct feeling that Hubbard, Ohio, had never seen anything quite like it.

In fact, I was counting on it.

Like the Red Sea in front of Moses, the crowds in the parking lot parted when I walked through, head up, shoulders back, and that gleam in my eyes that told them I owned the world and they'd better get used to it. The same thing happened on the sidewalk in front of the well-kept brick building where hundreds of the truly sorrowful and the plenty curious were packed like sardines waiting to pay their respects to Jack Lancer.

A little style, a little swagger, and a whole bunch of chutzpah, and I arrived at the front door, where a grim-faced man in a black suit spoke in hushed whispers.

"We're only allowing family and close friends in right now," he said.

I hoped my smile was bittersweet enough to pass muster. "Good," I told him, and walked right by him and into the building.

In fact, the arrangement wasn't just good, it was perfect. There was a cluster of a dozen or so people standing outside an open door where a nine-by-sixteen photograph of Jack Lancer was displayed along with a table full of local Emmy awards and testimonials from everyone from city council members to the mayor to someone named Clowning Carl, who'd written a flowery memorial poem that managed to rhyme *Lance* with things like *square dance, cash advance*, and *game of chance*, and signed it all with a smiley face complete with a big red nose.

Inside the room where a gleaming oak casket was displayed (closed, thank goodness) under dim, pinkish light, another twenty people were standing in small clusters and speaking to one another in hushed tones.

I made myself right at home and, believe me, I didn't waste any time. Once the guy in the black suit opened the doors to the public, I knew it would be impossible to speak to anyone. I did a quick scan of the room, chose my target, and closed in on a bleached blonde in a shape-hugging black dress with long, tight sleeves and a plunging neckline.

Why this woman?

I'd like to say I had a sixth sense about things like this.

Or that I was especially good at scanning a crowd and picking out those people I thought might be most helpful. But truth be told, the answer was far simpler than that: the woman's nose was wet and her eyes were red. In fact, she was the only one in the room who looked upset.

As if to prove it, just as I closed in on her, she pulled a tissue out of the box on the table near at hand and dabbed it to her blue eyes.

"It's terrible, isn't it?" I asked her, my voice as low as everyone else's in the room. "I'm Laurel."

She sniffed. "Maxine. Maxine Carmichael."

I don't think I was imagining it, she actually did say this like it was supposed to mean something.

I tried to look sympathetic when all I really felt was annoyed. These were the kinds of games actors played when they expected everyone to know each role they'd played and each movie they'd been in. I didn't expect the same sort of nonsense from a hometown woman whose lipstick was smudged and whose aqua eyeshadow practically screamed trailer trash. Believe me, I did not hold this against her. I'd been called that—and worse—back when I bounced from foster home to foster home, neighborhood to neighborhood, school to school. I knew what it meant. Trailer trash? Maybe. But that meant like me, she could be street-smart and plenty cagey.

I told myself not to forget it.

"I'm new in town," I said.

"But you were a friend of Jack's?" For the first time since I'd closed in on her, she gave me a careful look. Her eyes narrowed and her bottom lip jutted out like the prow of the *Titanic*. "How well did you know him?"

This was not a casual question. I knew this because Maxine's eyes shot blue fire in my direction.

"Not anywhere near as well as you obviously did," I said, and I guess I hit the nail on the head because she let go a long breath and took a step back and away from me. "I'm the one . . ." I glanced at the gleaming casket and at the floral tributes that surrounded it. "I'm the one who found Jack's body."

"Oh no!" Maxine's voice bounced along the walls with their tasteful paintings of flowers and forests, and she clamped a hand on my arm. "That's terrible."

I remembered to look upset, but while I was at it, don't think I didn't notice that everyone else in this company of family and close friends shot Maxine what I can only call death-ray looks. "It was," I told her.

"If only . . ." She ignored all those stares from all those people, raising her chin a fraction of an inch. "I should have been the one who found him," she said, and she pressed a hand to her heart. "Our lives were entwined. I should have been the one to escort him into the arms of Death."

She was being poetic. I was not when I asked, "So, you're telling me you didn't have anything to do with Jack's murder?"

Her shoulders shot back. "Who says I did? It was Jill, right?" Her top lip curled and she looked over her shoulder toward where a short woman in a navy suit was talking to two other ladies. "That bitch doesn't know when to keep her mouth shut."

"It wasn't Jill. I don't even know Jill." I felt this was important to point out before Maxine went to the other side of the room and gave Jill what for. "No one told me anything. Not about who might have killed Jack. I thought since you knew him so well—"

Maxine sighed. "We were soulmates. Our hearts beat as one. If you're looking for someone who had a reason to kill

Jack . . ." Again her gaze darted across the room at the three women.

"Jill?" I asked.

"Could be." Maxine's nose crinkled. "But it could be one of his other exes, too. You know, Tina or Deb."

This didn't exactly surprise me. After all, I'd lived six years in Hollywood, where the "until death do us part" line of the wedding vows was often omitted, simply because no one believed a marriage could possibly last that long. But I did need to be certain. "You mean, you think one of Jack's ex-wives might have killed him?"

"They hated him," Maxine told me in no uncertain terms. "And they hate me. Look at the way they're looking at me." As far as I could tell, Jill, Tina, and Deb weren't looking at Maxine at all, but that didn't stop her from harrumphing her opinion. "Jealous. Every single one of them. And it's annoying, you know? I mean, you probably don't. You probably don't know what it's like to have people watching your every move, keeping an eye on you, talking about what you're wearing and where you go and who you're with. But then, when you date the biggest celebrity in town—"

I had to be sure. "Jack."

"Of course, Jack. Who else could it be? I was always under a microscope. I still am. That's why they're watching me." She darted looks all around the room. "You know, people are jealous. Of me. Of what Jack and I had. Like the three of them." She tossed the exes a look of collective contempt. "Each and every one of them screwed it up big-time with Jack. It was only after he left them that they realized what they'd lost. But by then, it was too late. Jack wasn't the kind of guy who forgives easily. I was . . ." A tear trickled down her cheek. "I was a very lucky woman. There are few who know that kind of love."

Maybe, but don't think I'd forgotten what I'd learned about Jack from Kim and from Carrie. He was a man-about-town in a town where there wasn't much of anything to be about. I backed away from Maxine and headed over to talk to the exes.

"Friend of yours?" Jill asked with a look over my shoulder toward Maxine. She was a petite middle-aged woman with short, dark hair, and her smile was tight. "The grieving widow."

"Oh, I didn't know they were—"

"Oh, honey! They weren't!" Tina's hair was too red to be natural. She was as tall as I am, and as skinny as a green bean, and she wore a black sleeveless sheath that was both appropriate to the occasion and stylish. There were a dozen gold bangles on her left wrist and they clanged together when she barked out a laugh, then clamped a hand over her mouth to contain it. "But she sure would have liked to be."

"Idiot." Deb was the roundest and the oldest of the three women. Her silvery hair was cut in a stylish bob that brushed her cheeks when she bent closer and put a hand on my arm. She smelled slightly of scotch. "We don't know you, do we?"

"No, and Maxine, she doesn't, either." I thought this only fair to mention so they knew I wasn't one of the enemy. "I just stopped in to pay my respects. I'm the one . . ." I remembered Maxine's reaction to the news and tried to break it to them gently. "I'm the one who found Jack's body in the restaurant."

"You lucky dog!" Jill crooned.

Deb grinned. "What I wouldn't have given for a ringside seat for that event!"

"Not just on finding the body." Tina cackled and when she realized how loud she was, she lowered her head and

her voice. "It would have been way more fun to be the one
who killed the bastard."

"Amen." Deb raised an invisible glass to the ceiling.

"What?" When she saw my jaw go slack, Jill wrapped
an arm around my shoulders. "Are we shocking you?
We don't mean to, but, honey, if you were that close to Jack
there at the very end, the least you deserve is a little bit of
the truth. Girls?" She glanced around at the other exes.
"What do you say we take our new buddy here over to
McGee's?"

Deb looped one arm through mine. "Why not?" she said,
and started for the door with me in tow. "It's five o'clock
somewhere."

Tina fell into step beside us. "And now that Jack is dead,
we've definitely got something to celebrate!"

MCGEE'S WAS ONE of those places where they always keep
the lights low so patrons can't see the faded paint on the
walls or the gouges in the tile on the floor. There were
posters from beer companies up on the walls and a pool
table over in the corner next to a jukebox. Ten tables—I
counted them—and as many seats at the bar. A popcorn
machine, empty at this early hour, and an old guy down at
the end of the bar who looked like he'd been there forever.

What it lacked in ambience, the bar that sat across the
street and kitty-corner from the funeral chapel made up for
with down-home hospitality. A tall, thin man wearing a
white apron waved hello to us the moment we walked in and
told us to take a table along the far wall. From there, we
didn't have a thing to worry about. Deb—who apparently
spent a goodly amount of time there—ordered a pitcher of

margaritas, an order of onion rings, and a plate of nachos that turned out to be heaped with cheese, salsa, and jalapeño rings.

When the margaritas arrived, Tina poured and Jill raised a glass.

"To Jack Lancer," she said. "Lowest of the low."

"Nastiest of the nasty," Tina added.

"Dirtiest of dirty rats," Deb said, and took a nice, long drink.

I sipped, and realized that early hour or not, it was one of the best margaritas I'd ever had. When Tina handed around small plates, I took one and, like the other women, piled it with nachos. "It's odd," I ventured. "Three ex-wives drinking together. You're friends?"

"We sure weren't in the old days," Jill told me.

Tina laughed. "Jill was Mrs. Jack Lancer Number One." Jill was sitting next to her, Deb and I were across the table, and when Tina patted Jill's arm, those bangles on Tina's wrist added a *ching-a-ling* like castanets to her story. "When I started dating Jack—"

"While he was still married to me," Jill added for clarification.

Tina winced. "Well, let's just say that the first time I bumped into this lady here, Jack and I were coming out of a no-tell motel and she just happened to be running into the convenience store next door. It was not a pretty scene."

"Same here." Deb poured another margarita for herself. "Tina was Mrs. Number Two when I met Jack. He charmed me." She shook her head as if even now, she couldn't believe it. "What a blind idiot I was. He charmed me and I let it happen. Even though I knew about his reputation. But that's always the way it is, isn't it?" She glanced at her friends.

"We all believe we're going to be the one to change a man, the one who finally makes him settle down."

"Jack? Settle down?" Tina puffed out a breath of disbelief. "Once he pulled the same nonsense on Deb, well, that's when we all realized we had something in common."

"Good thing, too," Jill told me. "What you see here—our friendship—that's what's gotten each of us through the horrible experience that was Jack Lancer."

"To Jack!" Deb raised her glass again. "I'm so glad the creep is dead, if I had the energy, I'd do a little dance."

Their honesty was certainly refreshing. I only hoped if they were this direct when it came to their feelings about Jack, they'd be equally reliable when it came to the details of his life and maybe the reasons for his murder.

"So, I've heard . . ." There was gooey cheese on my fingers and I wiped them on a paper napkin that I plucked from the holder at the end of the table. "Somebody told me Jack used to have knock-down, drag-out phone fights with his ex. Which one of you was it?"

They threw back their heads and laughed so loud I couldn't hear the country song wailing from the jukebox.

"That was me," Jill confided.

"Or it could have been me," Tina said.

"Happened to me a time or two or three or four, too!" Deb howled with laughter.

"See, Jack . . ." Jill chomped into an onion ring and washed it down with a mouthful of margarita. "He was not an easy man to live with."

"Or not to live with," Tina added. "I think most of our fights happened once we were already divorced."

"Because . . ." I looked at the exes. "What did you fight about?"

"Alimony," Tina said.

"Child support," Jill admitted.

"Anything and everything," Deb put in. "That man didn't abide by anything in the divorce decree. He was supposed to make my mortgage payments."

"And never did," Tina said. "Mine, either. And he was supposed to pay for Jill's kids' private school."

"And never contributed a penny," Jill said.

It was a no-brainer, but as long as they were being so brutally honest, the least I could do was be just as aboveboard. "So, what you're telling me is that each of you had reason to hate Jack Lancer."

"Absolutely." Jill nodded.

"With a fiery passion." Tina grinned.

Deb took a drink. "With all my heart and all my soul."

"Did one of you kill him?"

Another round of laughs made even the old guy at the bar sit up and take notice.

"I wish!" Tina drifted a finger through the wet ring left on the table by her glass.

"If only I'd thought of it myself," Jill mumbled.

"We didn't do it." It was amazing that Deb could sound so stone-cold sober when it counted. "Not me, not any of us. And we didn't somehow work together to do it, either. It's kind of nice, though, isn't it, girls . . . ?" She looked at her friends. "It's kind of nice to know someone thinks we're clever enough to actually pull off a murder!"

I gave them a smile I hoped conveyed my apologies. "I never actually thought—"

"Of course you did!" Deb squealed. "And that's fine, really. That cop, that Detective Oberlin, he talked to us, too. Seems to me he didn't find anything suspicious about any of us, because we haven't heard from him since."

"So, if not the three of you, who?" I asked.

Jill shrugged.

Tina shook her head.

Deb poured another margarita.

"What about his work?" I waded into the subject carefully. I didn't want to put thoughts in their heads or words in their mouths. "Have any of you talked to Jack recently? Do you have any idea what he was working on?"

"I called him last week," Jill said. "The youngest needs braces. He blew me off."

"I talked to him last week, too," Tina said. "We shot the breeze for a while but he knew all along what I was calling about. He owes me a bundle of money and as soon as I mentioned it, he suddenly got all busy and had to go."

"You think his murder had something to do with a story he was working on?" Deb asked.

I had to admit I didn't know for sure. "I just wondered . . ." I grabbed another couple nachos. "Did he ever mention working on a story about the food pantry over at St. Colman's Church?"

Deb's eyebrows shot up while Tina and Jill exchanged looks.

I sat up like a shot, afraid to hear more, afraid not to ask. "He did? He really was working on a story about—"

"Even if he did . . ." Tina waved away the idea with one hand. "What difference would it make? Somebody leaves donations at the food pantry once in a while? That's worthy of a news story?"

"No way that could have anything to do with his murder," Deb said. "If you ask me, there's only one explanation for that."

Jill pushed the plate (now empty) from the onion rings

away so she could fold her hands on the table in front of her. "Maxine," she said.

"From the funeral home?"

I guess my question was a no-brainer because two sets of eyes were rolled toward the dingy ceiling.

Tina was even more direct. "Of course it was Maxine."

"But she told me stuff," I said, thinking back to what I'd learned over at Worth's. "About how their souls were entwined and their hearts—"

"Beat as one." It wasn't the margarita that made Deb pucker. "Whatever! That little tramp can say whatever she wants about how much she loved Jack—"

"But they've been seen duking it out," Jill confided. "More than once and—"

"Not that long ago," Tina added. "Why, it was just—"

"A couple weeks ago, remember?" Deb knew her friends did, so she went right on. "We were out to dinner. Our monthly Jack Lancer bashing. And who shows up in the restaurant but Jack and that little—"

"Well, we weren't about to get up and leave," Jill told me. "Not even when they were seated just a few tables away. And you'd think they'd actually have tried to behave, knowing we were there, but—"

"No." Tina somehow turned the word into two syllables. "They had a couple drinks. Then a couple more. Then that Maxine started in on him."

"About?" I asked.

"Everything. As far as we could tell," Deb said. "Something about Jack cheating on her. Jack cheating on her! Like she expected anything else from that low-down scumbag?"

I took a moment to process all this. "So, you think—"

"Maxine. Yep." Jill spoke, but all three women nodded in unison. "Maxine Carmichael definitely murdered Jack."

I WILL CONFESS, I did not return directly to the Terminal after my meeting with the Jack Lancer Haters Club. The margaritas made me sleepy and, besides, I wanted some quiet time alone to process everything the women had told me.

Could Maxine have murdered the Lance of Justice?

Honestly, to me, she didn't look smart enough to plan and cover up a murder, but I hoped it was true. If Maxine was our culprit, that meant Sophie was off the hook. Of course, that also meant figuring out how Maxine—who didn't seem to have the brains God gave a hamster—could have gotten a key to the Terminal, gotten Jack there, and covered up her crime with enough panache to keep the cops guessing.

I might actually have had time to consider the possibilities if, when I walked into Sophie's, a couple things didn't happen.

The first was an attack by a flying furry black-and-white creature who came screeching at me out of nowhere the moment I opened the front door. I ducked out of the way of Muffin's slashing claws, but not before the nasty critter caught and snagged the sleeve of my linen blazer.

I barked out a curse designed to get the feline version of Godzilla to back off and that's when I heard another noise out in the kitchen.

Like the back door banging open.

Yeah, yeah, I know what everybody says at the movies when some brainless heroine goes into a dark basement. Or a kitchen when she's home all alone and she's sure she's heard something she shouldn't have heard.

I should have known better.

I shouldn't have done it.

But if I didn't, I wouldn't have seen that the back door was wide open.

And I wouldn't have caught just a glimpse of a person in dark clothes just as that person slipped out of Sophie's backyard and took off running.

Chapter 16

I called the cops, who told me that, unfortunately, they saw this kind of thing all the time. Some bad guy checks out houses, finds the ones where everybody's working and nobody's home, and sees what he can scoop up. In fact, they informed me, if I read the police blotter in the local newspaper, I'd realize there was something of a crime spree going on in Hubbard at that very moment. They were hot on the trail of a burglar who was making off with everything from flat-screen TVs to computers to cell phones, things he could carry away and easily fence. Quick money, that's what the cops called it, though what kind of quick money some crook hoped to find at Sophie's modest bungalow was beyond me.

I am not easily frightened, but I'm not stupid, either. I had the two nice police officers check out the house from top to bottom and after they gave me the all clear and assured me that I was lucky (a) to have arrived home just in time to scare off the intruder and (b) that he *was* scared off by my yelling at Muffin and didn't decide to confront me, I called a locksmith and had dead bolts installed. On Monday, I'd get a security system put in, too, and tell Sophie it was a thank-you for letting me stay in her home.

By the time it was all over and the adrenaline had pumped its way out of my system, I felt like a wet rag. I changed into shorts and a T-shirt and set the alarm on my phone. I'd allow myself an hour's nap, then get back to the Terminal.

It was a great plan, but stress—and those early-afternoon margaritas—had a funny way of messing with my head, and in the end, the stress won out. I slept right through the alarm, and by the time I opened my eyes, the shadows outside the house were long and low, and I had been MIA from the Terminal nearly all day.

I have never been a slacker, and I wasn't about to earn that reputation now. I jumped out of bed, showered, changed, and headed back to Traintown as quickly as I could.

Once I got there, I wondered if I was still asleep, and dreaming to boot.

The street outside the Terminal was packed with cars, and not just the news vans that had made the place their permanent home since the murder. It was a sunny, warm, early evening and there were people everywhere. They strolled from Carrie's art gallery to John and Mike's bookstore. They gathered for pictures around the marker in front of the Terminal that declared the building a historic place. They wandered in and out of the restaurant, and in that moment between the time the door opened and when it slapped shut again, I heard music.

Boisterous, rousing, foot-tapping, blood-stirring, heart-pounding music.

Irish music.

Just inside the front door of the Terminal, I froze and
listened to the cadence of a muffled drum, the strum of a
guitar keeping the beat, the jaunty song of a tin whistle, and
the way a fiddle picked up the tune and ran with it. Through
the doorway that led into the restaurant, a couple whizzed
by, caught up in the rhythm of the dance.

Dancing?

In the Terminal?

I was just about to march in there and see what was going
on when Inez dance-stepped her way over to the cash
register. "Oh, good. You're here." She didn't sound like she
held it against me that I had not been there all day. In fact,
her words bumped to the beat of the music. "We called in
Judy, and she's been great, but we can use all the help we
can get."

With that, and with some customer's change in hand, she
danced back in the direction she'd come.

The song ended and a round of applause and cheers went
up. Curious, I edged into the restaurant, almost afraid of
what I'd see.

The first thing that caught my eye was Declan, wearing
a tailored charcoal suit, a white shirt, and a green tie with
shamrocks all over it. He smiled, waved, and headed my
way.

"What on earth . . ." I looked around at the tables, loaded
with patrons, and the four-man band that had set up outside
my office door. "What's going on here? Why are you here?
Shouldn't you be at that first communion party?"

The band started into another rousing song. I guess that's
why Declan thought it was necessary for him to lean in nice
and close so I could hear him. "We brought the party here,"
he shouted.

"But . . ." I saw Ellen Fury at a table over near the windows that looked out over the train tracks. She waved and so did the bearded man next to her, who I assumed was Declan's father, Malachi. "But you were getting ready for the party at your mother's and—"

"Truth be told . . ." If I thought he was standing close before, I was wrong. Because now Declan inched even closer and the scent of bay rum filled my nostrils and messed with my head. So did the way his words brushed my ear and tickled through my bloodstream. "Word is out, I'm afraid. My mother, she heard your stew is better than hers. She had to come try it, and then my father said of course, he'd come, too, and then Kitty and Pat agreed to ride along, and then . . ." He raised his arms and glanced around, taking in the scene in all its glory.

There were at least four dozen people—elderly men and women, others Declan's parents' age, teenagers, young children—at the tables that had been decorated with orange, white, and green Irish flags, sparkling rainbows, and those little pots of gold Declan had brought over earlier in the day. As I watched, a dozen of the patrons headed to the makeshift dance floor, a spot right in front of the band where the tables had been pushed back and the chairs cleared. They swung through the tiny area, feet stomping, hands clapping, and some of the people who sat and watched joined in on a song I didn't recognize, but they obviously did.

Still stunned by it all, I couldn't help but blurt out, "But there's a band!"

"And they're good, aren't they?" Declan laughed. "That's my brother, Seamus, on the fiddle. You met him at Mom's yesterday. And my cousin Jerry on the whistle. He plays the bagpipes, too, but I asked him to leave those home today. Bagpipes, it's my considered opinion, are a lot like bicycles—better outdoors than they are in."

"And the drummer and the guitar player?" I asked.

"My cousins Dan and Martin. Great guys. You'll like Dan and Martin."

"But . . ." I wasn't sure what I was going to say so I struggled with the words. "But how . . ."

"Never ask how or why. Not when the music is playing and the food is delicious and the beer is flowing like water." When he saw the look on my face that clearly said that was impossible since the Terminal didn't have a liquor license, Declan laughed. "Sorry, just being poetic. That's what happens when I listen to Irish music. That, and the uncontrollable urge to dance."

He didn't ask if I wanted to, he simply slipped a hand around my waist and pulled me onto the dance floor.

For a second, I was too surprised to do anything but stand there like an idiot, but when the first wave of our fellow dancers closed around us, I had no choice; it was move my feet or get mowed over.

"I don't know how to dance!" I yelled to Declan; this close to the band, the music was louder than ever.

"You're doing fine," he assured me, and as if to make sure of it, he tightened his hold and closed his left hand over my right.

He was a good dancer, and in spite of myself, I couldn't help but be caught up in the moment and in the effortless way he guided me around the floor. By the time the song was over, my head was whirling like the ceiling fans that turned above our heads.

He grinned. "Another dance?"

I fought to catch my breath. "I can't. I haven't been here all day and we're busy and—"

And what? I could possibly tell him that one more minute snatched up in the crook of his arm and inhaling the heady scent of his aftershave and I'd be a goner. Instead, I beat a hasty retreat and pushed open the swinging kitchen door.

George should have had plenty of warning that I was coming. After all, with the door open, the sounds of the crowd out in the restaurant flowed into the kitchen like the River Shannon. Maybe he didn't care. Maybe he just wasn't fast enough. Whatever the reason, just as I walked in, I saw him down a glass of amber-colored liquid. I saw the bottle nearby, too, that Irish whiskey I'd bought to add to the stew.

Even when he realized I was there, George didn't apologize or offer any excuses. He didn't look embarrassed, either. In fact, all he did was wipe the corner of his white apron across his lips, cap the bottle, and put it back up on the shelf. That is, right before he reached for one of the red and white mints like the ones we kept out at the register and popped one in his mouth.

I shouldn't have been surprised. After all, George admitted to having a drinking problem thanks to the Lance of Justice, and he said that he was trying to handle it by attending AA meetings at St. Colman's. There was no use making him feel any more guilty for giving in to temptation than he probably already did, and as I'd learned from sharing a couple of foster homes with a couple of alcoholics, there was no amount of pleading, lecturing, or shaming that was going to help, anyway.

Later, I would casually mention St. Colman's and tell him that if he ever needed a ride to a meeting, I'd be happy to take him. For now, my gaze swung from the bottle on the shelf to George. "Do we have enough stew?"

"Made another batch. It's going like hotcakes."

"What else are they ordering?"

He pointed to a soup pot on the stove. "That Declan Fury,

he said we should do something called"—George consulted the printed recipe hung nearby—"colcannon."

I nodded. "Mashed potatoes and steamed cabbage."

"And kale."

I remembered Declan's secret ingredient. "And kale."

"And corned beef and cabbage. That Fury fellow, he said it would sell, even though it's not a traditional Irish meal. Not in Ireland, anyway. Except I always thought it was." Considering this cultural conundrum, George rubbed a finger under his nose. "He was right. We've already gone through three corned beefs. Sophie, she lets me order from our supplier when we're low on things or when I need something special. Figured you wouldn't mind."

I didn't, and I told him so. After all, Sophie was the one who made the rules around here. I was just the bookmark, the person designated to keep her place until she was able to return and take control. And besides, from the looks of the orders lined up and waiting for George to plate them, the corned beef and cabbage was a mighty popular entrée.

"Don't need no desserts." As I'd already learned, George could only look me—or any woman—in the eye for so long, and it was usually about two seconds. He stared down at his shoes. "That Fury family, they brought the biggest sheet cake I've ever seen. Said to serve a piece of it to anyone who comes in and wants one. But that Declan Fury . . ." The way George's lips folded in on themselves, I couldn't tell if he approved or disapproved. "He says not to give anything else away, to make them all pay for their dinners, even himself and his family. Even though they brought their party here. I tried to tell him that, you know, that maybe they should get a discount or something, but he wouldn't listen."

Before I could remind myself to control the reaction, I

felt the edges of my mouth lift into a smile. "He never listens."

"So, you're okay with all of it?" George asked. "The cake and the corned beef and . . ."

I was, and I told him, then headed into my office to catch my breath and take a look at the day's receipts.

But not before I grabbed that bottle of Irish whiskey and took it with me to lock in Sophie's desk drawer.

I HAVE NEVER been a fan of traditional music of any kind, not because I think it's terrible, but because growing up, I'd never been exposed to it. Hip-hop, reggae, country. I listened to whatever kinds of music my foster families listened to and I never realized that traditional music—something I'd always pictured as being sung by men with beards and women with stringy hair—could be quite so infectious.

Or so memorable.

Even the next morning, the beat of the songs Seamus and his cousins had played still buzzed through my bloodstream, and when I got out of my car at St. Colman's Church, I was humming the tune of the last song they'd played the night before and thinking that I'd keep my Irish specials on the menu another week and invite the band to come back both the next Friday and Saturday nights.

Moving to the beat, I went around to the back of the car to open my trunk and while I was at it, I looked over the church. There was nothing grand about St. Colman's, that was for sure. It had been built of giant blocks of wheat-colored stone more than one hundred years earlier, and in spite of its vibrant stained glass windows and the army of purple and yellow pansies planted along the side of the

building that faced the parking lot, the church looked tough
and solid, as if it grew right out of the rough-and-tumble,
seen-better-days neighborhood that surrounded it.

I grabbed the first of the cartons of food I'd brought along
for the pantry and went inside, where one staircase led up
and into the church and another led down. From upstairs, I
heard a choir singing. The food pantry, I decided, had to be
down.

I found it along a dimly lit corridor where there was a
WELCOME sign outside an open door and a stack of plastic
grocery bags nearby.

"Grab a bag," a voice called from inside the room, "and
come on in. We've got a good selection today."

I hoisted the box I was carrying. "Not here for food," I
told the middle-aged woman stationed behind a table and
in front of shelves that weren't exactly overflowing. "I've
brought a donation. From the Terminal."

Her hands flew to her cheeks. "You're Sophie's niece!
She told us you were coming to town. Come on, honey . . ."
She patted the table in front of her. "That box looks heavy.
Put it down here."

I did, and went back to the car for the second box George
had packed.

When I returned to the pantry, the woman already had
the first box open. "I'm Jennifer," she told me, and stuck out
a hand. "Can't tell you how thrilled I am to see this many
cans of tuna. People love tuna. It's a nice, quick meal, and
nutritious, too. Now, if only we had a couple dozen loaves
of bread and some mayo." She looked up at the ceiling. Even
from here in the basement, we could hear the baritone
rumble of the priest's prayers and the voices of his
congregation as they responded to him. "When Mass is
finished, there will be a line out the door. It would be nice

if we could give them all the ingredients so they could make sandwiches."

I helped her unpack both boxes and went around to the other side of the table so I could put the things I'd brought on the shelves.

I glanced at the few cans of soup and vegetables and a dozen boxes of cereal and macaroni and cheese mix and thought about that line out the door she'd mentioned. "Will there be enough for everyone?"

Jennifer's nose crinkled. "There's never enough. But if there's one thing folks around here know about, it's how to make do. We've had to since most of the employers moved out of town. These days it's gotten to the point that Father David . . . he's our pastor . . . it's gotten to the point that he'll do just about anything to bring in some revenue so we can stock the shelves here. Had a spaghetti dinner a couple weeks ago. It was delicious! You'll have to come to the next one. We raised seven hundred dollars. Of course . . ." Her shoulders sagged. "That was the same week the thermostat went out at the school building so that money flew right out the window. But no worries!" I don't know if she was trying to convince me or herself, but Jennifer grinned. "Father will think of some other way to fatten our checking account. He always does."

I thought about what I'd heard from George. "Like using the church for AA meetings."

Jennifer's brow furrowed. "Here? At St. Colman's? We don't have an AA group that meets here."

I was sure I remembered correctly. When I asked George where he'd been the night the Lance of Justice was murdered, he said the AA meeting at St. Colman's. "Maybe there used to be a group that met here," I suggested even though in this case *used to* was only a week earlier.

Jennifer dismissed the thought with a shake of her head that made her shoulder-length salt-and-pepper hair twitch. "I've been a member of this parish for thirty years, and I've been on parish council the last ten. I can tell you, there's never been an AA group here. There's a Wednesday-morning meeting over at the Methodist church. I know because my uncle, he used to go. If you're looking for a group—"

"I'm not," I assured her.

Which didn't mean I wasn't looking for answers.

Thinking it over, I stacked a few more cans of tuna on the shelf.

An AA meeting. George told me he'd been at an AA meeting here at the church. George, the guy I'd found drinking Irish whiskey not twenty-four hours earlier.

"What is it?" Jennifer's question snapped me out of my thoughts. "You look like you're thinking about something real serious."

I was, but I couldn't tell her that. Because what I was thinking was that George hated the Lance of Justice.

And that George's alibi had just gone up in smoke.

"Oh, look at that, will you?" Once again, I was forced to abandon my thoughts when Jennifer spoke. "One more jar of spaghetti sauce left." She reached far to the back of a shelf in the corner. "Way back here. Oh, somebody's going to love this. Then again . . ." Her eyes twinkling, she grabbed the jar of sauce and tucked it under the table, then gave me a wink. "Old Mrs. Wyjacki loves spaghetti and she's always at this Mass. I'll slip it to her when she comes down here and no one else is looking!"

Though I'd been in Hollywood for six years, believe me, I didn't live under a rock. I knew there were plenty of people who were hungry, but nothing brought it home like looking at the half-bare shelves of St. Colman's food pantry or thinking that one jar of pasta sauce could be so treasured.

"I can bring more next week," I told Jennifer, even though I wasn't sure what might be left over or what George would find to pack. "Maybe bread. Or pasta."

"Or maybe our Robin Hood will show up again. We wouldn't even have this much if it wasn't for him."

The mention of the Food Pantry Robin Hood took my mind off George, the bottle of Irish whiskey, and the AA meeting that wasn't. See, Robin Hood was exactly what I'd hope to talk to someone about. I'd planned to choose my time carefully, but since Jennifer brought up the subject, I didn't have to worry about that anymore.

"Was Jack Lancer doing a story about the food pantry?" I asked Jennifer.

"The Lance of Justice?" Jennifer was a short woman, and as round as she was tall. She pressed a hand to her ample bosom. "Isn't it just awful what happened to that wonderful man? He was always so nice. Always so friendly."

"You knew him?"

"Well, he did a story on TV about the food pantry. Oh, I don't know . . . three or four years ago."

I wasn't exactly sure why this bit of news hit me somewhere between my heart and my stomach. I moved a stack of tuna cans from one side of an empty shelf to the other. "He wasn't working on a story now? He already did one?"

She nodded. "Like I said, three or four years ago. We just wanted to get the word out, you know, that we were here and that we were able to help people out. Father David, he called the station and they said they were happy to help. Weren't we all just knocked out of our socks when the Lance

of Justice showed up to talk to us!" All these years later, the
excitement lingered; she fanned her face with one hand.
"Such a nice man. Such a terrible shame what happened
to him."

"So, if he did a story about the food pantry years ago, he
wasn't working on another one now."

"Well . . ." I don't know how long I'd stood there thinking
all this through and holding a can of tuna, but it was
apparently too long. Jennifer plucked the can out of my hand
and placed it on the shelf. "Now that you mention it, it was
kind of odd. You see, about a month or so ago, the Lance of
Justice, he showed up here again. Weren't we all just thrilled!
But he never did run another story. Not about the food
pantry. And when he was here . . ." Thinking, she tipped
her head. "Well, all he really seemed to care about was
Robin Hood. You know, the person who leaves food for us
now and again. Shows up out of nowhere. Like a miracle!
Boxes and boxes of food. And nobody knows who drops it
off. We come in and there it is. One day it's a pallet of
canned chili. Another day, it's fresh veggies. Lots and lots
of them. And I'll tell you what, that's a real treat because
the people who get food here, they don't have the luxury of
buying a whole lot of fresh vegetables."

I thought this through. "When was the last time Robin
Hood left food here?" I asked Jennifer.

"Three weeks ago. No, two," she corrected herself.
"Twelve cases of peanut butter."

My head snapped up and my brain spun. Twelve cases
of peanut butter?

It wasn't the first time my questions about Jack Lancer
led me back in the same direction, and this time, like last,
I knew exactly where that direction would take me.

I left the church and headed over to Serenity Oaks.

Chapter 17

"**B**ingo!" Sophie grumbled the word, then glanced around to make sure Vi and Margaret, who were sitting at the table with her, weren't watching. She rolled her eyes at the same time she crinkled up her nose and made a face. "Can't say I like bingo much," she said, leaning in close so I was the only one who could hear her. "Boring game designed for old people. They make us play every afternoon."

"Incentive," I told her, talking out of the side of my mouth. It wasn't like I was afraid of what either Vi or Margaret thought of me, but hey, if Sophie was going for secrecy, I wasn't going to argue. Especially since secrecy was exactly what I'd come to Serenity Oaks to talk to her about. "The sooner you're up and moving on your own, the sooner you can leave. Then you won't have to play bingo anymore."

"Bingo? Everybody loves bingo!" Margaret was supposed to be hard of hearing, but the moment I saw the silvery-haired woman with the sharp dark eyes, I figured she was a shrewd old bird. She waved at the young woman at the front of the room who was calling out the numbers. "Hey, Melissa! We've got a visitor. Get her a card!"

"No. Really." I pushed my chair back from the table. "I've got to get over to the Terminal. I don't have time to—"

"Everybody has time for bingo!" Sophie was on my right, her friend Vi sat on my left. She patted my arm with one incredibly wrinkled hand. "So soothing. Don't you think, Sophie?" Vi's eyes twinkled with mischief. "Perfect for old ladies like us!"

Sophie's lips puckered. "Old ladies." She added a harrumph to make her opinion clear. "When I came here for rehab, I thought we'd have time for gossiping about the old days. And catching up on our soaps. And flirting with some of the fellas here." As if to prove it, she twinkled across the room at a guy with a receding hairline and flamboyant handlebar mustache who grinned back at Sophie like a teenager at his first mixer.

"But no!" Sophie dragged out the last word to emphasize her point. "They keep us busy all day long. Meals and bingo and therapy and more meals, and the food isn't anywhere near as good as it is at the Terminal. They treat us like we're old! I can't stand it. I'm not old. I run my own restaurant, don't I? I haven't lost my marbles and I haven't lost my energy, even if this dumb knee . . ." She glared down at her right leg. "Even if it isn't working quite right yet. It will be. Soon. Then watch out, world!"

I had no doubt she'd make good on the promise, but for now I was grateful that she was something of a captive audience. I popped out of my seat and grabbed on to the back of Sophie's wheelchair. "Let's go outside," I suggested, and I never gave her time to object. "There are some things I need to talk to you about."

"Thank goodness," Sophie said once we were out of the activity room and in the garden behind Serenity Oaks. It was a pleasant space shaded by broad trees and dotted here and there with pots of pink impatiens and white begonias. There were benches along a brick path, and I parked the wheelchair next to one and sat down. The better to look Sophie in the eye.

"Thanks for saving me from bingo, kiddo," she said.

"That's not why I'm here," I told her.

"You want advice. About the restaurant." Sophie was so sure of this, she nodded. "I can understand. I know you have experience, but cooking for those highfalutin Hollywood stars, that's different from actually running a restaurant with real food and real customers."

"I don't need advice about the restaurant," I said. "In fact, the Terminal's been doing really well. We had more customers last night than we've had in the last month."

All the days of the last month combined.

I didn't bother to point this out since I didn't want Sophie to feel bad.

"So, if you don't want to talk about the restaurant . . ." Sophie's cheeks shot through with color and her eyes flew open. "It's got to be love! It's Declan, isn't it? Well, if you want my opinion—"

"I don't," I assured her with a little too much oomph in my voice to convince either one of us. "I'm not here about the restaurant. And I'm sure not here because of Declan. I'm here about peanut butter."

She did her best to play it cool, but don't think that I didn't notice that all that color drained out of Sophie's face in an instant. Stalling for time, she cleared her throat. "Do you like peanut butter? I do. Extra crunchy."

"Peanut butter and I don't exactly get along," I told her, and I didn't bother to explain that was because I'd once lived with a foster family who fed me nothing but peanut butter sandwiches for breakfast and lunch every single day of the six months I was with them. "But that doesn't matter. I'm not here because I eat peanut butter."

"You're looking for recipes! To add to the menu at the Terminal!" Relief washed through Sophie's expression. "Peanut butter pie would be good. People love peanut butter pie, especially when it's drizzled with chocolate. Or peanut butter cookies. That might be a nice addition to the lunchtime menu. Or there's—"

"There's twelve cases of peanut butter on our inventory list and not one jar of the stuff in the restaurant," I said, and before she could offer up some lame excuse designed to throw me off the scent, I was sure to add, "And St. Colman's just got twelve cases of peanut butter from the Food Pantry Robin Hood."

"Twelve cases! How generous of someone. But you can't possibly think that I have anything to do with—"

"What's the big deal?" I jumped to my feet and turned to face her, my fists on my hips. "It's a wonderful thing that you're doing. And it's incredibly kind, too. And, believe me, I don't care if you're spending the profits of the Terminal on filling the shelves at the food pantry, I've been there. I've seen it. I—"

"You took today's donation? That was awfully nice of you."

Probably not, since I'd had an ulterior motive for going to St. Colman's all along.

"I really don't care if you're the Food Pantry Robin

Hood," I told her, sure to keep my voice down. After all, Sophie obviously wanted the truth of the matter kept secret, otherwise she wouldn't make sure the food showed up out of nowhere. "I do care that Jack Lancer was working on a story about you."

"About me?" Her hand flew to her heart. "Oh no. No, no, no. That's wrong! He couldn't have been."

"But he was. I've heard it from one of his coworkers, and I heard it from one of his ex-wives, and I heard it from Jennifer at the food pantry. He was snooping around. He was asking questions about the Food Pantry Robin Hood. And if you wanted to make sure the truth didn't get out . . ."

Sophie was breathless. "You think I killed the Lance of Justice?"

"I think you were at the Terminal earlier that Monday evening, before I arrived in town. I think you parked out front. I think you let yourself in at the front door. Then I think—"

"Whatever you think after that," she said, "it's wrong."

"But I'm not wrong about you being at the Terminal, am I? I'm not wrong about how you used your key and walked in and—"

"No." She shook her head. "You're not wrong about any of that. But I can't . . ." Her shoulders rose and fell. "I can't tell you any more than that. It's not my secret to keep."

"Then whose is it?" I stopped just short of screeching, and when she clamped her lips shut, I gave in and grumbled. "This is important, Sophie. And it's better for you to tell me the truth than it is to have the cops show up here."

As if they already had, her head snapped up and her gaze shot to the door. Her voice trembled when she asked, "You think they know?"

"I think if I found out, they're going to find out, too. And if they do, they're going to talk to you. They're going to want answers, and so do I. I can understand if it was an accident of some kind. Or if you were defending yourself. But if you had anything to do with Jack Lancer's death—"

"I didn't. I swear." She held up two fingers, like a Boy Scout taking an oath. "You've got to believe me. But . . ." She swallowed hard. "That's all I can tell you."

I flopped back down on the bench and ran a hand through my hair. "It's not as easy as that, Sophie. There's been a murder, and the cops aren't going to ease up on investigating it until they have some answers. So what if you're taking every penny the Terminal ever makes and—"

Her lips folded in on themselves. "Well, that's just it, isn't it, dear? You've got it all wrong. And if that's what the police think, then they'd have it all wrong, too." She looked away and I knew when she made up her mind, because after a minute, she glanced back at me. "You know so much already, I suppose there's only one thing to do. You've got to talk to the only person who can tell you the truth."

THE IRISH STORE wasn't open on Sundays, but as soon as I got back to Traintown, I knew Declan was around because I saw that smokin'-hot motorcycle of his parked at the side of the building. There was a chance he was across the street at the Terminal, looking to make my life miserable and far more complicated than I imagined it would be when I got in my car back in California and made the trip to Ohio, but I knocked on the front door of the gift shop anyway.

A moment later, I saw him in the doorway of his office at the back of the shop. He closed the door behind him before he walked up front.

"Good morning!" Declan stepped back so I could walk into the shop and, while he was at it, he looked over my shoulder at the Terminal. "I see you've got a good crowd for brunch this morning."

I'd noticed that, too, but since I wasn't there to talk about restaurant business, I slipped into the Irish store and waited until he closed the door behind me.

"Coffee?" he asked.

"I'd rather have the truth."

He was dressed in khakis and a white shirt that was open at the collar, and he stepped back and studied me. "What are we talking about?"

"What do you think we're talking about?"

"Well, that's the thing, isn't it?" He scraped a hand through his hair, further mussing it in a way that made it look as if he'd just rode in on that motorcycle of his. "I asked you about coffee, and you said—"

"That I'd rather know the truth. Are you the Food Pantry Robin Hood?"

He was too smart to let anything as small as an expression or a gesture give away whatever it was he was thinking. Instead, he offered me a dazzling smile. "You've been talking to my mother. She swears I'm a superhero. But then . . ." The shrug was far too contrived to look innocent. "I suppose that's how all mothers think of their favorite child."

"You? Ellen's favorite?" I crossed my arms across my chest. "Seamus plays a damned good fiddle."

"And Claire and Bridget are saints because they're nurses, and Aiden is an angel of mercy—he's a paramedic, you know—and Brian is changing the world because he's a teacher, and Riordan . . . !" As if to prove there was no arguing with his mother's opinions, Declan threw his hands in the air. "Well, soldiers have a way of melting women's hearts, especially if those hearts belong to their mothers. But none of that keeps my mother from being extra fond of me. I'm the youngest, you know. So I have a special place in her heart."

"Really? And your mother, she thinks you're the Food Pantry Robin Hood?"

"Not really." He grinned. "But it's just the kind of thing she would fantasize about. Mom, she's imaginative like that."

"So, are you the Food Pantry Robin Hood or aren't you?"

He scrubbed his hands over his face. "I don't know about you, but I stayed up late last night. It was a heck of a party, wasn't it? And I got up early this morning so I could get to church. I really do need a cup of coffee." He marched to the back of the store and when I didn't budge, he never even bothered to look back at me.

He brought out one mug of coffee for himself and another for me. Since I still had my arms hugged around myself, he set my cup of coffee on the nearest counter. "Who have you been talking to?" he asked.

"Kim Kline, for one," I told him. "She tells me the Lance of Justice was working on a story about the Food Pantry Robin Hood."

Thinking, he sipped his coffee. "I don't see why. There's nothing very sensational in it, is there? Somebody leaves food at the pantry now and again."

"The same somebody who orders the food through Sophie's suppliers."

His eyebrows rose a fraction of an inch. "She told you that?"

"She didn't have to. I'm pretty smart."

"And pretty nosy. The emphasis being on the pretty."

I blew out a breath of frustration. "If you think I can be so easily distracted by your lame compliments, you can think again. I know Sophie was at the restaurant the night of the murder."

"Sure she was. She was with you when you found the body."

"Before I got here." I stared at him hard when I said this, the better to let him know I wasn't about to put up with his attempts to distract me with his charms or the chemistry that bubbled between us like Irish stew on the boil. "She came early. She parked out front. She walked in through the front door."

"And you think she, what, invited Jack Lancer to meet her and killed him once he got there?"

"I can't imagine Sophie killing anyone." It was the truth, so of course my voice rang with conviction. "She's not that kind of person."

"And why would she feel the secret of the Food Pantry Robin Hood was worth killing for, anyway? Whoever Robin Hood is . . . well, he must be a wonderful guy, don't you think?"

Yes, I noticed that his shoulders shot back a fraction of an inch when he said this. Since I didn't acknowledge the question, Declan went right on.

"He must be generous and charitable. Practically a saint! If he's paying for the food and Sophie is ordering it for him and then he's sneaking it over to the church . . . I don't know about you, but I'm thinking the guy is like Mother Teresa and Gandhi all rolled into one. With just a touch of Pope Francis thrown in for good measure."

"And a great big dose of hogwash!"

He laughed. "You think?" he asked, but he didn't give me a chance to answer before he asked another question.

"Why would someone so wonderful and generous and kind and compassionate and—"

"Cut the bull."

His expression sobered. "Consider it cut. So, why would someone like that kill Jack Lancer just because Lancer was thinking about doing a story about him?"

"Exactly what I've been asking myself."

"And the answer you've come up with?"

I grabbed my coffee cup and took a good, long drink before I said any more. Between my early-morning visits to the food pantry and Serenity Oaks, the Irish music that raced through my bloodstream all night long, and the fact that I didn't get much sleep thanks to being nervous about that attempted break-in at Sophie's, I needed all the time I could get to clear my head.

"You're right," I finally said.

Declan's expression brightened. "Two little words I thought I'd never hear from you."

"And you might not hear them again. But this time, you are right. As much fun as it might be for Jack Lancer to expose the Food Pantry Robin Hood, it's not exactly a story that would make or break his career. And it's certainly not worth getting killed over."

Satisfied, he nodded. "Exactly."

"So, there has to be more to the story than just that."

He was just about to take another sip of coffee, and over the rim of his cup, his eyes flickered to mine. "You think?"

"Oh, I've been thinking a lot. About what Sophie was doing at the restaurant early that evening. About how you just happened to arrive on the scene once we got there. About how someone is using her suppliers to order goodies for the food pantry. And about Jack Lancer."

I strolled to the front of the shop and looked across the

street at the Terminal. "You know, he'd been coming in every afternoon for pie and coffee."

"Sophie has great pie."

Declan had come to stand at my side, and I slid him a look. "That's not why he was there."

"The coffee's not that good."

I ignored the comment. "Jack sat at the same table every day," I said.

"A creature of habit. I think habits are boring, don't you? Me, I'd rather be spontaneous. You know, passionate."

I ignored this, too, because it was an attempt to knock my train of thought off its tracks and because I knew if I let that happen, it would lead to a train wreck. "The table Jack sat at"—I pointed out—"from there, he had a perfect view of this place."

"Really?" Declan pursed his lips. "What do you suppose that means?"

"That he had a line on something interesting. That he was watching you. He knew you were the Food Pantry Robin Hood and I think he knew something more, like maybe about how you were funding your little charity project. There's plenty of speculation around here about you and your family, especially your uncle Pat. If Jack Lancer knew—"

"First of all," Declan was quick to point out, "Jack Lancer didn't *know* anything. He might have suspected a thing or two, but truth be told, he wasn't a good enough reporter to really find out anything of value. He was a hack, a showboater. And even if he did uncover anything interesting . . ."

It was Declan's turn to take a walk around the shop. He straightened the plaid kilts where they hung near CDs of Irish music. He grabbed a feather duster and danced it over the top of a glass display case. He moved a gorgeous pair of Waterford wineglasses to make sure they were sitting square under a spotlight so that when it was turned on, the light would ignite the hundreds of facets cut into the glass. When he was all done, he grabbed something out of a pretty glass bowl, and when he came back, he dropped those somethings on the counter nearby.

"Irish pennies," he said, running his hand through the little pile of copper coins. "Look, there's a harp on this one. That's the national symbol of Ireland, you know. Here's a fairly new penny with a picture on it from the Book of Kells, and here's an older one." He held the coin between thumb and forefinger. "It's got a hen and chicks on it because farming is Ireland's chief economy."

"And Irish pennies have what to do with Jack Lancer?" I asked.

"Nothing at all," he admitted with a chuckle. "But let's just say . . ." He whisked his fingers across the coins, neatly dividing them into two piles, one with just a couple pennies in it and the other one piled high. "For argument's sake, let's examine the scenario you just mentioned. Let's say that this pile of pennies . . ." He touched a finger to the smaller of the two piles. "Let's just say that this is the money the food pantry has for operations. Not much, is it? Not nearly enough to serve all the needs of the people who come looking for food. What are they going to do?"

I looked over his little example. "Take money from the other pile?"

"That would not be keeping with the idea of charity, that's for sure." He tapped the larger pile. "But let's say there is someone with all the money the food pantry needs. Here it is. Only this money, it's not so easy to spend, if you know what I mean."

I didn't.

Declan chose his words carefully when he explained. "Let's pretend this money came to the person who owns it by means that are . . . well, let's just say that they're not exactly legal."

Instantly, I thought about everything I'd heard about Declan's Traveller family and especially his uncle Pat Sheedy, the purported leader of the local Irish mob. He must have known it, because he jumped right in with a disclaimer.

"Not that I'm saying anyone's done anything wrong," he said. "Or that anyone has gotten money by illegal means. You understand, this is all just for illustration purposes."

Oh, I understood, all right. And he understood that I understood. I knew this because he nodded once and went right on.

"Let's say the person who has all these pennies wants to make sure that everything he has is safe and that no one knows about what he's doing or how he's getting the pennies he has. He has to protect it, right?" He took some of the pennies and built a third pile. "He has to put it somewhere."

I pushed that third pile farther from the other two. "You mean like offshore accounts. We're talking money laundering."

He winced. "Such ugly words. But if that's what you want to call it, sure. We'll call it money laundering. For illustration purposes. Now, let's say that there's someone who's supposed to take care of the details for the person who has all this money."

I watched him carefully. "You."

Declan rolled his eyes. "It can't be me. Because it's not real. It's just an—"

"Illustration. Yes, I know. So the person who's made all this money wants it taken care of."

"And the person who's taking care of it decides it can be put to better use than just sitting in a bank account somewhere."

I looked from what was still the largest stack of pennies to that stack I'd sent to an offshore account. "Doesn't the person who owns the pennies want to know what's happening to all his other pennies?"

"He does." Declan put one finger on the newest stack of pennies and glided it closer. "He hears all about it from the person he's put in charge of taking care of it for him. And someday . . ." One by one, he flicked the pennies off the counter and into his hand. "Someday when the FBI starts asking questions and the person with all those pennies is backed against a wall . . . well, if the money was in an offshore account or if there was anything havey-cavey going on, then he'd be up a creek. But this way . . ." He had all the pennies from the largest stack in his hand and all the pennies from the newest stack, too, and with a *chink* he added them to the pile he'd used to represent the food pantry.

"Someday when he's up against a wall, the person who owns all this money will thank the person he put in charge of it," Declan said. "Because the authorities, they won't be able to prove a thing."

I ran my finger through the coins, spreading them out on the counter. "So, if a reporter found out about the pennies, and the person in charge of those pennies thought the truth was going to come out—"

"The reporter didn't find out, and the person in charge of the pennies was never worried," he assured me. "Besides . . ." He swept up the pennies into his hand, dropped them back in the bowl they'd come out of, and came back to the front of the shop, brushing his hands together.

"It's all hypothetical, anyway. Just an example."

"An illustration."

"Exactly." His eyes gleamed. "But if it was real and if someone found out . . ." The *someone* he was talking about now wasn't Jack Lancer. I suspected it from the start, and my suspicions were confirmed when he tapped the tip of my nose with one finger. "Well, it would be a shame to reveal the secret to the world, wouldn't it? And what good would it do, anyway? The only people who would suffer are the ones who come to the food pantry and find the shelves empty. It would be a shame to reveal the Food Pantry Robin Hood and spoil things for them, wouldn't it?"

I gritted my teeth and smiled. "Not if it meant catching a killer."

He puffed out a breath of annoyance. Or maybe it was a sound of surrender. "All right, since you know Sophie was at the Terminal early on the night of the murder, you should know that I was, too. We were discussing the details of something we were working on together."

"Ordering from her suppliers for the food pantry."

"I didn't say that. I'm not going to say it. I will say that when I was there, I had a list of sorts with me, you know, things we were going to talk about, and when she realized how late it was and how she had to get home because you were scheduled to arrive, she hurried me out and I left my list behind."

"That's what you were looking for when you came over to the Terminal once Sophie and I arrived!"

"It's not like it was incriminating or anything," he told me. "But I couldn't take the chance of someone finding it. Turns out I didn't have to worry, because Sophie scooped up the paper and took it with her. Only I didn't know that, not then."

"And if someone did find it?"

"You mean, like Jack Lancer?" Declan whisked my coffee mug off the counter and took it to the back room. I heard water running and a minute later, he was back.

"No secret is worth the price of a human life," he said.

"So you didn't kill Jack Lancer."

"I'm glad you finally realize it."

"And Sophie didn't kill Jack Lancer."

"I think we can both be pretty sure of that."

"So we're back to square one."

"Not exactly. We have made some progress today. We know each other a little better. And that makes me wonder . . . if I really was the Food Pantry Robin Hood, that dashing, daring superhero . . . would you have a drink with me tonight?"

The man was exasperating beyond belief.

Which didn't explain why there was a spring in my step when I walked back to the Terminal.

Or what on earth I was thinking when I agreed to meet him for a drink that evening.

Chapter 18

At least I found a distraction right from the start on Sunday evening—and it wasn't Declan's easy smile or the way he made me feel as if I were the only one on the planet with him.

It was the restaurant he chose to take me to.

Linen tablecloths.

Flickering candles.

A wine cellar I could see at the far end of the spacious room with its stone floors, its rustic (but not kitschy) barnwood walls, and two walls of windows that looked out onto what seemed to be a never-ending expanse of trees, their new, fresh foliage glimmering in the last of the evening light.

I breathed in the heady scent of garlic and sherry and shallots. I listened to the clink of ice cubes in glasses, the satisfying swish of a wine cork being pulled from its bottle, the respectful rumble of a waiter's voice as he tossed a

Caesar salad at the table nearest where we stood waiting to be seated. Oh yeah, I took it all in.

And my shoulders sagged.

"What?" Declan didn't miss a thing. His gray gaze shot my way. "You don't like it here? We can go somewhere else."

"It's fine." Truth be told, it was more than just fine. The Rockworth Tavern was the kind of restaurant where I could picture myself comfortably ensconced: showing patrons to their tables, making wine and dinner suggestions, smoothly and efficiently handling the staff in their black pants and crisp white shirts.

It ought to be. It was the restaurant that Sophie had shown me pictures of over the years, the one I thought I was coming to Hubbard to manage.

Once we were seated at a table next to the windows and had drinks in front of us—cab for Declan and a caipirinha for me that (in the great no-man's-land somewhere outside of Hubbard!) even included authentic cachaça, a liquor made from sugarcane juice—I told him the story. To his credit, he laughed.

"Sophie's really something. She's got the energy of a woman half her age. I bet she'll be back at the Terminal in no time at all."

I took a sip of my perfectly prepared drink. "The sooner the better."

He sat back and studied me. "When she comes back, you're leaving."

My shrug should have said it all. "I never intended to stay. She knew that from the start."

"Where will you go?"

"I've got a couple options." This was not technically true. Not unless *a couple* translated to "I have no idea." Declan didn't need to know that. "I haven't decided yet."

"And if the murder isn't solved by then?"

This time, my shrug packed a little more punch. "It's not my job to make sure Jack Lancer's murder is solved," I reminded him.

"But you're the only one who seems to be making any progress on the case."

I doubted this was true. "I'm sure Detective Oberlin is working very hard."

"Gus Oberlin has been over to my mother's twice this weekend to talk to Owen. He keeps asking the kid the same questions over and over, waiting for him to slip up. Gus is stuck in a groove—he's such a stubborn son of a gun. There's not one fingerprint upstairs that puts Owen on the scene, but Gus being Gus, he doesn't much care. He's not going to look any further. Not unless you show him that there are other places to look."

"Apparently not at the Food Pantry Robin Hood." He didn't rise to the bait I hoped would get him talking more about what he'd told me that morning, so I went right on. "And thank goodness, now that the whole food pantry idea is off the table, Sophie as a suspect is, too."

"You can't think she actually might have done it."

"Not really. But that's the thing, isn't it? You can't really know people. Not wholly. Not completely. And you can't really know what they would—or wouldn't—kill for. If Sophie had a strong enough reason . . . well, I don't know. I suppose if there was something she believed in enough or something she wanted to protect or some secret she had to make sure didn't get revealed, then, yeah, I suppose she might kill for it. I suppose any of us would."

"Even you?"

I laughed. "I don't have any secrets," I told him, and, yes, I did emphasize the *I* just so he'd know that I hadn't forgotten what he'd told me about the Food Pantry Robin Hood. "My life's an open book."

"But not everyone's is."

He was right. He was also hungry, and while he looked over the menu and ordered appetizers—mussels with miso sauce and wonton wrappers baked into crispy little boats and filled with pulled pork and candied jalapeño peppers—I thought about what else I'd learned back at the food pantry, namely that there was not now and never had been an AA group that met at St. Colman's Church.

"You're thinking about the case." Declan's voice snapped me to. "You've got that look in your eyes. Like you're putting two and two together."

"And coming up with five," I admitted, and hated doing it. "George lied to me about his alibi for the night of the murder."

"He's got every reason in the world to hate Jack Lancer."

"Agreed. But . . ."

He sipped his wine. "But?"

"I can't imagine George actually killing someone." I drowned the thought with a sip of caipirinha because actually, yeah, I could imagine George as a killer. It was because he never looked me in the eye for long, and because he was always so darned surly. It was because I knew he hated Jack Lancer. He admitted it.

But he wasn't the only one who had a motive to off the newscaster.

"And then there's Maxine, of course." I filled Declan in on what Jack Lancer's exes had told me about his current girlfriend. "If they're right, she could have been angry enough to want to do Jack in."

"See, you are getting somewhere." Our appetizers arrived and he bowed his head for a second, then dug in. "Mussels?"

"We were only supposed to be coming for drinks."

"You might be serving Irish food over at the Terminal, but you have yet to learn nearly what you need to know about the Irish character. You don't just go for drinks. You drink. You eat. You talk. A lot. It's all part of an evening out, and when I'm with a date—"

In spite of the fact that I'd just taken a drink, my mouth went dry. "Is that what this is? A date?"

"If you're afraid your Hollywood friends will find out you've gone out with a lowly attorney from Hubbard, Ohio, I can be sworn to secrecy."

He was kidding. Maybe. I wasn't when I told him, "That's not it at all. For one thing, I don't have any Hollywood friends. Not anymore. And even if I did, who I choose to date—"

"See? It is a date!" The argument settled   at least in his mind—he piled mussels on my plate and with the tip of his fork, urged me to start eating.

Since the mussels were fabulous and the wonton wrappers had just the right amount of crunch and the filling was delicious, I was glad I did. I finished the mussels and spooned a few more from the serving platter onto my plate. "I may have found my new favorite restaurant."

"Not the Terminal?" His eyes sparked with mischief.

"I have you to thank for giving me the idea for the Irish food," I admitted.

His smile was as genuine as it was enticing. "I'm glad. If there's ever anything else you'd like my help with, you'll let me know, right?"

There was something about the purr of his voice combined with his shimmering smile that made my knees weak. I guess that means it's a good thing that I didn't have much of a chance to think about it. There was a bar at the far end of the restaurant, a little jut-out to one side of the wine cellar, and from in there, we heard a whoop.

"You hear that?" a man's voice called out. He stuck his head out of the bar so everyone in the restaurant could hear him. "We've got the TV on in here. Just saw a report. Kim Kline, she's going to announce it on the news tonight. She says she knows who killed Jack Lancer!"

A buzz of excitement ran through the restaurant, and I guess I could see why. Upscale or not, the patrons of the Rockworth Tavern were as caught up in the drama of the Lance of Justice's murder as the rest of us.

Declan and I exchanged looks. "What do you think?" he asked. "Is there any way she could be that far ahead of us?"

I thought about Kim of the too-shiny hair and the too-big nose. She was young, sure, but she must have had some qualifications to land the job she had. If she had the reporter's instincts to go along with them . . .

Suddenly, the mussels and the wontons didn't taste so good anymore. I pushed my plate away. "She said Jack might have been looking into the story of the Food Pantry Robin Hood," I told Declan. "She knew that Jack Lancer sat at the same table every day and that he had his eyes on your place. What if she decided to run with the story? If she breaks the news that—"

"Impossible." His voice rang with conviction, but he pushed his chair back from the table and offered me his hand. "Come on," he said.

"We're going? Where?"

We couldn't see into the bar from there, but he glanced that way, anyway. "We've got to talk Kim Kline out of airing some story she shouldn't. If she blows the cover of the Food Pantry Robin Hood, she's not only going to accuse somebody who shouldn't be accused, but a lot of hungry people are going to suffer, and Uncle Pat . . ." He whistled low under his breath. "If Uncle Pat catches wind that his ill-gotten gains are going toward spaghetti sauce and Cheerios, he's going to be one pissed-off Irishman!"

IF KIM KLINE was planning on breaking a big story about Jack Lancer's murder on the eleven o'clock news that night, I figured she'd be at the station.

I was right. Sort of. The receptionist at the desk in the lobby of the offices of station WKFJ told us that Kim would be back, but that she'd left there a couple hours earlier after she'd recorded that snippet about breaking news we'd heard at the Rockworth. She'd gone home to freshen up and get changed.

"You heard her spot earlier, right?" The phone on the receptionist's desk rang off the hook. No doubt, there were plenty of people as excited about what they'd heard from Kim as we were. All for different reasons. "We're going to scoop all the other stations tonight. Kim, she's going to be a star because of this. You watch. You'll see."

I told her I had no doubt of it and shot Declan a look. "We need to talk to her," I told him on our way back to the car.

"Already working on it." He tipped his phone so I could see the text message he'd just received. "Kim Kline's address," he informed me.

I glanced up at him. "How did you—"

We got into his car. "Let's just say that there are a couple cops around here who owe me favors."

"Let's just say that makes me a little nervous."

"What?" Declan laughed. "You don't think an attorney can be on the right side of the law?"

There was no use arguing the point with him so I didn't bother to answer. Instead, I watched the scenery zip by. The offices of the TV station were in Youngstown, the region's biggest city and, like so many northern industrial cities, Youngstown's glory days were long gone. We passed closed factory after closed factory, shuttered buildings, and neighborhoods of homes that looked as worn-out as the area's economy. Farther from the center of town, the lot sizes got bigger, the homes were better kept. Still, the whole area seemed as if it were holding its breath, waiting for the world to change back to the way it was when American steel was king and the men who worked to manufacture it lived the good life, thanks to overtime pay, fat benefit packages, and pension plans they thought would take them through their golden years.

In the meantime, cities struggled and made do with what they could to cobble together some kind of economic viability for their residents. In Austintown, near where Kim lived, there was a new racino, and the parking lot was packed. Driving by, I could just about feel the vibes coming off the place like smoke from a three-alarm fire.

Hopes and dreams.

The chance to hit it big.

The opportunity to turn lives around.

I guess there's no better place for dreaming than a town where so many dreams had already been dashed.

Seems like Hollywood and Youngstown have a whole lot in common.

"This is her street," Declan said, drawing me out of my thoughts at the same time he made a left turn. I admit I was a tad disappointed when he'd picked me up at Sophie's in a late-model Infiniti instead of his Harley. Then again, the leather seats were cushy. I sunk back and, through the growing darkness, helped him read the addresses on the mailboxes out near the street.

Kim's house was a single-story brick ranch with geraniums planted out front around a lamppost and a red Cooper Mini in the drive.

The front door was wide open and light spilled from inside and onto the front step. One look and relief washed through me.

"She must still be home. She's probably just leaving. Now all we have to do is think of what to say, what to tell her so that she doesn't run that spot about Robin Hood."

When I got out of the car, Declan did, too. "You could present your theories. You know, about other suspects. Once she realizes Robin Hood couldn't possibly have killed Jack Lancer, maybe she'll decide not to say too much too soon. If you get her excited about those other suspects . . ."

His words dissolved and, as if we'd choreographed the move, we both stopped cold five feet from Kim's front door.

It was wide open, all right, and there was a pool of something fresh and wet and very red on the beige carpeting, and Kim Kline lay right in the middle of it.

Her arms were thrown out to her sides and those glossy ringlets of hers were a mess. Her eyes were wide open. They stared up at the ceiling, cold, unseeing, and very dead.

ONE MURDER IS more than enough for one lifetime.

Two in one week is just plain wrong.

I leaned against the blue and white patrol car that had come racing to Kim's when Declan called. Someone—maybe one of the paramedics who was now bent over Kim's body?—had thrown a blanket over my shoulders, and I tugged it tighter around myself and watched the cops go

through the motions of the beginnings of their investigation.
Declan and I had already answered what questions we
could—who we were, what we'd seen, how long we'd been
there—and now, Declan spoke to a detective who stood
nearby. They knew each other. I could tell from the easy
way their conversation bounced back and forth, and when
they were done, Declan came to stand next to me and slipped
an arm around my shoulders.

"You okay?"

If I hadn't been toughened by a lifetime of empty
promises and by hoping to see the best of people and then
seeing those hopes squashed by reality over and over, I think
I actually might have shed a tear.

"She was awfully young."

He settled next to me, his hip brushing mine, and slipped
his arm around my shoulders. "If it's any consolation, Charlie Martin, the guy I was just talking to, he says it looks like
she was hit from behind. Her skull was crushed."

I had enough presence of mind to give him a scathing
look. "That's supposed to be consolation?"

"Charlie said she went fast. She never knew what hit her."

"What did hit her?"

I felt rather than saw his shrug. "Something big and
heavy, and whatever it was, it doesn't look like the murderer
left it behind."

"How long—"

"They don't know yet. Not for sure. But I heard one of
the techs tell Charlie that he figures it's been about an hour."

Honest, I didn't mean to sigh with relief.

"What?" Declan unwrapped his arm from around me
and took a step forward so he could pivot to face me. "What's
that supposed to mean?"

I could have denied knowing what he was talking about

but, hey, we'd just found a dead body together. We owed each other something, and we might as well start with the truth.

"It means you didn't do it," I said.

He bit back whatever words were going to fly out of his mouth and chewed them over for a moment before he asked, "Did you really think I did?"

"No." That was the truth, too. "But, hey, it doesn't hurt to eliminate suspects."

"And I was a suspect."

"You know you were. Not a serious one," I added quickly when he made to walk away. Just to be sure he didn't, I put a hand on his arm. "But I had to consider all the possibilities. You have to admit, you were acting mighty fishy the night I found Jack Lancer's body."

"I explained that. Sophie and I were talking. About business."

I nodded my understanding. "And I believed you. But this . . ." From inside the house, we saw the paramedics lift the body and put it on a gurney. "This sort of seals the deal."

"It did for Kim Kline."

"Do you suppose . . ." The thought had been niggling around inside my brain since the moment we saw the blood and the body, and now I took a moment to let it settle. "Whoever killed her, I bet he saw the same promo spot we heard about back at Rockworth. She said she was going to reveal who killed Jack Lancer."

We watched the paramedics wheel the body to a waiting ambulance. "Looks like somebody didn't want that to happen."

Chapter 19

"So I know you didn't kill Kim, because we were together last night at the time of the murder, and I know Sophie didn't kill Kim. And before you ask," I added, glancing across the stainless steel counter in the Terminal kitchen at Declan, "I know this for a fact because I called over to Serenity Oaks last night and double-checked. According to the woman at the front desk, Sophie was in the lounge all evening for oldies night. With that guy. The one with the fancy mustache. She never left so she couldn't possibly have killed Kim."

"Well, I'm relieved to know we're officially off your suspect list." He'd brought something all wrapped in foil into the Terminal with him that Monday morning and he set the roundish package on the counter and unwrapped it.

"Bread?" I leaned over for a better look and, while I was at it, I took a deep breath of the wonderful aroma that only fresh homemade bread has. "What kind?"

I would have thought an attorney was beyond the whole rolled-eyes thing, but apparently Declan felt he had just cause. "Soda bread, of course. You really need to add it to your Irish menu. I made a couple loaves when I got home last night and—"

"You bake bread?"

"I bake Irish soda bread." The way he said it made me realize that in his mind, there was a very real difference. "I couldn't sleep last night and—"

"You, either, huh?" I wasn't going to mention it because really, if I did, I'd have to admit that every time I tried to close my eyes the night before, all I could see was that pool of blood soaked into Kim Kline's carpet and Kim in the middle of it, her eyes staring up at the ceiling.

I wrapped my arms around myself. "It's hard to get that kind of thing out of your head."

"Which is why I resorted to baking." He found a bread knife and sliced into the squat, round loaf. "There's no yeast in soda bread so you don't have to wait for it to rise, but still, it took me a couple hours to get all the ingredients together and get it mixed and baked. It was better than thinking about—"

"Yeah." I wished I'd thought of baking. Instead, in the hours when I couldn't sleep, I'd paced Sophie's living room, dodging Muffin's bared claws and ignoring Muffin's disapproving meows. As if to prove it, I stifled a yawn and checked out the thick slab of bread he put on a plate and handed to me. "No raisins?"

"Not in my recipe!" He made it sound as if just asking was an insult, but since he smiled when he said it, I didn't take it too seriously. "However . . ." With the tip of the knife, he pointed to the incision at the top of the loaf. "I always follow the tradition of putting a cross in the top of my soda bread," he told me. "Some people say it helps the bread grow. Others believe the tradition started either to ward off evil or to let the fairies out."

I slathered butter on my bread and took a bite. It was soft and crumbly, the best soda bread I'd ever tasted. "Which do you believe?" I asked him before I took another bite. "Are there fairies?"

"Of course there are fairies and don't you believe anyone who tries to tell you there aren't. But this loaf . . ." He took a bite, chewed, and swallowed. "When I cut that cross, I thought about warding off evil. The way things have been going around here lately, I'd say that's our best bet."

"You got that right!" I finished my piece of bread and accepted another one when he offered it.

"So?" he asked. "You going to add soda bread to the menu?"

"Are you going to give me your recipe?"

He whisked the already typed-up recipe out of his pocket and handed it to me.

"You're pretty sure of yourself," I told him.

It was very early and the sun was just starting to creep through the windows high up on the wall to my left; the kitchen was filled with shadows. Declan's smile brightened each and every one of them. "One thing I've never been accused of is a lack of self-confidence."

This, I was sure of.

I got us cups of coffee and when he offered another piece of bread, I was tempted. I opted for half a piece, instead, at the same time I hoped he was planning on leaving what was left of the loaf at the Terminal. I was already dreaming of soda bread along with an afternoon cup of coffee.

"So . . ." I broke off a piece of buttered bread and popped

it in my mouth. "If Sophie didn't kill Kim and if you didn't kill her, who did?"

He brushed crumbs from the front of his black T-shirt. "Good question. And here's another thing to think about. We can be reasonably sure the story Kim was going to break on the eleven o'clock news wasn't the story about the Food Pantry Robin Hood because Sophie and I are the only ones who would have cared if that news came out, and since you've so graciously"—he gave me a quick little bow— "eliminated us as suspects, there has to be something else Kim was about to reveal."

"About someone else who didn't want the story to get out." I scooped up our dishes and took them to the sink along with the knife he'd used to slice the bread. "She said she was going to break the case wide open, right? She said she was going to reveal who the killer was. If it wasn't you and it wasn't Sophie, then it was someone else." That was obviously a no-brainer, and thinking about it, I drummed my fingers against the counter, and the noise they made against the stainless steel added a thrumming beat to the pounding already going on inside my head.

"What we really need to do," I said, "is look through Kim's reporting of the murder. Maybe she said something somewhere along the line. You know, gave some sort of clue that no one paid any attention to because it was small and didn't seem to matter. I wonder if the station would let us look through their tape archives."

"I wondered the same thing." Along with the soda bread, he'd brought his iPad into the kitchen with him, and now Declan tapped the keyboard and crooked a finger so that I would come around to the other side of the counter and stand next to him where I could see the screen.

There was Kim Kline's face, right at the center of it.

"You got the tapes of Kim's reporting?" I shot him a look. "How?"

He tried hard not to smile. "I know a woman who works down at the station. In accounting. And she knows people in production. She's pretty persuasive."

"I'm sure you are, too, and I'm not going to ask what you promised in return for these."

"Hey, it's not like they're top secret or anything. Most of this stuff is what's already been on TV. Although there is one segment . . . Well, you'll see."

Like Declan, I stood and watched the recorded segments. There was one from right outside the Terminal the night Jack Lancer died. Another the next day with Kim looking as if she hadn't gotten much sleep. A little shorter story from the next night. All of them pretty much reported the same thing: Jack Lancer, hero of the people, was dead. There was mention of Owen's arrest and later, of his release. There was talk of a reward for information, of dead ends when it came to suspects, of all the good Jack had done for the community and how much he would be missed. There was footage of his wake and the crowds of people outside the memorial chapel.

In the midst of it all, reporting and commenting and looking suitably morose, was Kim Kline.

"Poor Kim." I shivered. "It's hard to watch. I mean, with what we saw last night."

"Shhh! This is the part I think you'll want to see."

He was right. The next segment on the tape was one that hadn't aired on TV. I knew this for a fact because there was no setup, no banner with Kim's name on it across the bottom of the screen. Instead, it opened with a shot of Kim asking her cameraman if he was ready, he said he was, and then she—

"She's tucking a little camera in his lapel," I said, pointing to what was happening like Declan wasn't looking exactly where I was looking. "It's a little surveillance camera. And then they're walking into—"

I felt the blood drain from my face.

"That was the day she came in here for dinner!" This time when I pointed at the screen, my finger trembled. "She's . . . she's taping me!"

"My guess is she had something up her sleeve. Like maybe doing a story about you somewhere down the line, you and your Hollywood connections."

"If I knew that," I grumbled, "I might have killed her myself."

Side by side, Declan and I watched the rest of what the cameraman had caught with his hidden camera. If you asked me, it wasn't much and it sure wouldn't have made for interesting TV viewing. The cameraman (I remembered his name was Dustin) turned briefly toward the front door when Denice raced in, apologized for being late, and tucked her Terminal polo shirt into her black pants. Just like I remembered, her son, Ronnie, was with her, and he sauntered by and went to sit at a table along the far wall to wait for his daily supply of free coffee.

Not knowing I was being recorded, I handed Kim and Dustin the menus I'd handwritten, the one that featured my new brainstorm, ethnic foods.

"Irish stew?" Kim crinkled her nose.

I darted a glance across the street toward the Irish store. "A neighborhood family recipe," I told her, and added, "Though I've changed it up a bit, made a few modifications."

"The Fury family?" Kim sat up and looked across the street, too. "All right, I'm game. I'll give it a try. Denice . . . I'll try the stew and, Dustin . . ." She looked his way and the picture wobbled when he nodded. "Make that two."

"That's pretty much it." Declan stopped the videos. "I don't know about you, but to me, there doesn't look like there's anything there worth killing for."

My mind working over the problem, I kept right on staring at the blank screen. "I don't suppose while you were charming your way into your TV station friend's heart, you managed to get a look at Kim's story files?"

"You think I can be charming?"

It was my turn to roll my eyes. "Not what we were talking about."

You wouldn't know it from his grin. "But we could."

"Except we shouldn't."

"Why not?"

I was so busy hating the fact that I let out a sigh, I didn't have time to consider if it was one of annoyance or surrender.

"I don't do relationships," I told him.

"Because . . . ?"

I threw my hands in the air. "Because I don't. Because I never have. Because I don't know how. You, you've got all that . . . family . . ." I'm not sure how I thought throwing out my arms and wiggling my fingers in the direction of the Irish store explained either his family or what I thought of the crazy, wonderful, musical lot of them and how much they terrified me at the same time they made me as jealous as hell. "You've got all those people around all the time and you always have and so you know how to relate to people. And me, I've . . ." I dropped my arms to my side. "I've never had that. I never will. And it's fine, really," I added quickly when he stepped forward and I got the sneaking suspicion that he actually thought it might be a good idea to hug me. "But what it means is I don't do relationships and, correct me if I'm wrong, but I'm thinking that's the only thing you do. Relationships. You're not a one-night-stand sort of guy."

Too bad the kitchen was such a mishmash of light and shadows. Otherwise, I might have been better able to read his expression. It was too rock steady to be considered bittersweet, and besides, he wasn't the bittersweet type. He raised his eyebrows. "I could learn to be."

I had a feeling he was half-serious so I played it cool and boffed him on the arm. It was that or admit that just the thought made me feel as if all the air had been forced out of my lungs.

"There you go," I said, "trying to be charming again."

"And it's"—his shoulders sagged—"not working."

"It's not going to." I was so sure of this, I lifted my chin. I pointed to him. "Relationships. Family. Stability." I swung my finger around to myself. "Not so much. I can't give you what you're looking for, Declan, and you, you've got too much to give me. Besides, once Sophie gets back, I'm outta here. And, admit it, the last thing you want is an outta-here kind of girl. Isn't that what you told me? You're one of the settled ones."

He let the message sink in, then stood tall and inched back his shoulders. "That's good. That's great that we're clear about all that. It's good to get that sort of thing out of the way right from the start, don't you think? It's like—"

"Like something they'd ask you on one of those surveys from an online dating site," I put in and, yeah, like his, my voice was a little too light and airy and my smile was a little too broad. "It's one of those things that exes out two people from ever being a couple."

"Absolutely." He grabbed his iPad and went to the door.

"Positively," I called after him.

He backed up to the door and bumped it open with his butt. "Glad we got it out in the open."

"Me, too. Thanks for the bread. And the recipe."

"Anytime," he said, and he was gone.

And me? I was thrilled, right? Well, of course I was. I knew everything we'd just said was true, and like Declan, I was grateful to get it all out in the open.

I told myself not to forget it and while I was at it, I grabbed the salt shakers that needed to be filled and got to work. A moment later, I realized the sun had inched up enough over the roof of that nearby factory to stream through the windows and flood the kitchen.

Funny, though, it felt as if those long, dark shadows were still all around me.

IT WAS THAT kind of Monday. We were reasonably busy for lunch and dinner and for that, I was grateful, but not nearly as grateful as I was to finally get home that night. It was nearly eight and already dark by the time I pulled into Sophie's driveway, and I braced myself for what was sure to be another ugly encounter with Muffin.

I dragged to the front door, poked my key into the lock, and when it didn't slide in easily, I grumbled a curse.

"New locks," I reminded myself. "Wrong key."

Though I thought I'd left the front porch light on when I left that morning, I had apparently been in too much of a hurry. It was dark there on the stoop, and I fumbled to figure out which key on the Swarovski crystal keychain I'd gotten from the salesman when I picked up my BMW Z4 was the one given to me by the locksmith on Saturday.

And, in hindsight, I guess that was a very lucky thing.

That meant I was still outside and the door was still locked when an arm went around my waist and a gloved hand covered my mouth.

"Open the door," a man's hot, wet voice hissed close to my ear. "You make one funny move, and you're dead."

My breath caught behind a ball of panic in my throat at the same time an idea burst into my head with all the subtlety of a Fourth of July rocket.

One funny move and I was dead, huh?

No funny moves, and I'd be alone in the house with a stranger, and the door would be closed behind me.

Before I could tell myself it was probably a very bad idea, I cocked my elbow and jabbed it as hard as I could into the guy's ribs.

Years of working in restaurants lugging trays laden with glasses and dishes had done a lot for my muscles. And I had the added advantage of surprise.

Chalk one up for funny moves. He was just surprised enough to loosen his grip and step back an inch or two, far enough away from me to allow me to twist out of his grasp.

But not for long.

A second later, his knee slammed into the small of my back. Pain shot through my legs and radiated up my spine and I let out a yelp. While I was at it, I kept right on yelping, too. I had yet to meet any of Sophie's neighbors, but this seemed as good a time as any. I turned to face my attacker and, with the clarity that often comes at times like this, I evaluated the situation and the man whose eyes burned at me from behind a black ski mask.

Five-ten. Whip thin, but plenty strong.

Jeans. Dark sweater, hood up and over a ball cap. A logo on it I couldn't see because of the dark.

And something in his right hand. Something sharp and shiny.

I didn't need to see any more. I screamed until my lungs hurt.

"Shut up!" He tried for a backhand slap, but, hey, years in the system and some really bad placements had taught me to be quick on my feet; I ducked under his arm. That's when I remembered I still had my keys in my hand, and I poked them up through my fingers, and closed my fist around my key fob. The next time he got within striking distance, I jabbed the keys into the man's stomach.

He let out a grunt and made a grab for the keys. He wanted me in the house, and I knew I had to do everything in my power to make sure he never got the door open.

When he gripped my arm, I kicked and punched and when I finally managed to squirm away far enough so that I could get a good windup, I threw the keys as far away as I could. They landed in the shrubbery, the geraniums, and the petunias outside Sophie's living room window.

My attacker looked at the dense undergrowth and he knew exactly what I knew: it would take too long to find the keys.

With a curse, the man slapped me across the face. Then he turned on his heels and ran.

EVEN THOUGH THE pulsing lights of the police car roll bar flashed in my face and practically blinded me, I knew when Declan arrived. The whole vibe of the scene out on Sophie's driveway changed. I recognized him immediately silhouetted against the light, all rigid shoulders and raised chin and a jaw held so tight, even before he was in my face, I had a feeling it just might snap.

"What the hell!" He grabbed my shoulders, which wasn't so great an idea considering that I'd just been attacked by a stranger and so wasn't in the mood for close contact. Not with anyone.

Which made it perfectly justifiable for me to haul off and punch him in the nose.

"What the hell!" Declan jumped back and fingered the bridge of his nose, but, truth be told, there wasn't much damage; I was pretty worn out from all the fighting I'd done with the man who tried to get inside Sophie's house.

"Hey, you two!" Gus Oberlin stomped over. "Is there a problem over here?"

"No problem." Declan knew better than to try for another hold on me. He backed up a step, gave me a quick once-over, and glanced at Gus. "Just making sure Laurel's okay."

"Laurel's more than okay." I thought Gus would have known better; he clamped a hand on my shoulder.

I wiggled out from under the hold.

"She fought back like a trouper," Gus told Declan. "Not always the smartest thing for a woman to do, but in this case, it worked."

"He wanted to get in the house." My throat was raw, my voice was hoarse. "If he just wanted my purse or the car, he could have taken it. But he wanted . . ." When I gulped, my throat protested. "He wanted to get inside the house."

"Just like someone wanted to get inside last Saturday?"

The question from Declan made my head snap up. "How did you know . . . ?"

"A better question," he growled, "is why didn't you tell me?"

"You?" This time, I snapped my gaze to Detective Oberlin. "You really think you should share that kind of information with—"

At one time in his career, Gus must have been a traffic cop. He stopped me with arm extended and his hand out. "Hey, it's all public record and, besides, I thought it was only fair to let Declan know what was going on. Chances are, it's one of his relatives behind this burglary ring."

"And you think that's what happened here? An attempted burglary?" I had to give Declan credit; though his voice simmered with anger, he ignored Oberlin's dig and went straight to the heart of the matter. "Think again, Gus. From what I've seen, none of the other reports say anything about the burglar confronting the homeowner. Why should he? He comes in when people are out of the house, he rips off whatever's worth taking, then he disappears. There's less chance of getting caught that way, less chance of being seen. What happened here—"

"It fits the pattern." When one of the uniformed officers called Gus over to the front door, he turned and walked away. "You'll see, counselor. When all the pieces fall into place, I'd bet any money we find a Fury at the bottom of this burglary ring."

"Son of a . . ." Declan scraped a hand through his hair. That is, right before he said, "Sorry. For . . . you know . . . for grabbing you like that. I should have known—"

"Knee-jerk reaction," I told him. "You want to come in the house? We'll get some ice for your nose."

Since the cops were still busy poking around out front—they found my keys, hurray!—we went around to the back door.

"Looks like he tried to get in here first," Declan said, checking out the scratches on one side of the jamb.

"But not tonight." A block of ice formed in my stomach. "The other day . . . I heard a noise . . . I thought it was the cat."

"So, someone's been trying to get into the house for a few days?" This time, he placed a hand gently on my elbow and I didn't fight back. We walked into the kitchen and I flopped into the nearest chair.

Declan turned on the ceiling fan and the second the light was on, I saw a black-and-white flash head out from under the table and down the basement steps.

He dropped into the chair next to mine and I saw the red blotch on the left side of his nose. At least there was no blood.

I popped out of my chair, got ice from the freezer and put it in a sandwich bag, then wrapped the whole thing in a kitchen towel and handed it to him.

He accepted the icy package but he didn't put it up to his nose. Instead, he laid it on my cheek.

I winced. In all the excitement, I'd forgotten my attacker had slapped me.

"You sit here for a couple minutes and catch your breath." When I lifted the ice pack from my face, Declan put his hand over mine and put it—and the ice—back on my cheek. "Then you can gather up some things and we can get going."

"Going? Where?"

"You don't think I'm going to let you stay here another night, do you? You're going to my mom's house."

It was the smart thing to do. I knew that the moment he suggested it.

Just like I knew I wasn't going to budge.

"No." I got to my feet, the better to stand my ground. "I don't need you to take care of me."

"Hey, you're the one who called me."

"I did." It was too late to tell him it had been a mistake. Besides, the way he was acting pretty much proved it. "I didn't know what else to do. I don't know anyone else in Hubbard and—"

"And I'm glad you did." He stood and took the ice pack out of my hands. "And, believe me, I'm not trying to butt in and I'm not trying to take over. I just want to help. My mom won't mind. She's got plenty of empty bedrooms. You'll be more comfortable there."

"Thank you." Why did those two words always seem to stick in my throat? I cleared away the uncomfortable feeling with a cough. "But I'm staying here."

"I can't let you."

"You can't stop me."

"Laurel, you don't have to prove how tough you are. You already did that. You fought off the guy who jumped you. You gave the police as good a description as you could. You've already been a hero tonight. You don't need to prove yourself again."

"No, I don't." I backstepped away from him, gathering my thoughts. "But see, here's the thing, and maybe you won't understand, but it's the truth so just hear me out. I've spent my whole life being shuffled from one family to another, from one home to another. I'm not going to let it happen again. Nobody's going to push me around. Not anymore. Nobody's going to say where I can live and where I can't and where I can sleep and where I can't. Nobody's going to make me stuff everything I own in a big, black garbage bag and drag it along to another place. Not anymore. I'm staying, Declan. I'm staying here. No guy in a ski mask is going to make it so that I can't."

He gave in with an almost imperceptible nod and grabbed his phone and walked into the living room to make a call. Within fifteen minutes, his cousins Martin and Dan showed up along with brothers Seamus and Brian, and Declan informed me that they'd be stationed outside the house all night long.

I protested. Long and as loud as I was able to, considering the condition of my throat.

Martin, Dan, Seamus, and Brian didn't even bother to listen. They went outside to let the cops in on what Declan had planned.

"You guys can't stay outside all night!" I insisted.

"Those guys can!" Chuckling, Declan strolled into the living room, fluffed the pillows from the couch, and plopped right down. "I'm the one who thought of the plan. That means I'm the brains of the operation. I'm sleeping right here!"

I suppose I could have argued but, truth be told, I was dog tired. I got a pillow and a blanket and a sheet and I made him move so that I could lay it out on the couch. I put the pillow on the couch and dropped the blanket next to it.

"Why?" I asked him.

Declan spread the blanket out. "Why . . . what?"

"Why here? What's so special about Sophie's house that a guy . . ." I couldn't help myself, even though I knew that the police were still out front, that Martin and Dan and Brian and Seamus were on guard duty, I looked over my shoulder at the front door. "Why was he so dead set on getting in here?"

"That's what we've got to figure out." Declan sat down and patted the patch of couch next to him. I sat down, too.

"Someone tried to break in here three times that we know of." I told him about the first time when I'd heard the noise in the kitchen and figured it was the cat. Then about the attempted break-in the Saturday before. "Three times—that's no coincidence. They were looking for something. And it can't have anything to do with Jack Lancer's murder. Or with Kim Kline's. It doesn't make any sense."

"It doesn't, but you know . . ."

I knew what he was going to say. I must have. Otherwise, my blood wouldn't have run cold. I put a hand on Declan's arm.

"That day at the Terminal. That's what you were going to mention, wasn't it? You were going to remind me about that day someone went through the Dumpster."

Declan nodded. "I sure was. Somebody's searching for something, Laurel. And it looks like they're willing to do anything to find it."

Chapter 20

I knew for a fact that the man who attacked me outside Sophie's house wasn't George. He wasn't tall enough to be the Terminal cook. He wasn't bulky enough. He didn't smell like fried onions.

No way was my attacker Maxine, the late, great Jack Lancer's most recent girlfriend, either, and besides George of the phony alibi, she was the only other person on my way-too-short list of suspects. It was a man's voice that warned me I'd better not make any funny moves, a man's strong arm that grabbed me around the waist, a man's hand that left an angry red mark on my cheek that still stung the next day.

I was back to square one, or at least I would have been if I could start thinking about the case dispassionately and stop thinking about everything that happened out in front of Sophie's house the night before and everything it meant.

Was the masked man the same one who'd gone through the Terminal trash?

And why?

Was he the same man who killed Jack Lancer? And Kim Kline?

And was I next on the hit list?

I promised myself I wasn't going to obsess about it, but sitting in Sophie's office at the Terminal, I just couldn't help it. Less than twenty-four hours after the attack and my knees still felt rubbery and my heart fluttered around in my chest.

If I hadn't fought back. If I hadn't thought to throw the keys where the man couldn't find them. If I hadn't been lucky in a way neither Jack nor Kim was . . .

The very thought made my stomach do flip-flops, and in the hopes of getting it to settle down, I did my best to concentrate on the stack of receipts in front of me, the ones I had yet to enter into the computer program Sophie used to keep the business of the Terminal in order. She'd be disappointed when she found out the truth—I'd been so busy concentrating on the investigation, I'd been ignoring the day-to-day details that were so important to keeping a restaurant going.

"No more," I vowed, and I grabbed the pile of receipts and got to work.

The distraction was successful. At least for a little while. Not only did I get caught up, but I was gratified to see that my ethnic foods idea was starting to pay off. In the last few days, we'd sold lots of Irish stew and our colcannon orders outweighed the ones for french fries.

I was just about finished with the receipts when there was a knock on the office door.

George toed the line between the restaurant and the office.

"Can I . . ." He looked up at the ceiling. Down at the floor. "I wondered if I could . . ." He cleared his throat. "It's Tuesday and it's almost four thirty and we close in just a little while. I was thinking . . ." He scrubbed a finger under his nose. "Can I leave a little early today? I've got something special going on, an extra sort of . . . an extra sort of meeting."

I am not a hard taskmaster, but I'm not a pushover, either. I was just about to remind him that there was no telling what kind of business we'd get between now and when the Terminal closed at five and then relent and let him leave when George spoke up again.

"I gotta . . ." He shuffled his feet. "I gotta get over to my AA meeting at St. Colman's."

That nice speech I had prepared froze on my lips. An AA meeting at the church, huh? The AA meeting that did not now and never had existed? The one that was George's alibi?

In a split second, I came up with a plan.

Was my smile convincing? I liked to think so. After all, I'd learned phoniness in the phony capital of the universe. "Of course you can leave early, George. Your meeting is important and I'd hate to see you miss it."

I paused here and gave him a chance to come clean, and when he didn't, I kept my smile firmly in place. "As long as there's enough Irish stew ready in case anyone orders it."

He assured me there was and backed out of the office.

I gathered up my purse and, since it was chilly, a light jacket, and waited for George to leave the restaurant. When he did, I left instructions with Inez and Denice, hopped in my car, and followed him.

Whatever I had expected, it wasn't the building where

he stopped his clunker of a Pontiac and went inside, the one he walked out of an hour and a half later.

When he did, I was waiting at the door.

"Oh." George's cheeks were flushed and the golf shirt he'd put on instead of the white T-shirt he usually wore in the kitchen had traces of sweat on it. "What are you . . ." The hard-soled shoes were a new addition, too, and he shuffled them against the sidewalk. "What are you doing here?"

"I guess that's the question I need to ask you. You told me you had an alibi for the night of the murder, George. You told me you were at St. Colman's. But that was Monday night, and this is Tuesday night. And this sure isn't St. Colman's."

"Last week? I was at the church. Sure. Yeah. Of course I was. My meeting was at the church last Monday, and today . . . well, like I told you before, this is something special, something extra." I don't think I'd ever seen George smile before, which made it all the more disturbing. "I just stopped in here today. You know, to see a friend."

I backed up a step and looked at the window of the establishment he'd just walked out of.

"Jerome's Dance Studio." Since the neon sign glowed at us from not three feet away, I really didn't need to read it, but I figured it proved my point. "Ballroom dancing lessons."

I swung away from the sign to pin George with a look. "What's really going on?"

There is nothing more pathetic than the surrender of a really big guy. George's wide-as-a-barn shoulders sagged. His smile wilted and the color in his cheeks intensified.

"I couldn't tell you the truth," he muttered. "I couldn't let anybody know I was taking . . . you know, dancing lessons. That's why I said I was going to an AA meeting."

Grinning would be an insult, so I controlled myself. "Dance lessons are nothing to be ashamed of."

"People, they'd make fun of me if they knew. If they knew why I wanted to."

I thought the probing look I gave him would have been enough to get my unspoken question answered, but when it wasn't, I pressed him. "Why are you taking dancing lessons?"

George squeezed his lips together. That is, right before he let out a long sigh. "It's Denice," he said. "I've been wanting to . . . that is, I've been sort of thinking about . . . I thought maybe one of these days I might—"

"You want to ask her out on a date."

He was so relieved at not having to say the words himself, this time, his smile was genuine. "I know she likes to dance and I thought if I could . . ."

I almost told him it was sweet but the way I figured it, George wasn't the kind of guy who wanted to hear things like that.

He wasn't the kind of guy who lied about his alibi because he'd killed Jack Lancer, either, I realized, and smiling, I told him to have a good night and went on home, humming the tune of a waltz and picturing George out there on the dance floor, Denice caught up in the crook of his arm.

THAT TUESDAY MORNING before I'd left for work, I told Declan I didn't need him or his family at the house that night.

I did not tell him—at least not in so many words—how comforting it was when I was up in bed on Monday night and knew that his family was stationed outside and he was down on the couch. I had felt cared for a time or two in my

life, mostly by Nina, who'd waded through the minefield
of my teenage years with me. I had felt valued, too, at one
time, for my skills as a chef and for my ability to juggle
Meghan's diet regimen with her obsessive-compulsive need
to fit into the smallest bikinis and the tightest of tight
evening gowns.

I had never felt truly safe.

Not that I was about to confess all that to Declan. I
thanked him, of course. I told Martin and Dan and Seamus
and Brian to stop into the Terminal anytime for a meal on
the house.

To me, that meant the matter was over and done with.
Not so with the Fury boys.

They were all waiting for me when I got home from
Jerome's Dance Studio that Tuesday.

"You can't," I said the moment I was out of the car and
my feet touched the driveway. "You can't all stay here
again."

"It's not like we really want to." Seamus poked his hands
into the pockets of his jeans.

"Yeah," Brian added, "it's not like we think it's the best
idea in the world."

"But Declan here . . ." Like I didn't know Declan was
standing there grinning at me, Martin looked his way. "The
way we figure it, if he's alone in the house with you—"

"Well, you're new in town and you don't know the boy's
reputation," Dan told me, shaking his head as if it really was
a pitiful confession. "It's not you we're here to keep an eye
on, it's him!"

It was hard to argue with logic like that.

Rather than even try, I made grilled cheese sandwiches
for everyone and since it was late and I didn't know I was
having company, I managed strawberries and fresh whipped

cream for dessert. While my outside guests got settled in their sleeping bags, Declan helped with the dishes.

"You can't keep doing this," I told him.

"Drying the dishes? Why not?"

A click of the tongue should have told him all he needed to know, but if there was one thing I'd learned about Declan, it was that he sometimes needed to be hit over the head with the obvious. "You know what I'm talking about. You all can't keep staying here. Don't your cousins and your brothers have jobs?"

"Of course they do. What do we look like, riffraff? And we're not going to stay here forever. Just until we figure out what's going on and why someone keeps trying to get into the house."

I finished with the dishes, rinsed down the sink, and told myself that before I left town, I would order a state-of-the-art dishwasher for Sophie. "It doesn't make any sense," I grumbled.

"Them working? Or someone trying to get into the house?"

Since he knew exactly what I was talking about, I didn't bother to answer. Instead, I got a glass of ice water for myself and poured coffee for Declan, who said he didn't mind the caffeine because he'd want to stay alert all night, anyway.

And that only made me feel more guilty about having him there.

I turned and leaned against the sink. "Do you suppose it all has anything to do with the murders?"

He finished with the last of the dishes and draped the red-and-white-checked cotton dish towel over the counter. "I wish I knew."

"Maybe if we watched those tapes of Kim's again . . ." Inside my head, it had sounded like a good suggestion, but the moment the words were out of my mouth, I couldn't help but think how lame it was. "We watched them once. We didn't see anything useful."

"Which doesn't mean we can't give it another try."

We went into the living room together and Declan tossed aside the pillow he'd used the night before so we could sit side by side on the couch when he got out his iPad. For the second time, we watched Kim's reporting of Jack's murder.

"It's all the same old, same old," I said halfway through. "Photos of Jack. Kim looking somber, reporting the facts."

"And that crazy segment with her secretly taping you."

We were just at that particular segment and together, we watched the action unfold on the screen in front of us.

"There's Denice walking in with Ronnie," I said, my voice as dull and heavy as the dead-end feeling in my stomach. "There I am handing out the menus with the Irish stew special."

"And Kim is going to place two orders."

We watched her do it.

"I'll give it a try," Kim said. "Denice . . ." She called the waitress over. "I'll try the stew and, Dustin? Make that two."

There was nothing there. Nothing unusual. Nothing telling. Certainly nothing suspicious.

I asked Declan to replay the segment anyway because as weird as it seemed, that nothing felt very much like something.

Again, we watched the scene.

"I'll give it a try," Kim said. "Denice . . ."

I sat up like a shot. "That's it!"

Declan paused the video. "And it is what?"

"Back it up a little," I instructed him, and when he did, we watched Kim and Dustin get settled. "Kim said she'd never eaten there," I told Declan. "I swear she told me that.

But when Denice arrived she called her by name." We watched it all happen again.

"Your waitresses wear name tags," Declan reminded me. "It all makes perfect sense."

I wasn't so sure. I asked him to back up the video again and this time, to enlarge Denice when she came on the screen and to play the tape in slow motion. "She's running late. Her shirt isn't even tucked in. And look!" This time I didn't bother to point, I poked my finger into the screen right at the spot where the Terminal was embroidered on Denice's shirt, and Declan saw what I saw.

Denice hadn't put on her name tag yet.

Declan sat back and looked at where he'd paused the video, right on Denice. "What do you think it means?"

"For one thing, it means Kim was lying."

Declan's nose was hardly red at all. Still, he fingered it, no doubt because he remembered what happened the last time he said something he shouldn't have. He inched away from me. "Maybe she just didn't want to admit she'd eaten at the Terminal before. You know, on account of the restaurant's reputation for—"

"What?" I demanded.

"Good food. Great service." His smile didn't convince me.

Exactly why I didn't acknowledge it.

"Let's watch the rest of what they caught on tape that day," I suggested instead. "Maybe there's more."

And guess what, there was, though on first glance, it sure didn't seem like much.

Dustin the cameraman had kept the hidden camera rolling through dinner and though I enjoy good food and appreciate other people's love of a well-cooked meal, I can't say it was especially interesting to watch Kim slurp down the Irish stew, even though she commented more than a time or two about how delicious it was.

"He's a good kid." In the background of the scene, Denice zipped by with a tray on her shoulder. I think she was talking about her son, Ronnie. "And it's not like he's taking up a table where customers would be sitting. Well, not usually, anyway. Am I right, Marvin?" She raised her voice enough to be heard by Marvin, who was seated two tables away. "My Ronnie, he's a good kid, right?"

Marvin—the man I would always remember as the one who ordered the only lentil quinoa salad I'd ever sold at the Terminal—answered. "The best. He should be on TV!"

"Yeah!" We couldn't see Denice on the video, but she was standing close enough to Dustin so we could hear her loud and clear. "Imagine him on the big screen. You know, one of those flat-screen TVs like they hang on the wall, forty-two inches wide."

"Forty-eight inches," Ronnie called out. "I'd look way better on a screen that was forty-eight inches wide."

"Forty-eight inches." Marvin chuckled. "Yeah, that sounds good."

There was more background chatter after that, more small talk between Kim and Dustin and—thank goodness—more compliments for the Irish stew. Watching it all was a bit like watching paint dry.

Then I brought over complimentary slices of chocolate pie, and there was Kim giving me an intense look from across the table. "The story of the Lance of Justice's murder has local Emmy written all over it," she crooned. "You know I can't give away the details. They're just too delicious."

"Then, you do know something?" I asked.

Denice came over to collect the dishes just as Kim said,

"Not only do I know something, but I have a line on who killed the Lance of Justice, and why."

"That's it, Declan!" I grabbed on to his arm with both hands, so excited I could barely sit still. "Kim did know who killed Jack Lancer. And you know what? I think that now I do, too."

Chapter 21

Nobody knows how to throw a party like I know how to throw a party.

I should. For six years, I'd made sure that Meghan Cohan was the toast of Hollywood. I knew the food and I cooked it like a wizard, and I knew the party planners who could work their own special magic and make sure Meghan's Pacific Palisades mansion looked even more spectacular than usual.

Meghan wanted an Arabian Nights theme?

We pulled it off, complete with tents on the lawn, an oasis around the pool, and a variety of foods that would make a sultan swoon.

Meghan was in the mood for something more medieval?

Believe me, I wasn't thrilled about planning a menu that included turkey legs guests would eat without silverware, but I endured and even got a chance to watch jousting on the back lawn.

What I had planned for the Terminal, needless to say, was a little less epic scale and a little more down-to-earth.

A party after the restaurant closed on Wednesday.

And staff, neighbors, and some customers were invited.

"You're sure about this?" It was almost time for our guests to arrive and Declan looked over the restaurant and nodded his approval. In honor of our Irish specials, we'd gone all out with the "old sod" theme: there were green streamers hanging between the ceilings fans, a rainbow made out of multicolored balloons over the front entrance, and even green cloth napkins on every table. The band was here, too—more for backup than music—and I'd invited a couple special guests who were going to stay put in the kitchen until I told them it was time to come out.

"I'm sure." I scraped my palms against the skirt of the taupe, cream, and black colorblock sheath dress I was wearing. "I think."

"Well, the Terminal looks wonderful!" He was trying to cheer me, trying to calm me, and for that, I was grateful. "You know, you might think about turning this into an Irish pub."

"Sophie would have my head! And, speaking of Sophie . . ." We saw a van pull up to the front door and I hurried that way to help Sophie out of it.

"Well, isn't this just . . ." She looked around at the decorations and spent a moment listening to Seamus tune up his fiddle to help pass the time, and when she looked my way, she blinked as if she'd been asleep for a hundred years and she wasn't quite sure where she'd woken up. "We're an Irish restaurant now?"

I put a hand on her shoulder to reassure her. "We've got a few Irish specials on the menu. The decorations . . . well, most of the decorations are just for tonight."

266 Kylie Logan

"Just for the party."

It wasn't a question, so theoretically, I wasn't required to answer. Instead, I helped Sophie over to a chair I knew would be at the center of the action. The Terminal was her restaurant—her life—and I owed her a ringside seat.

"Our guests will be here in a minute," I told her and Elvis, the man who'd brought her over to the Terminal—the one with the luxurious mustache.

"What are we celebrating?" he wanted to know.

I knew someone was bound to ask, and I was all set with an answer. "Sophie's recovery, for one thing," I told him. "And the chance we've had this last week to get to know our neighbors better. They're all here. Look." I glanced toward the door just as Carrie from the art gallery and Bill and Myra and Barb from Caf-Fiends and John and Mike from the bookstore showed up. They were followed by Kitty and Pat Sheedy, who'd brought Owen along—even though the kid looked as though he would have liked to be anywhere else—and a minute later by Inez, who apologized for running late again and then paled when she realized Sophie was there and heard her, and by Denice, whom I'd told to bring her son, Ronnie, along. George stepped out of the kitchen.

Denice looked up at the bouquet of shamrock-shaped Mylar balloons that floated overhead. "You worked hard once we left today! The place looks amazing."

"It's the least I could do." I sat Denice and her son next to a table with Kitty and Pat. "I wanted to thank everyone for helping me feel so at home this past week."

"Did you? Feel at home?" Sophie clapped her hands to her heart. I swear, the woman could cry at the drop of a hat. A fat tear streaked down her cheek. "I'm so happy you're settling in. It's beautiful, isn't it, Elvis?" The man with the mustache—who did not look like an Elvis to me—nodded. "It's so nice to know you're going to call Hubbard home."

I had never said this, but I wasn't about to argue. Not right then. Our next batch of guests arrived—Stan and Dale and Phil and Ruben took their usual table. Marvin, he of the lentil quinoa salad, started for his usual spot across the room, but Declan deftly ushered him to a table closer at hand and he sat down, looking mighty confused about what was going on and what he was doing there.

Once everyone was settled, I stepped to the center of the room. "Welcome. I have a feeling some of you might be wondering what's going on here tonight. Like I just told Sophie, we're here to celebrate her recovery!" There was a round of applause. "And her continued rest and relaxation," I added because I saw the way she was checking out the stack of menus that had been left on a nearby table, and I had the distinct feeling she was going to pop up and go get a damp cloth so she could wipe off the plastic-coated pages.

"We've got Irish food for dinner and Irish music after." I lied like a pro to put our guests at ease, and gestured toward the band. There was another smattering of applause, the loudest from Kitty and Pat, but then, Dan and Martin were their sons. "But first . . ." Hey, I'd learned a thing or two in Hollywood. I drew out the drama by pausing for a moment or two. "First, I think it's important that we talk about murder."

This time, the applause was replaced by a murmur of voices and a shuffle of feet. Ronnie grumbled a word he shouldn't have used in front of Sophie. Marvin still looked confused and our four regulars sat up in their chairs, eager to hear more.

"You want to serve something while you're talking about

all this?" Denice asked me, and took a step toward the
kitchen. "I can get fried pickles."

Fried pickles were one of our most popular appetizers,
but they could wait. By the time we were done, I wasn't sure
anyone would have much of an appetite. "I'd like you here,"
I told Denice. "And I'd like you all to see something."

That was Declan's signal. He started up the video. I'm
no whiz when it comes to technology, but he'd figured out
a way to project the video onto the wall, and together we all
watched Kim's secret tape and saw ourselves, bigger than
life, up there on our makeshift screen.

We watched Kim Kline get settled, and we watched
Denice race into the restaurant. We heard Kim call Denice
by name.

Just as we'd discussed, Declan paused the tape right
there.

"Weird, isn't it?" I asked no one in particular, but I looked
at Denice. "She knew your name."

Denice's nose twitched. "Of course she did. We all wear
name tags, don't we?"

"You weren't wearing one. You hadn't put it on yet that
day," I reminded her, and every single person in the room
looked up at the picture on the wall and saw that it was true.

Denice shrugged. "Then, she knew me because she'd
been here before. What's the big deal?"

"The big deal," I told her, "is that Kim had never been
here beforc. Isn't that right, Sophie?"

"Never." Sophie was sure of this. "At least not until she
showed up here the night of the murder to interview us. I'd
remember a big star like that coming into the restaurant."

"And I'd remember it if Kim ever interviewed you about
the murder, Denice," I added, "but she didn't. I should know.

I watched the tapes of her reporting of the case a hundred times over the last few days."

"So?" Denice was a wiry woman and when she twitched, she reminded me of a fidgety little mouse. "That doesn't mean anything."

"It really doesn't," I conceded. "Not on its own. Except there's more on this tape."

"And I don't see why I have to sit here and watch any of it!" Marvin popped out of his seat. "You're wasting my time."

"I'll try to make it quick," I promised him, and he sat right back down again. Believe me, I didn't have any illusions (or delusions) about my ability to convince him; I'd stationed Brian and Seamus at the front door, and Marvin knew there wasn't a chance they were going to let him leave.

"Here's what really put me on the right track," I said, and motioned to Declan. He restarted the video and we heard Denice's conversation with Marvin and Ronnie about the big-screen TV. Then we heard Kim tell Denice that she knew who killed Jack Lancer.

"Don't prove nothing." Ronnie folded his hands over his chest, sat back in his chair, and stuck his legs out in front of him. "Bunch of bull, and none of it, it don't mean nothing."

"It wouldn't," I told him. "If I didn't have this."

Like a magician pulling a rabbit from a hat, I reached to the table behind me for the receipt I'd left there.

"Lentil quinoa salad," I said, looking at Marvin. "You're the only one who's ever ordered it. Here's the receipt."

He raised his chin. "So?"

"So I was thinking about that day, and it's a shame Kim wasn't here secretly taping me then, because then we'd have video that shows how very much you wanted to make sure

Denice took the money for your lunch. But it wasn't the money you were worried about, was it, Marvin?"

His eyes narrowed and he sat up when I produced a second piece of paper. This one was tucked into a police department plastic evidence bag.

"You didn't care if Denice got the tip you left for her," I told Marvin. "What you really cared about was this piece of paper, the one you slipped under the receipt. To me . . ." I didn't need to see it again, but remember, I was being all about drama. I gave the piece of paper a careful look. "It doesn't look like much to me. A square drawn on a piece of paper. A few tick marks on one end of it. A list of numbers on the side." Not that they could see it very well from where they all sat, but I showed the bag and its contents around. "Fortunately, the police are a whole lot better at figuring out this kind of thing than I am."

Oh, I said the magic word, all right, and at the very mention of the police, Marvin jumped out of his chair again.

Not to worry, that was the exact moment Gus Oberlin stepped out of the kitchen.

Marvin ran his tongue across his lips. "That don't prove nothing," he said.

"It wouldn't. If there wasn't a burglary ring operating in town. That's why you were so desperate to get this piece of paper back, isn't it"—I swung my gaze over the crowd—"Ronnie?"

The kid went as white as a sheet. "I don't . . . I don't know what you're talking about."

"You must, otherwise you wouldn't have gone through the trash here at the restaurant to find this piece of paper. And when you didn't, you thought I might have taken it home. That's why you were trying to break in. You were right, you know. I found it in with a bunch of receipts I was going to enter into Sophie's computer at home. I've been so busy, I didn't get around to it, otherwise I would have seen this piece of paper then."

"Somebody broke into the house?" Sophie fanned her face with one hand.

"Tried to break in," I repeated. "And no worries, the locks have been changed and you're getting a security system installed next week. Not that you'll need it now. The cops have this piece of paper, so Marvin and Ronnie, they won't have to try and get it back again."

Kitty Sheedy shifted left and right in her seat for a better look. "What is it?" she asked. "Why is it so important?"

"You want to tell them, Ronnie?" Since he clamped his lips shut, I had to. "It's a map of the Tollifer Electronics Warehouse over on the other side of town. And the security codes Marvin managed to get from one of the employees there."

"Don't bother to try and deny it." Detective Oberlin stepped forward. "We talked to a guy, Marvin. He admitted that he sold you the codes. You and Ronnie here were going to use them to break into the warehouse, and I'm guessing you were all set to do it this week when the new shipment of some big video game system arrives. Something all the kids have been talking about."

"You can't prove I had anything to do with it," Ronnie snapped. "Maybe he"—he stabbed a finger in Marvin's direction—"maybe he had that there map, but you can't prove I had anything to do with—"

"With the burglary ring?" I gave Ronnie a long look. "Maybe you weren't watching the video like we were, Ronnie. Or maybe you just thought no one would notice. Declan . . ." I looked his way and he knew exactly what I wanted. He queued the tape and played the scene.

"Imagine him on the big screen." On-screen, we watched Kim eat her Irish stew, but we heard Denice's voice in the background and we knew she was talking about Ronnie. "You know, one of those flat-screen TVs like they hang on the wall, forty-two inches wide."

"Forty-eight inches," Ronnie called out. "I'd look way better on a screen that was forty-eight inches wide."

"Forty-eight inches." Marvin chuckled. "Yeah, that sounds good."

Declan put the video on pause.

"You were putting in your order, Marvin. For a TV. Detective Oberlin here tells me there was a forty-eight-inch flat-screen taken from a home just the night before."

"There are plenty of TVs in the world." Marvin waved away my words. "That don't prove a thing."

"Your fingerprints on this map do." Gus took the evidence bag out of my hands. "Put that together with the guy over at Tollifer's who gave you the security codes and we've got you, Marvin."

Marvin swallowed so hard, I heard him gulp. "But not for murder. Nobody ever said anything about murder."

"Kim did," I reminded him, and once again, we played the tape. When it was over, I said, "You saw it right there and then. Kim says she knows who murdered Jack Lancer. And she didn't say it for my sake, did she? She wanted the murderer to know she was onto him. So, was it you, Marvin?" I asked, then swung the other way. "Or was it you, Ronnie?"

Color shot into Ronnie's face. It was an ugly shade of maroon. He jumped to his feet. "No way you're going to pin that murder on me," he said. "I didn't do it. It wasn't me. No way I'm going down for something I didn't do. It was her. My mom!"

Okay, I admit it, I'd been so convinced that either Ronnie or Marvin was our perp, I was as completely at a loss for words as everyone else. Well, everyone except Denice.

I will not report the first words out of her mouth. She was no less angry when she lashed out at her son. "You ungrateful little creep. After all I've done for you!"

"And you want me to take a murder rap for you? She did it," Ronnie said, looking around at everyone gathered there in the Terminal. "She did it because she said Jack Lancer knew about what me and Marvin were doing, about how I was taking stuff out of houses and Mom was fencing it here through the restaurant."

"Oh my!" Sophie got so pale I hurried and got her a glass of water and waited until Elvis helped her drink a few gulps before I said, "You thought Jack Lancer was doing a story on the burglary ring?"

"Well, he was." Denice crossed her scrawny arms over her chest. "He told me so himself. He said that's why he was here every day. He said something hot was going on and he was going to break the story. What else could he have been talking about?"

Declan and I exchanged looks.

"She was afraid she'd end up in jail." By now, Ronnie was shaking. He braced his hand against the table to keep himself upright. "She said we had to do something about the Lance of Justice. She told him she had information for his story, and she told him to meet her here that night and she has a key, you know. She had it made a couple years ago."

"Shut up, Ronnie!"

Her son paid no attention to her. "She killed Lancer, not me," Ronnie said. "And that stupid Kim, that stupid woman, it turns out was following Lancer because she was trying to find out what story he was working on. She took a picture. Of my mother. My mother and Jack Lancer."

"She wanted money." I practically groaned. "That's why Kim Kline made such a big deal about knowing who the murderer was. She was blackmailing you, wasn't she, Denice?"

Denice pressed her lips shut. "Not saying another word."

But then, she didn't have to. It didn't take a Hollywood scriptwriter to imagine the rest. Kim had proof of the murder, Kim wanted money, Denice took care of Kim.

"A big TV star like that." As disgusted as the rest of us, Sophie shook her head. "What would a young woman like that need money for? Why would she take that kind of chance, just to blackmail someone?"

Denice barked out a laugh. "All you had to do is look at the chick. She said she wanted the money for a nose job. So she could be on network news!"

By now, the other cops who'd been in the kitchen with Gus Oberlin had Marvin, Ronnie, and Denice surrounded. They slapped the cuffs on all three of them and led them out the door to where three police cruisers waited.

"We did it." I felt as if all the air had been let out of me, and I dropped into the nearest chair and took Sophie's hand in mine. "It's all settled. There's nothing to worry about, Sophie. Not anymore."

"I'm so glad, dear." She smiled. "I'll sleep better tonight, and I know you will, too."

Before our guests filed out the door, we heated up a big pot of Irish stew so we could officially celebrate and the band played a couple tunes. When we were done, Elvis took Sophie back to Serenity Oaks, Inez left to pick up her son, George shuffled into the kitchen.

I stuck my head in there. "You okay?" I asked him.

"Sure. Why wouldn't I be?" He grabbed his jacket and headed out the door.

Declan and I watched him go. "Funny," he said, "George doesn't look okay."

"No, I don't imagine he is. George has still got the music of that waltz going on inside his head. And Denice, the only dance she's going to be doing is the jailhouse rock."

Recipe

ELLEN FURY'S
GRANDMOTHER'S IRISH STEW

1¼ pounds chuck beef stew meat, cut into 1½ inch
   chunks
3 teaspoons of salt (more to taste)
¼ cup olive oil
6 large garlic cloves, minced
4 cups beef stock or broth
2 cups water
1 cup Guinness Extra Stout
1 cup hearty red wine
2 tablespoons tomato paste
1 tablespoon sugar
1 tablespoon dried thyme
1 tablespoon Worcestershire sauce
2 bay leaves

2 tablespoons butter
1 large onion, chopped (1½ to 2 cups)
2 cups ½-inch peeled carrots cut in pieces
3 pounds russet potatoes, peeled, cut into ½-inch
    pieces (about 7 cups)
½ teaspoon freshly ground black pepper
1 cup parsnips, peeled and cut in pieces

Sprinkle the salt over the beef. Heat oil in a large pot and brown the meat. Add garlic and sauté for 30 seconds.

Add beef stock, water, Guinness, red wine, tomato paste, sugar, thyme, Worcestershire sauce, and bay leaves. Stir. Bring to a simmer, then reduce heat, cover and cook for 1 hour.

While that is cooking, melt the butter in another pot and add onions and carrots. Sauté until onions are golden, about 15 minutes. Add to beef along with the potatoes after the beef has simmered for one hour. Also add black pepper and salt to taste. Simmer until vegetables are tender, another 40 minutes or so. Because they're delicate, add the parsnips during the last 30 minutes.

Enjoy!

Serves 6.

"**B**one sue war!"

I was putting the last touches on the quiches about to go into the oven, so I didn't turn around when someone bumped through the kitchen door of Sophie's Terminal at the Tracks and called out the greeting.

I didn't need to.

I'd recognize Sophie Charnowski's voice—and her lousy French accent—anywhere.

Then again, I should. It had been six months since I'd left California and arrived in Hubbard, Ohio, to run what I thought was Sophie's white-linen-and-candlelight restaurant while she had knee replacement surgery. Six months since I found out that the elegant restaurant she'd lied about for years was really a greasy spoon in an old train station that anchored a battered-but-trying-to-gentrify part of town.

Six months since I'd been embroiled as much in murder as I was in cooking.

The thought hit and a touch like icy fingers squirmed its way up my back. I twitched it aside and called over my shoulder. "*Bonsoir*, Sophie. Any sign of Rocky yet?"

"No! She is nowhere to be seen, yes?" Sophie tried for a French lilt that pinged around the tile and stainless steel kitchen and fell flat. With her usual good humor, she laughed it away and came up behind me so she could stand on tiptoe and peek over my shoulder at the six quiches on the counter.

"Oh, Laurel, they look fabulous!" Sophie breathed in deep. "Think six will be enough?"

I wiped my hands on the white apron looped around my neck. "We've got three more in the fridge and George will pop them in the oven if we need them," I told Sophie at the same time I glanced across the kitchen. George Porter was leaning back against the industrial fridge, his beefy arms crossed over his massive chest and a scowl on his face that pretty much said all there was to say about what he thought of quiche.

In spite of the scowl—or maybe because of it—I gave him the kind of smile that said I was sure he was on board with my plan.

George didn't smile back.

But then, what did I expect?

The Terminal's long-time cook was a mountain of a man with more tats on his arms than I had fingers and toes, a meat-and-potatoes kind of guy who was as happy as a cholesterol-challenged clam cooking up the fried eggs, fried bologna, fried steak, and fried chicken that for years had been the staples of the Terminal menu. That is, before I arrived and started introducing healthier dishes and, in a flash of inspiration, featuring ethnic specials.

We'd started with Irish and that summer had tried Japanese (sushi did not exactly go over big with the Hubbard crowd) and Italian (popular, but there were plenty of Italian places in town and I gave up on a menu that seemed to me to be déjà vu all over again). Now, in honor of a town celebration commemorating the day the French presented the Statue of Liberty to the people of America, we'd decided to go with the Tri-Color flow. French food, but not the fussy kind that's so off-putting to so many people. We were sticking with French country, French bistro. Delicious, accessible, and easy for a man like George to handle. Even if in his heart-of-fried-food hearts, he didn't want to.

I sloughed the thought aside and reminded Sophie, "There are tartines, too."

"Tartines." Her sigh hovered in the ether somewhere between Nirvana and Utopia. In the weeks since we'd started planning our French menu and I'd introduced her to tartines, she'd become something of an addict. And who could blame her! The knife-and-fork open-faced French sandwiches are delightful.

"We're going to use some of the heirloom tomatoes still coming in from the local farmers," I told Sophie. "We'll put those on some of the tartines along with eggplant. Then for others, we've got ham and Gruyere, and toasted Camembert, walnut, and fig."

"Walnut and fig."

I ignored George when he grunted.

"Now all we need . . ." I glanced at the quiches that looked decidedly naked. "Did Rocky say what time she'd be here with the herbs?"

"I'm late. I know. I'm sorry!"

For the second time in as many minutes, the kitchen door swung open and this time, Raquel Arnaud bumped into the room. Rocky was a friend of Sophie's but there couldn't be two women who were more different. Sophie was short, plump, and as down to earth as her sensible shoes. Her hair was the same silvery color as Rocky's, but while Sophie's was short and shaggy, Rocky's was long and sleek and as glorious as the woman herself.

But then, Rocky had the whole French thing going for her, including just a trace of an accent that hadn't disappeared in spite of the fact that she'd left her native country nearly fifty years earlier.

Rocky was almost as tall as my five-nine, willowy, and as elegant as her clothing. She was a farmer—herbs and speciality vegetables—a woman whose life revolved around the seasons and the weather and the acreage thirty minutes outside of Hubbard where she grew some of the best produce in the state, yet anyone meeting her for the first time would think she'd just stepped out of the house to shop on the Rue de la Pax.

Well, except for that Friday night.

I did a double take.

That evening, graceful and refined Rocky looked . . .

She was wearing the black A-line dress she claimed was a fashion must, but Rocky's hair was uncombed and her lipstick was smudged. Sure, she was running late, and that might account for the slapdash grooming, but nothing I knew about Rocky could explain—

Sneakers?

Before I came to Hubbard, I'd worked as a personal chef in Hollywood. Believe me, I knew fashion trends, fashion faux pas, and plain ol' fashion disasters.

I'd never known Raquel Arnaud to dare something as unfashionable and as downright un-French as to wear tennis shoes outside of the house. Especially ones that looked to be encrusted with a week's worth of garden goo.

"I knew I was running late so I chopped the thyme at home."

Before I could even think of what to say or how to ask Rocky if she'd completely lost her mind, she raced over and put a basket on the countertop beside me. There was a white linen towel thrown over the top of it and when Rocky whisked it away, I forgot all about her smeared lipstick and her tennis shoes.

But then, who can resist the heavenly woody/lemony aroma of fresh thyme!

I took a deep breath and automatically found myself smiling.

"Always has that affect on me, too." Rocky gave me a playful poke in the ribs at the same time she reached around me to sprinkle thyme on the quiches. "I brought griselles, too," she said. "But since you're already done with these, they'll have to wait for tomorrow's quiche."

I stepped back to admire the finished quiches. "Bacon, onion, and Swiss today," I told Rocky. "Pretty traditional, I know, but I thought that might be easiest if we get a crowd after the book signing. Tomorrow after the big parade, we'll mix it up with spinach and the shallots in some of the quiches." I peeked at the French shallots—what Rocky called griselles—and took another deep breath and I swear, I could still smell the scent of autumn earth that clung to the shallots.

And to Rocky.

Carefully, I took another sniff.

A fragrant cloud of Chanel No. 5 usually enveloped Rocky.

That night, she smelled more like wet soil. And red wine. Lots of red wine.

I guess Sophie noticed, too, because behind Rocky's

back, she raised her eyebrows and gave me That Look. The one that said I was supposed to ask what the heck was going on.

Before I could, Rocky pulled a bottle of wine out of the basket she'd brought with her.

"We need to have a glass before we head out, eh?" She didn't wait for us to agree, but reached for the corkscrew she'd also brought along and opened the bottle. "You have glasses, George?" she asked and since we didn't have a liquor license and there weren't any appropriate wineglasses around, he brought over water glasses. Four of them.

Rocky didn't mind sharing. She poured into each of the glasses and she was just about to take a drink when Sophie stopped her.

"What about a toast?" Sophie asked. "We always have a toast."

"Oh." As if this was a new thought, Rocky blinked and stared into her glass.

This time, Sophie augmented That Look with a scrunched up nose and a tip of her head in Rocky's direction.

I knew a losing cause when I saw one.

I put a hand on Rocky's arm and couldn't help but notice that when I did, she flinched.

"Are you all right?" I asked. "You seem distracted."

She made a face that would have been convincing if I hadn't spent the last few years of my career as the personal chef of Hollywood megastar Meghan Cohan. I knew actors. Good actors. Bad actors. Rocky fell into the latter category.

"I get so flustered when I'm running late." I guess Rocky forgot all about the toast, because she downed her wine. "We should probably get going, huh? We don't want to miss the book signing."

"Imagine, Aurore Brisson here in Hubbard!" It looked as if Sophie knew a losing cause when she saw one, too, because she gave up on the toast, took a quick sip of wine, and set down her glass. She stepped up beside Rocky. "How exciting it must be for you to have a Frenchwoman here in town. And such a famous one! That book of hers—"

"*Yesterday's Passion*. Yes, yes." Before Sophie could pilot her to the door, Rocky poured another glass of wine and slugged it down. "I'm anxious to read it. I've always been interested in my country's history but really, I don't know all that much about the Middle Ages. The story sounds so . . . so romantic. Knights, ladies, castles—"

"And that gorgeous hunk, Sam Baker, who's going to play the lead role when the book's made into a TV series!" Sophie grinned and leaned closer to Rocky, speaking in a stage whisper I couldn't fail to hear. "Laurel knows him."

Rocky raised her eyebrows.

"Not well," I admitted because it was better than letting anyone know that Sam Baker had once had an affair with Meghan Cohan and had come onto me one morning while I was getting breakfast ready for the two of them down in the kitchen of Meghan's mansion. "We've met."

"Is he as gorgeous in person as he is in the movies?" Rocky asked.

He was, and I admitted it. Without adding that he was also a little too much into recreational drugs and other men's wives.

"It's only natural that he's playing the lead. Isn't that right, Laurel?" Sophie asked. "Meghan Cohan herself is producing and directing and starring. She's playing Cecile. The tabloids say they're having an affair, Meghan and Sam." Sophie paused, waiting for me to fill in the blanks. When I didn't, she breezed right on. "Oh, I can't wait to read the book and see the show and see if they stick to the original story. Is that how it works, Laurel? When they make a film or a TV show, do they usually stick to the original story?"

In this case, only if the original story involved late-night fights of epic proportions, accusations thrown back and forth like rocks from a catapult, and a huge and ugly breakup the tabloids had yet to get wind of. No doubt the network had squelched the truth to get as much mileage as they could out of what they were touting as both an on-screen and an off-screen romance.

"Well, I'm buying a copy of the book, that's for sure," Sophie told us. "And I can't wait to get Aurore Brisson's autograph. How clever it was of John and Mike over at the Book Nook to get her here just in time for the Statue of Liberty celebration. She's such a superstar, so young and pretty. I bet there will be a line out the door of the book store. Let's get over there fast."

Fast, of course, is a relative word when it comes to Sophie, who always has a patron to stop and say hello to or a neighbor to greet. Then, of course, there was the matter of Sophie's knee. Oh, she didn't move at a snail's pace because of that replacement surgery back in the spring. She'd recovered from that and gone through rehab and all was well. At least for a few weeks. That's when she twisted her knee. While she was on a Mediterranean cruise. On an island. Drinking ouzo and doing the Zorba—the Greek dance—with some hunky fisherman who e-mailed her regularly now and called her his little baklava and promised to come visit some time soon.

To say this new injury annoyed me no end makes me look small-minded when, in fact, it makes sense that I'd be irritated. See, I had no intention of staying in Hubbard and

I'd told Sophie that from the start. I promised I'd stay only until she felt better and could take over the management of the restaurant herself again.

Only that didn't look like it was going to happen any time soon.

I held on to my temper along with the thought that this, too, would pass. And when it did . . .

We had just walked out the front door of the Terminal and a brisk autumn breeze ruffled my hair along with the French flag we were flying from a post out front, and I made sure to keep a smile off my face.

Sophie had an uncanny way of reading into my smiles and for now, what I knew about how long I was staying and where I might be going when I waved adios to the town that time forgot was my business and mine alone.

We fell into step behind the throngs of people milling in front of the bookstore and slowly making themselves into some sort of orderly line, and while Sophie and Rocky chatted about people I didn't know, I had a few minutes to look around. What was now called the Traintown neighborhood had once been at the heart of Hubbard's industrial center. There were railroad tracks that ran along the back side of the restaurant and six times a day, a train still rumbled by and shook the Terminal to its nineteenth-century foundation. Across the tracks was a factory, long shuttered, just one of the many businesses that had gone south/closed their doors/ given up the ghost in what had once been a vibrant community.

Fortunately for the people of Hubbard and the small-business people who wanted so desperately to make a go of life there, Traintown took shape from the battered landscape. It was only one street, anchored at one end by the Book Nook and at the other by the Irish store, a charming little gift shop run by Declan Fury, who was even more charming than every last little stuffed leprechaun he kept in stock.

And he knew it.

Automatically I glanced down the street toward the green shamrock that danced above the shop's front door in the autumn breeze. There was no sign of Declan and while I couldn't say if that was good or bad, I wasn't surprised. Not only was *Yesterday's Passion* the biggest thing to come out of New York publishing since Scarlett lifted her fist to the sky, it was historical romance in all its over-blown, trashy, bodice-ripping glory. Traintown fairly gushed estrogen and no self-respecting guy would be caught dead in the crowd.

We crossed to the other side of the street and the end of the line that snaked out of the bookstore and past Caf-Fiends, our local coffee shop, and all the way over in front of Artisans All, a craft and gift shop with decent merchandise and prices that made this California girl think she'd died and gone to heaven. There we stopped behind three young women wearing medieval attire: long dresses, wimples, and veils. Though I am certainly no historian, I was pretty sure the tattoo on one girl's wrist wasn't exactly authentic to the period.

"Oh, I forgot to give you the CDs of French music!" Rocky passed a hand over her eyes. "Silly me. You'll find them, Laurel." She put a hand on my arm. "In the basket with the herbs. I brought you Piaf and Maurice Chavalier and of course, Téléphone!" When Sophie looked at her in wonder, Rocky managed a laugh that for a second, erased whatever it was that was bothering her and transformed her into the vivacious Rocky I knew. "Hey, back in the day, they opened for the Stones!"

The doors of the Book Nook swung open and a buzz of feminine excitement filled Traintown as we surged forward and closer to the shop and to Mike and John, who stood on either side of the front door.

The Guys, as they were affectionately known throughout Traintown, were personal as well as business partners. They were middle-aged, both tall and thin and they both wore wire-rimmed glasses and had receding hairlines. Mike, dressed tonight in a dapper suit, favored herb teas and had been the first in line when we introduced sushi at the Terminal. John, who sported a beret and a red cravat, adored the strong coffee I made for myself (and shared with him when he stopped in). That evening, he had a cup from Caf-Fiends in one hand and when we finally got close enough, he raised it in greeting.

"Fabulous turnout." Not that he needed me to tell him. I tried to glance over the crowd and into the shop. "And the guest of honor?"

Behind those wire-rimmed glasses, John rolled his eyes. He looked around to make sure no one was paying attention to us when he mouthed the words, "Prima donna."

This didn't surprise me in the least. But then, I had previously lived and worked in a place where prima was never prima enough and every last donna thought she was God's gift.

A few minutes later we were in the shop and just a bit after that, directly in front of the table where Aurore Brisson, blond, plump-lipped, and curvy, looked very bored and very eager for the harried assistant at her elbow to grab the next book, open it, and slide it in front of her so she could scrawl her signature and move on to the next fan.

"*Bonjour.*" When Rocky greeted her, Aurore glanced up, but only for a moment. "*Bienvenue a* Hubbard!"

The author's smile was tight.

"Next!" the assistant called out.

Rocky stepped aside and Sophie took her place. "So much for trying to be friendly," I said to Rocky, but she was hardly listening. She'd already flipped open the book and stepped to the side. The last I saw of her, she was headed down an aisle between two bookshelves marked *Crafts* and *Cooking*, her nose in the book.

"I'm afraid it's my fault." Sophie side-stepped her way around the three medieval maidens who were busy trying to find the best angle for selfies that would include Aurore Brisson in the background. "Rocky's worried. She's nervous. You know, about the symposium over at Youngstown State."

It took a moment for the pieces to fall into place in my brain. "The peace symposium? Rocky's speaking at it, I know, but how is that your—"

"I talked her into it." Sophie's shoulders hunched. "She didn't want to do it, and I talked her into accepting the invitation. In fact, I volunteered her when I heard Professor Weinhart was putting together the symposium. I told Rocky I thought it was important for people to hear about her experiences on the front lines of the peace movement back in the sixties and seventies."

Though Rocky had never said a word to me about her hippie days, I'd heard the story from Sophie before. I knew that Rocky had once been involved in a group devoted to ending the Vietnam War. While they were at it, they did their best to spread peace, love, and joy throughout the land. Now, like I always did, I marveled at the very thought. The only thing Rocky Arnaud was radical about these days was the quality of her produce.

"She has so much valuable information, so many interesting experiences with community organizing and lobbying," Sophie said, glancing toward the aisle where Rocky had disappeared. "They were peaceniks, you know. They were sure they could change the world through their message of love and tolerance. Young people need to hear the story these days and it wouldn't hurt for some of us old-timers to be reminded, too. But ever since she agreed to speak at the symposium, Rocky's been . . ." Sophie crinkled her nose. "Well, when she first heard Aurore Brisson was coming to town, she couldn't wait to get over here and meet her. And last time I talked to her about it, she was just about jumping up and down with excitement about the big parade tomorrow and the talk that Statue of Liberty expert is giving over at the library. But the symposium is getting closer and closer and now tonight . . ."

"She'll be fine," I assured Sophie. "Maybe it's just a case of the jitters."

Sophie cradled her copy of *Yesterday's Passion* to her broad bosom. "Well, I hope so. At least she's excited about reading the book. I mean, she must be, right, because she couldn't wait to open it and get started. That's a good thing, right? Maybe it will take her mind off that symposium and speaking in front of an auditorium full of people."

Another group of people—all clutching the book—moved away from the signing table, and I grabbed Sophie's arm to get her out of the way. But then, the last thing I wanted to do was see her take a fall and end up in rehab again. "Caf-Fiends is serving cookies and coffee," I told her. "Let's get some."

If the crowd hadn't been so heavy, there was no way Sophie would have agreed. See, in her book, Caf-Fiends is an affront to humanity, a place that adulterates coffee with things like whipped cream, sprinkles, and flavored syrups. Then they have the nerve to charge more than three dollars a cup for it. Back when I first arrived in Hubbard, there had been plenty of tension between Caf-Fiends and the Terminal because the Terminal was losing business to the new coffee shop with its wraps, its fancy sandwiches, and its killer key lime pie. The good news was that these days with the ethnic specialities on our menu and our crowds up, the Terminal and Caf-Fiends were learning to peacefully co-exist.

Well, some of us were.

I stepped up to the dessert table and came eye to eye with Myra, the Caf-Fiends waitress who made no secret of the fact that she had her eye on Declan Fury and that she didn't like it one bit when she saw the two of us together. Hey, I wasn't the one who was going to tell her that she had nothing to worry about. Declan and I, we were—

"Coffee?" Myra held out a cup toward Sophie and pretended I didn't exist. "We've got cookies, too. John and Mike had us bring lots of cookies." When she swiveled to look my way, her chestnut-colored ponytail twitched. "Ours are the best."

"I have no doubt," I said, scooping a cookie from the table even though I didn't want one. I chomped into it, turned my back, and made my way over toward the cash register so Sophie could pay for her book. After that, it was all a matter of waiting. Once the crowd of book buyers dwindled, we were told that Aurore Brisson, she of the too-yellow hair and the too-white smile, would be giving a little talk.

I found Sophie one of the last chairs in the shop and stood behind it, waiting for the big moment, and I have to say, once it came, I was a tad underwhelmed.

Aurore, who spoke decent-enough English, didn't have a whole lot to say other than that her book, it was fabulous and the cable TV series that was about to premiere . . . well, it was nothing short of *extraodinaire*!

When she was finished singing her own praises, we
clapped politely and Mike moved to the front of the room.

"We've only got a few minutes," he said. "But I think . . . I
hope . . ." He smiled at the author who did not smile back.
"Ms. Brisson has been gracious enough to say she would
answer a few questions."

"Questions? Questions?" Where Rocky came from, I
couldn't tell. I only knew that there she was, out of whatever
hidey-hole she'd gone into to read, standing at the center of
the room with her arms pressed to her sides and her cheeks
flaming and for a moment, I saw a glimpse of the peace
crusader she had once been.

Rocky's head was high. Her shoulders were steady. Her
voice rang through the shop like the first strident, brilliant
chord of Jimi Hendrix's "Star Spangled Banner."

"I've got a question for you, Aurore Brisson!" Rocky held
her copy of *Yesterday's Passion* to the sky and used her other
hand to point a finger at the author. "How did you . . . Why
did you . . ." Rocky's voice broke and she pulled in a sob.
"How can you stand there and let these *mensonges* . . . these
lies . . . leave your lips? Why did you steal Marie Daigneau's
book?"

Kylie Logan is also the national bestselling author of the League of Literary Ladies Mysteries and the Chili Cook-off Mysteries.